A FAMILY SHATTERED

MICHAL'S DESTINY SERIES - BOOK 2

USA Today Bestselling Author

ROBERTA KAGAN

ISBN (eBook): 978-1-957207-69-8
ISBN (Paperback): 978-1-957207-70-4
ISBN (Hardcover): 978-1-957207-71-1

DISCLAIMER

This is a work of fiction. Names, characters, businesses, places, events, and incidents are either the products of the author's imagination or used in a fictitious manner. Any resemblance to actual persons, living or dead, or actual events is purely coincidental.

Title Production by The BookWhisperer

prologue
Reichskristallnacht

THE DAILY TELEGRAPH correspondent wrote of events in Berlin:

"Mob law ruled in Berlin throughout the afternoon and evening, and hordes of hooligans indulged in an orgy of destruction. I have seen several anti-Jewish outbreaks in Germany during the last five years, but never anything as nauseating as this. Racial hatred and hysteria seemed to have taken complete hold of otherwise decent people. I saw fashionably dressed women clapping their hands and screaming with glee while respectable middle-class mothers held up their babies to see the 'fun.'"

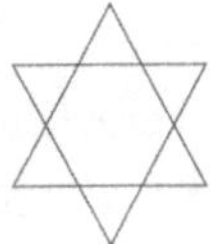

one
Michal

Berlin, Germany,
1938. The morning after Kristallnacht, the night of the broken glass.

MICHAL GATHERED her long black curls into a knot at the nape of her neck. She wore a modest dress, kissed her two daughters goodbye, and then steeled herself for whatever lay ahead. Her husband, Taavi, had been arrested the night before when a gang of hoodlums had attacked the neighborhood. These men had broken windows and beaten innocent men and women on the streets. Alina's boyfriend, Benny, was walking her home from dinner at his house when the two were attacked. Taavi heard his daughter screaming and ran outside. He tried to defend Benny but was too late; Benny had been beaten to death. And then, instead of arresting the perpetrators, the police arrested Taavi. The Nazis claimed that this attack on her little neighborhood was a punishment for something that happened in France.

Michal knew better. She had lived through a pogrom, and she was no stranger to anti-Semitism. The sector of the town where she lived was all Jewish. The thugs had written messages of hatred for the Jews all over the buildings. Then, when the police arrested Taavi instead of the gangs of wild brutes, she knew this was a deliberate attack on Jews. She had no idea what she would face at the police station, but she had to try to reason with them and somehow get her husband released. She walked five blocks through the Jewish neighborhood where she lived. Instead of the quiet residential community she knew and had come to love, the streets looked like a war zone. The windows of the businesses were busted out. The streets were filled with shards of glass and broken wood from the doors that had been smashed with clubs. Dark pools of blood coagulated in nauseating amounts, turning from red to black on the pavement. Insults to Jews were splattered in red paint on the doors and buildings of Jewish-owned shops. Everywhere she looked, there was something derogatory about Jews. Michal squared her shoulders. She had to find her husband, no matter the danger.

Fear gripped her as she took a deep breath and entered the closest police station. It was likely that he'd been taken there. Her fingers twisted and wrung the fabric of her coat as beads of sweat dripped down her forehead. The station was crowded. Overhead hung a sign that read 'The Police, Your Friend, Your Helper.' Michal looked up at the sign and wished she could believe what it said. People were every-where, moving to and fro. She was out of place as she waited to speak with an official. Every instinct inside of her wanted to cry out to the officers at the police station. *Hurry, please; my husband has been taken away for no reason at all. I need help. Please give him back to us. He has a family. He didn't do anything wrong. I swear it to you.* But she restrained herself. They would be less likely to help her if she was aggressive or demanding. *I must wait quietly until someone gives me permission to speak.*

There was a line of people in front of a small inquiry hatch. She held her breath, waiting as each of them was attended to.

"What do you want?" the police finally asked Michal through the small hole in the wall opening.

"My name is Michal Margolis. I have come to ask about my husband, Taavi Margolis. He was arrested last night. Can you help me, please? Can you tell me where he is? What has happened to him?"

"Sit over there, and someone will be with you when they have time," a police officer with thick grey eyebrows said to Michal. He pointed at a row of chairs with his pointer finger.

Michal did as she was told.

The hands on a black-rimmed, moon-faced clock that hung in the police station moved slowly around in circles. Michal's breath was shallow, and she wanted to scream. But she didn't. Instead, she continued to wait. Sweat had begun collecting under her bra. As she sat on the hard wooden chair, waiting for an audience with someone of authority, she watched three other women who had come together searching for their husbands. These women had been more aggressive than Michal. Each of them insisted upon speaking with someone immediately. The officer spoke harshly, clearly annoyed, as he told them to sit down and wait, but they would not be silenced. One of them cried out in anger, demanding to see someone immediately. They were all talking at once, screaming for answers. The officer at the desk called for another policeman from the back room. He came out and told them to leave before he made them sorry they came. Two of the women left. The third did not leave. She was the one Michal would not forget. She was tall, attractive, and used to having her own way.

She stood up straight and unafraid, "I will see someone of higher authority right away." She commanded. Her shiny dark hair was wrapped into a perfect twist, and she wore a white mink coat. Large diamonds sparkled from her neck and fingers. Michal watched her. From how this woman carried herself, it was obvious that she had commanded the subservience of those around her for many years. She would not accept being put off by any of these civil workers in the *Ordnungspolizei*. After all, they were nothing but workers, but she was a woman from a wealthy family. They were here to serve her. In her station in life, she was above them.

"I want you to find someone to see me right now. My husband and son were arrested last night for no reason at all, and I want to know where they are."

The woman pointed her finger at the face of the policeman who was sitting at the desk.

"And you." She pointed at the officer. "I want to see your superior."

The skin of the officer sitting at the desk turned blood red. His thick eyebrows knitted to become a single dark caterpillar above his angry eyes.

The police officer glared at the woman. She'd embarrassed him in front of the others. She'd made him look unimportant.

"You say you are looking for someone? Is that correct?" The police officer had a club in his hand. He was rhythmically beating it against the side of his body.

"My son and my husband. I demand to know where they are. There was no cause to arrest them."

"Really, you demand? Do you?"

"I am not going to stand here and argue with you. I am looking for my family. I've told you I don't want to talk to you. I want to see your superior officer."

The man smiled at her. "I see." He nodded.

She still stood waiting. She was not returning his smile. Then he took the back of his hand and slapped her hard enough across the face to make her head jerk. Her nose and mouth began running with blood. The blood dripped onto her coat. The contrast of the red blood on the white fur caused a shiver to run up Michal's spine. The bleeding woman was shaking with anger. "I have friends. Important friends… I'll have your job for this!"

The police officer hit her face with the club. Her cheek was a bloody mess as he threw her out the door of the building. Then he wiped the blood that had spilled onto the floor and the wood of his desk. "Schwein," he said under his breath. Calmly, he began to sort through a pile of papers again, organizing them into smaller groupings.

It was very late that afternoon when Michal was finally called in to see Hauptmann Schteck. An officer Michal had not seen before came out from a room somewhere in the back of the building and walked over to her.

"Follow me; the Hauptmann will see you now."

Michal nodded. She thought of the woman she'd seen earlier who had spoken out and been beaten for it and reminded herself to hold her tongue. Even as angry and frightened as she was, she knew she must be as respectful as possible.

Michal held her breath as she walked into the office. On the wall, she saw a framed photograph of Adolf Hitler. A large mahogany desk was facing away from the window. It had been decorated with beautifully framed pictures of a smiling blond woman with three small children. A beautiful family, to be sure. Michal gazed at the faces in the photograph and told herself that a family man like this must be a good man, a kind man. After all, he had children and a wife of his own. The Hauptmann, who sat behind his desk, looked to be in his late thirties, attractive and well-groomed.

"You may sit," he said. Michal nodded and sat down. "Now, how can I help you?" he said, leaning back in his chair and looking her over.

"My husband was arrested last night. A mob of criminals came through our street, destroying businesses and beating up innocent, defenseless people."

"Oh, so that's why you are here?" He smiled again and lit a cigarette. "You know the *Führer* disapproves of smoking. I really must quit." Then he nodded as a wicked smile fell like a mask over his face. "So… let me guess? You're a Jew? Am I right?"

"Yes," Michal said in a quiet voice.

"Do you realize why this happened to your people?"

Michal shook her head. She'd heard something about a problem in France but decided it was best not to bring it up. She would sit quietly and allow him to speak. The man looked nice and refined; his pictures with his children seemed wholesome. Yet, when he uttered the word 'Jew,' a hatred came over his face that made him look like someone else, someone terrible.

"Ah, so you don't know why this thing happened. Well then, let me tell you. A Jewish criminal murdered a German official in France.

Now, as you can well imagine, that made the German people very angry. Very angry indeed."

"But my husband had nothing to do with this man in France…"

"You did say that you are Jews, didn't you?"

"Yes…" Her voice was small. She wondered if she should have lied to him and told him that she wasn't Jewish at all. She remembered the pogrom on that terrible day when the Cossacks invaded her home in Siberia when she was still living in Russia. It seemed like a lifetime ago. This Hauptmann's eyes reminded her of the Cossack that killed her first husband. They had come out of nowhere for no reason at all to destroy the small Siberian village, and all because the people there were Jews. It seemed to Michal that it had happened so long ago. It was before she and Taavi had come to Berlin and married. But the effects of what happened to Michal during that pogrom were burned into her heart and mind, and she could never forget them.

The Hauptman wore a clean, pressed white jacket that fit his slender body as if it had been custom-made. He put out his cigarette, then got up and stretched like a cat. With his eyes fixed on hers, he sauntered to the front of the desk. Then, without speaking but wearing a wicked smile, he reached over and grabbed her breast in his fist. At the same time, he gripped her buttocks with his other hand.

Michal winced in pain.

"No!" Michal screamed. She couldn't help herself because she was reliving the day that the Cossacks had come. Since that fateful day, she'd tried everything to bury the memory of being raped. But now, this moment brought it all back to her. Being a beautiful woman was nothing but a curse for a Jew. Someone had told her that once when she was much younger. Her poor, precious daughters. They were lovely young girls, and neither she nor her husband had the power to protect them from whatever fate had in store for them. After all, they were Jews.

The Nazi reached up into her hair and pulled her closer, tugging so hard that her head ached. Her hair fell out of the bun and hung loose. She tried to push him away. "What a feisty little Jewess you are." He laughed. "I like that." Then, he pressed his lips against hers until she could feel his teeth. It was early morning, yet he smelled and tasted like bitter beer. Michal gagged. She felt the vomit rise in her throat, then spew out of her mouth all over the Hauptmann's uniform. Anger flashed in his eyes, and fear came over her. He was clearly disgusted by the mess she'd made of him, and he slapped her face so hard that her head felt like it was going to fly off of her neck. Then, something inside her mind snapped.

The memories of the rape so long ago were suddenly as clear as if it had happened yesterday. For a moment, the past and present forged together so tightly that she forgot that she'd promised herself she would control her temper. And in her moment of madness, something made her lash out. So he wanted to kiss her? Well, she would show him. She reached up, and it seemed to him that she would kiss him passionately. His face told her he was amused. But then she bit his lip. Blood ran down the Nazi's face, and his eyes flew open wide. He was startled by the pain, and he tried to push her away, but her teeth were sunk deep into his lip, and for several seconds, like a dog with a locked jaw, she wouldn't release him. Then, she was sobered by the salty taste of rushing blood. Suddenly, she realized the magnitude of what she'd done and was frightened by her actions, terrified by what he might do to her.

"Bitch!" he screamed, slapping her hard across the face, the blood from his lip still running down his chin. "I could kill you right now. Right now, do you hear me? And nothing, nothing at all, would happen to me. You are a subhuman. I was kind enough to let you come in here and speak to me on your husband's behalf. Now, I see that you are a pig. All Jews are swine." He took a clean white handkerchief out of his breast pocket and began to mop up the blood and vomit that had already stained the front of his uniform. His eyes looked fiercely at her, and she saw the unbridled cruelty in them. "But, my little Jewish swine, I have decided that I am not going to kill you. That would be too easy for you, too good. No, you Hebrew demon. I have something much better in store for you. By the time I'm done with you, you'll wish I'd killed you."

Michal was paralyzed by fright. What was she thinking when she attacked this man? She'd gone out of her mind, temporarily insane. But the truth be told, he had power over her life. When he said he could do as he pleased with her, she knew it was true. *Oh God, what have I done?* The Hauptmann was angry with her, and all she could do was pray that by some miracle, God would touch his heart and he would be merciful. And to make matters worse, how was she ever going to find Taavi?

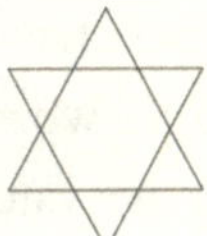

two

November 1938

TAAVI MARGOLIS WOULD HAVE FOUGHT BACK at the police station when he was arrested the day after *Kristallnacht* if the young boy who sat beside him on the bench had not coaxed him to silence. The boy was a stranger, just a young Jewish boy on the brink of manhood. He reminded Taavi of Benny. Poor Benny had died on the street the night before, beaten to death by a gang of thugs. Taavi had been in his apartment with his wife and daughter Gilde when he heard his older daughter Alina screaming outside. He looked out the window and ran out of the building to help Benny. What else could he do? Could he let a bunch of hoodlums kill an innocent boy and stand by and do nothing? What kind of man would that have made him? He rubbed the bump on his head where an *Oberleutnant* had struck him with a club. It was crusted with blood, as was his face. Taavi had overheard that he was being sent to a work camp. A work camp? Where? For how long? What would become of Michal and his two precious daughters, Alina and little Gilde? How about his business and his business partner, Lev? Once he realized his predicament, he swallowed his pride for the sake of his family and begged the policemen to let him go home. He apologized profusely for his behavior the previous night. He even promised that he would adhere to any demands they made. Pride meant nothing to him at that moment. All he wanted was to see his family again. There was no doubt in Taavi's mind that Michal and his daughters would be frantic by now. He wasn't worried about them having enough money. Lev, his best friend and business partner, would support them if worse came to worse. Taavi could count on his oldest and dearest friend. But he knew Michal and was sure she would not sit at home safely and wait for his return. Quite frankly, he was afraid of what she might do. She never ceased to amaze him. When he'd met Michal, she'd been an innocent religious girl from a small Jewish settlement in Siberia. But when they'd come to Berlin and gone through a period of separation, she'd grown into a strong and capable woman. And the woman she'd become was a fighter. There was no doubt that Michal would try to find him. Taavi was quite sure of it. If she came to the police station, the bastards might hurt her, and he would not be there to protect her, to stop them. This angered and frustrated him beyond measure. As he sat watching the policemen, he was unaware that both hands were in fists.

A group of *Oberleutnants* came with guns pointed at the prisoners and loaded them into the back of an open truck. They were surrounded by armed guards, and Taavi rationalized that there were too many armed men for him to attempt to overpower them.

The truck headed north and stopped in front of a building surrounded by a large gridiron gate. Taavi looked around him; an icy fingernail traveled up his spine, and he trembled slightly at the thought of being trapped and caged like an animal. Barbed wire surrounded the building in front of him, making escape almost impossible. His heart began beating hard and fast.

"Come on, let's get moving." The guard held a gun pointed at the prisoners as he yelled in German, "What are you waiting for?" As they got off the truck, the guard nudged them forward with the butt of his rifle. "Let's go, or I'll shoot you dead on the spot."

The prisoners were running, but they could not move fast enough to please the armed guards who were pointing guns directly at them. Taavi was running, too. He didn't even realize that he was running. He had become part of a herd of broken men being led like cattle, probably to slaughter. Once inside the gates, Taavi heard the iron doors slam shut behind him. It was the most profound and terrifying sound he'd ever heard. Above him, he saw a sign that said, "Work Makes You Free." A few of the prisoners had begun to cry. They were terrified. But their whimpering disgusted Taavi. Taavi would not cry. He would never give these bastards that satisfaction. He would rather die.

Next, the guards used their rifles to direct the men. Those who were too weak or old to work were forced into one line. Taavi and the stronger men were sent into another. The separation became apparent as the weaker men were led away. Some were begging; again, Taavi had to turn away. He knew that their begging would not help them. Whatever the guards had in store was out of the prisoners' control. Pleading would only humiliate them further, and Taavi couldn't bear to watch.

When Taavi got to the front of the line, he was stripped of his clothes. As he stood naked, his strong, muscular body taunted one of the guards, who was consumed with jealousy because he was fat and white like a doughboy. The doughboy hit Taavi in the face with the butt of his rifle. Taavi's hand formed a fist for a moment, and he drew his arm back. If need be, he was ready to fight to the death. Then he remembered Michal and his daughters. His hand unclenched. He felt the blood pour down his cheek and across his chest, but he didn't raise his hand to wipe it away. Taavi just glared at the guard, but he continued to walk in the line and do as he was told. Next, his thick, golden brown hair was shaved off completely, and then he was sent to a shower where he was deloused. Next, Taavi was ushered into another line, where he was handed a black-and-white striped uniform.

"*Mach Schnell*," another guard yelled as a group of men dressed in a large room. Taavi put the uniform on and followed the rest of the group.

He did what they commanded, not because he was afraid of dying, but because he was waiting for the right moment and opportunity to escape. There had to be a way out, but it was not through that barbed wire. He'd seen that even if somehow he was able to get through the fencing, there was a watchtower with guns pointed directly at the front. No, that wasn't the way out. But he would keep searching until he found a way. He had to get back to his family. They needed him, especially with all the hatred towards Jews that was exploding in Germany right now. Visions of his family, alone and unprotected, sent waves of panic through him. However, he kept reminding himself: *Taavi, stay calm, watch, wait. The right time will come.* Taavi was shoved along with the rest of the group into a room filled with bunks. There was not much space. The prisoners were piled together. He was surrounded on both sides by men. The room was overfilled, and it stunk of sweat and filth.

On one side of Taavi was a man in his late teens; on the other was a middle-aged man closer to Taavi's age of forty-two. It was hard for Taavi to keep his head. He wanted to overpower one of the guards, take his gun, and begin shooting. He'd kill as many as he could. But the chances of his getting out alive were slim, and he knew it.

"I'm Yigal," the younger man said to Taavi.

"Taavi."

"I'm Ber," the middle-aged fellow Taavi's age introduced himself. "How long do you think they intend to keep us here?"

"I don't know." Taavi was irritable. He didn't feel like talking to anyone. "I have a wife and two daughters who need me, so I hope they let us out soon," Taavi said, then he turned away, letting the men know he wasn't interested in having a conversation.

There were men everywhere, scrunched together on the bunks, spread on the floor. A scraggly man with collarbones and cheekbones jutting out of his skin and a red, angry rash covering his arms said to Taavi, "There's an epidemic of lice here. That's the worst part of it."

"Thanks for letting me know," Taavi answered.

"I'm Fredrick," the man said. "I'm a political prisoner." Then he laughed. "That means that I'm a communist, and I hate Hitler."

"I'm a Jew. That makes me a criminal." Taavi laughed, too. There was something about Fredrick that made him smile.

One of the other Jewish men who'd been arrested on *Kristallnacht* gave Taavi a look of disdain. "And that's funny to you, that being Jewish makes you a criminal?" he said.

"We can try to make jokes, make this easier. Or we can feel sorry for ourselves. I prefer to tell jokes. A smile can make the day a little brighter," Taavi said.

"I prefer to get out of here," the other Jewish man said.

"That goes without saying," Fredrick answered. "But until we do, I have something I'd like to discuss with you." He looked directly at Taavi.

"Why me?"

"Because you're big, you're healthy, and you're strong."

"I want to stay out of trouble. I am not looking to join in any kind of a revolution. I have to get home to my wife and children."

"You think you are going to get out of here?"

"I hope so," Taavi said. "I am not looking to join any groups."

"Let's see if you still feel that way in a month or two."

A loud bell rang.

Two guards carrying rifles entered and demanded that the men move quickly and line up outside for roll call.

Discreetly, Taavi glanced at the lines of men in black-and-white striped uniforms and wondered what was in store. How long would they keep him imprisoned? He had no idea how many men there were, but it looked like hundreds. From what he gathered in the half hour that he had been in the barracks, most of the men were either political prisoners or Jews who had been arrested during the demonstration the night he had been arrested. When he'd first arrived at the camp with a truckload of other Jews, he was stunned to see how many other men had been sent to the camp with him.

There were plenty of armed guards as well. They patrolled the men to prevent an escape. Taavi's eyes darted through the crowds, looking for a way to break out, but it was far too well guarded. From where he stood, he could see a watchtower with three men inside...

their guns aimed directly at the men in case anyone should attempt to escape.

"You will line up every day when you hear the bell. If you are not here when your name is called, we will hunt you down, and you will be shot. It's that simple. If you will notice, there is a watchtower. You are under surveillance at all times. Try to run, and you are dead," the guard said. He was a heavyset man with the perfect posture of one who was confident in his work. Back and forth, he paced, well-armed, well-fed, clean, and well-dressed, an absolute contrast to the men he lorded over.

It was late afternoon. The sun had begun her descent in the west, sending out her last rays of golden light before the moon hovered in the sky and the darkness and shadows began to appear.

Another bell sounded. The men lined up for dinner. It was a long line. Each of the new men was given a bowl and a spoon. "Don't lose that," Fredrick said. "You won't get another one."

Fredrick was behind Taavi. When they reached the front of the line, they were each doled out a ladle of liquid with a quarter of a potato and a few dead insects floating on top of an oily broth. Then, they received a crust of stale bread.

"This is disgusting," Taavi said, looking at the soup and feeling like he might puke.

"Eat it. You'll need the nourishment. They'll have us in the brick-works in the morning, and the work is hard. Let me tell you. Take any food you can get. It will keep you alive."

"I can't eat this," Taavi said, shaking his head.

"Then give it to me. I'll eat it."

Taavi handed Fredrick his bowl. Fredrick drank the soup without using the spoon. Taavi thought of the insects he'd seen floating in the greasy water. His stomach lurched, and he looked away.

That night, Taavi slept surrounded so closely by other men that he could not move his body. It was hard to determine when these men had last bathed. They did manual labor every day, and the strong and terrible smells on either side of Taavi were inescapable. He'd never felt so closed in, so trapped, and it was well after midnight that he finally drifted off into a light sleep.

Before sunrise, the alarm bell sounded. A loud, clanging, high-pitched noise shook the barracks. "Come on." Fredrick pulled Taavi's arm. "Get up."

Taavi's back and shoulders were stiff from sleeping in such confined quarters, but he shook the haze of sleep from his head and rose. One of the guards entered the room, pointing a rifle at the men, and demanded that they get in line for roll call.

"*Schnell. Schnell,*" he yelled.

This time, a tall scarecrow of a guard with thinning hair combed over his balding scalp walked the length of the lineup. Several other men stood holding guns aimed at the prisoners in case anyone should decide not to cooperate.

"It seems someone has stolen half of a loaf of bread from the kitchen. Do you know what that means? It means that there will be no bread today for anyone unless you can tell me who the thief is." He paced, his eyes like those of a panther, back and forth, glaring at each man, studying him to see if he was weak, if he was prey. Taavi noticed that none of the men let their eyes meet the guard's eyes. They all looked down at the ground, but no one dared speak.

"So, you are protecting your fellow inmate, the criminal? I think I know who might have done this," he said, pulling a young man out of the crowd.

"Was it you?"

"No, no..." The man shook his head. Taavi watched the guard poke him with the rifle butt. Looking closer at him, Taavi saw that he was barely a man, still closer to a boy.

"Then was it you?" the guard put his gun against an old man's chest.

"No. No, it wasn't me."

"Then it was him, am I correct?" The Nazi pushed the gun into the old man's chest as he asked if it was the younger man he'd questioned initially.

"Yes, it was him." The old man's body was shaking. He was clearly weak and afraid. The guard was enjoying this. He was smiling, waiting to see if the old man would sacrifice a young life for his own life. "Yes," the old man said, "it was him."

"Point to the thief. So we can all see that you are turning this criminal in for his crime," the Nazi said.

The old man bowed his head and pointed to the young man.

The Nazi turned the gun on the younger man and shot him directly in the face. "This is what happens when you steal."

The old man began to cry. He fell to his knees. He knew he had caused the death of another because of his own fear, and he was heartsick. He was old and feeble, and Taavi wondered how he had ever gotten through the initial inspection when they first arrived. All the men who had been unable to work had been taken away, taken somewhere else.

"Get up, old man," the guard said. The prisoner standing beside the elderly man helped him to his feet. But the guard laughed, and then he shot the old man and the prisoner who'd tried to help him.

"He was a useless eater," the guard said, smiling at the others who stood trembling in line, praying that the Nazis would not take a special interest in them.

"We've been wasting time playing games here with these two. There will be no bread today. You have your fellow prisoners to thank for it. Go now, and get in line for food. Let this little demonstration be a warning to anyone who thinks they can steal."

Again, the men were fed, but this time, it was just a bowl of oily water with a bit of carrot.

Taavi still could not bring himself to swallow the dirty water. He took a sip, but once the foul-smelling liquid was in his mouth, he gagged and spit it out on the ground. Then he turned and gave his bowl to Fredrick.

They were given fifteen minutes to eat, then they were lined up, and the entire group began to march.

"Where are we going?" Taavi whispered to Fredrick, who he knew had been in the camp for several months.

"To the Brickworks. Don't you know, we're creating Speer's vision of building a new Berlin."

"We are being sent there to work?"

"Oh yes. To work and the job is hell."

"Shut up back there. No talking," One of the guards said. He was a pimply-faced boy who looked like he could still be a teenager. They walked for six grueling miles. Taavi had not slept well and was already exhausted when they arrived.

Taavi was a strong man, and he was used to manual labor. But never in his life had he worked so hard. The weather was cool, but the sun scorched his face as he broke rocks with a pickaxe for fifteen long, endless hours without a short break. Then, when the sun had gone down and the brisk temperature of the autumn night began to drop, the men were instructed to carry the large bricks on their backs as they walked the six miles back to the camp.

The armed guards watched the men keenly, waiting for one to fall or try to escape. Their faces told Taavi that they enjoyed the power. Taavi still couldn't see any possible escape, so with the heavy load on his back, he labored his way to the camp.

That night, when the men were fed, Taavi ate. He was hungry enough to eat anything, so he gulped down mouthfuls of what had passed for soup. He swallowed whole pieces of stale and moldy bread, soaking them in oily water to soften them because they were too hard to chew.

What was in store for him? Would he live to see another year pass? Would he ever see his children again, his beautiful and precious wife? Then, an idea came to his mind. Perhaps he might have a chance to get out if he could somehow get word to his old boss, Frieda. The cabaret that Frieda owned had grown in popularity before the rise of the Third Reich. Many influential people came and went through the doors of Frieda's cabaret, and many owed her favors. He had not been there in the years since Hitler took power, but if she still had control of her business and had her prior connections, there was a good chance she could help him. It was not for sure, but it was a chance.

The only problem was that Frieda was angry with him. In the years that he and Michal had been separated, Taavi had been Frieda's lover and the manager of her nightclub. He doubted she'd ever loved him, but she depended on him. And that had been fine with him. For several years, he lived in an apartment in the back of the cabaret, enjoying a hefty salary, large tips, and a life of wild debauchery. At the time, he was young, and he enjoyed those years. But he always loved his wife, and even during this time with Frieda, he missed Michal. So when Michal came to him wanting to try again, Taavi was willing to give up everything to go home and be a husband to Michal. But that was not all Michal told him.

While they were apart, she had given birth to his child. He had a little girl whom he had never seen. He remembered how his heart swelled when he learned not only was he going to have his precious love back, but he'd also been blessed to be a father. Frieda had been livid when he told her he was leaving and going home, but his mind was made up, and he walked out. Now, he needed Frieda, and he doubted she'd forgiven him. But he also doubted that she would want to see him dead. And besides, she was his only chance. Frieda was the only Aryan person he knew with friends of influence in the Nazi party who could possibly be of any help. So, Taavi began to wonder how to get a message to Frieda. Whether she could or would help him or turn her back on him remained to be seen. First, he had to find a contact, one of these bastards who would be greedy enough to risk his life.

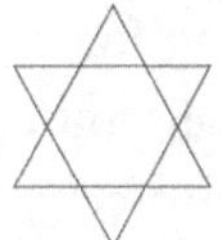

three

December 1, 1938
The First Kindertransport

GILDE MARGOLIS STOOD beside her sister, Alina, at the train station. Her arms were folded across her chest, and her small black valise sat on the ground beside her. It was that eerie time of morning before the sunrise, when the shadow of the night had not yet begun to lift, and the world was still cloaked in darkness. A dusting of snow fell like ashes on her hair, appearing more pale grey than white in the limited light of the station. Even though she was bundled up with a heavy coat over an itchy wool dress, thick black stockings, and long underwear, the icy fingers of winter reached deep under her clothing and into her skin. At twelve years old, Gilde was still a child, but circumstances forced her to embark on a journey that would lead her far away from everyone she knew and loved.

"Gilde, look at me and listen to me, please…" Alina, her older sister, bent to look into Gilde's golden brown eyes, glazed with tears. Alina was shaking. Her trembling hands were raw from the cold as she brushed a strand of blond hair from Gilde's eyes. Alina forced a smile, and trying to keep the fear out of her voice, she continued to speak. "Gilde, I know you don't want to go to Britain; believe me, I don't want to let go of you." Alina put her hands on both of Gilde's shoulders. "Since the day you were born, we have been inseparable, and I already miss you terribly even though you haven't left yet." Alina cleared her throat and mustered a half smile of encouragement. "But I know getting out of Germany right now is the safest thing for you. And you have to realize, Gilde, that it's harder for me than you can imagine to let you go so far away without me. I want to protect you the way I always have. But, I've turned this over in my mind a thousand times, and you see, sweetie, I truly believe you will be safer if you get out of Germany."

"Why can't you just come with me?"

"We've been over this, Gilde. I am too old. I can't go. The authorities won't allow it. This program is for children only. But you are lucky to have been chosen to be a part of it. Thank God you will be out of Germany and far away from Hitler."

"I don't feel at all thankful. I want to stay with you and Lotti and Lev and wait for Mommy and Papa to come back."

"Gilde, we don't know when they will return. For now, you will be in good hands in Britain. A family has agreed to care for you until everything settles down here in Germany, and then you'll be able to come back home, and it will be safe."

"I'm scared, Alina. I don't want to go all alone. I will be so far away from you, and I won't be here when our parents get back."

"I know, Gilde. I wish I didn't have to send you," Alina said. *If our parents ever come back. God help us.*

"You don't have to send me," Gilde said. Her voice was firm and angry.

"Yes, I do!" Alina took off the gold Star of David necklace she'd received as a gift from her parents for her fifteenth birthday and slipped it over her little sister's head. "Wear this until we are together again."

"But Alina, Mommy, and Papa gave that to you. I know how much you love it. I couldn't take it."

"You're not taking it away from me, Gilde. You're just holding on to it for me until we are together again."

"Please, don't make me go." Gilde reached up to her neck, gripped the Star of David, and held it in her small hand.

"You have to go, Gilde. I love you, and that is why I am insisting on this. Please, trust me." Alina made her voice as firm as possible.

Lotti and Lev were waiting on the other side of the station. They wanted to give Gilde and Alina a few minutes alone to say goodbye. Lotti walked over with Lev at her side. She hugged Gilde, and then Lev hugged her as well. Tears stained Lotti's cheeks, and her eyes were red and swollen. They had been friends with the family for many years. After Gilde and Alina's parents had been arrested by the local police, Lotti and Lev insisted that the two girls stay with them. It had all begun on the most horrible night of Gilde's young life when bands of wild ruffians had attacked the neighborhood where the Margolis family lived. They'd come through the streets, looting and killing anyone who was outside. They shattered the windows of all the Jewish-owned shops. Alina had been on her way home with her fiancé Benny when he was attacked. Taavi Margolis, Gilde, and Alina's father heard Alina screaming and ran out of their apartment to help Benny. He'd demanded that Alina get inside the apartment with her mother and sisters. The three females watched in horror as Taavi tried to stop the angry mob from kicking and hitting Benny with clubs. But the thugs were relentless. Then the police came, and Taavi, not the attackers, was arrested.

The police took him away in a black car that made a terrible, alarming sound. The two girls and their mother stayed up all night, waiting and praying for Taavi's return. When he'd not returned by the following morning, Gilde's mother had gone to the police station to beg for her husband's release. That was over two weeks ago, on a night that would become known as *Kristallnacht*, the night of the broken glass. Neither of Gilde's parents had been seen since then.

Before *Kristallnacht*, Lotti and Alina had been involved in running an orphanage for Jewish children as part of a group. After *Kristallnacht*, the orphanage received an offer from the British government. They had arranged for the transport of Jewish children from the orphanage to be taken to Britain to live with British families who had volunteered to take them and keep them safe. As soon as Alina and Lotti heard about the program, they begged the authorities to take Gilde along with the group. After many meetings and begging, Alina and Lotti successfully secured a place on the transport for Gilde. Gilde was going to live with a family in London, where she would be taken care of until the end of the war.

And now the time had come to leave Germany. Gilde stood at the train station as a frozen breeze swept across her face. With her knees quaking and tears freezing on her cheeks, she held on desperately to Alina's hand for the last few minutes before she boarded the train into the unknown.

Alina knew that if it weren't for the fact that Lotti had been volunteering at the orphanage for many years and then gotten Alina a job there, it was doubtful that Gilde would have been able to join the rest of the children on this rescue mission.

"It is for the best, isn't it?" Alina had asked Lotti on the day Gilde received her acceptance letter. Lotti had assured her that it was, but the question still plagued Alina, even now, even after she'd made the decision to send her sister on the transport.

"Gilde!" A heavyset boy of fourteen came loping over to Gilde. As he ran towards Gilde, he slipped on the ice and fell. His friend Elias, another orphan of the same age who'd been walking with him, laughed loudly.

"You've always been so clumsy. Come on, let me help you up," Elias said, giving Shaul his hand.

Shaul's face was red with embarrassment.

"Good morning," both Shaul and Elias said to Gilde.

"Good morning," Glide said without enthusiasm.

Elias pushed back the dark hair that was falling over his forehead. *Even at fourteen, it was already obvious that he was destined to be handsome.*

One of the teachers came over and handed Gilde and each of the boys a square of cardboard that had been made into a large necklace with two pieces of thick string. Numbers were written on the front of each of the cardboard tags. Gilde looked at the number.

"What is this for?" she asked.

"So that your new family can find and identify you when you get to Britain. They have a card with your number. That's how you will know each other," the teacher said.

"I don't need a new family," Gilde said, tossing the card back at the teacher.

"I'm sorry," Alina said, picking up the identification number and putting it over Gilde's head. Shaul read it. "Your number is twenty-four, Gilde. I'm eighty-two, and Elias is seventy-nine."

"Now we are nothing but numbers," Gilde said sarcastically, shaking her head.

"Please, Gilde. Don't fight this. I know it's hard. But you have to go," Alina said. She had been trying so hard to stay strong, but now she was crying too.

"All right, children, form a single-file line and say your goodbyes. It's time to board the train." One of the nurses Alina had become friends with during the years she'd worked at the orphanage was organizing the children for boarding.

"Come on." Shaul took Gilde's hand, but she shook him off violently. Then, she stood steadfast and would not move.

"Alina? Do I really have to go? Really?" Gilde's eyes were wide and pleading.

Alina nodded. "Yes. But don't forget to write. Write often."

Gilde's shoulders began to shake as she cried silent tears.

Elias put his arm around Gilde. "Let's go, Gilde. You'll sit with me. This is going to be a great adventure. You'll see." He carefully led Gilde into the line, and after a few moments, it was their time to board.

Elias took Gilde's suitcase and carried it up the stairs, then extended his hand to help her. Gilde turned to look back at her sister and Lotti with one more pleading glance.

"Don't make me go," Gilde said. Alina could hear the pain in her sister's voice.

"I love you," Alina said. "Write to me. Don't forget."

Shaul boarded behind Gilde.

Alina stood on the platform and watched her sister through the train window. Her heart ached. *Dear God, I hope I am doing the right thing.* Gilde's pleading eyes almost brought Alina to her knees. She turned and whispered to Lotti, "I want to get on the train and take her off. Whatever happens, at least we'll be together."

Lotti held Alina's arm. "Let her go," Lotti said, her voice gravely with held-back tears. "She'll be safe. I know it's hard. But let her go, Alina."

Alina saw Gilde wipe the tears from her cheeks with her thumb, and Alina began to cry.

Then, a loud whistle sounded, and the engine roared to life. This was the final second, the last moment to change things. If she didn't jump on the train at this very minute and grab her sister, Gilde would be gone. Somehow, Lotti knew what Alina was thinking, and she held fast to Alina's arm, restraining her.

Then, the train rumbled to life and began to move out of the station. Alina ran down the platform as far as she could to see the train until it disappeared into the horizon. When she could no longer see the train, Alina fell to her knees on the wooden platform and wept.

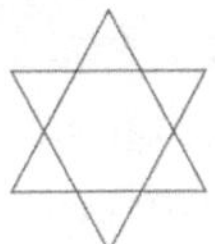

four
Alina

LOTTI AND ALINA had lost their jobs. They'd worked at the orphanage, and now that the children had all left for Britain on the Kindertransport, there was no more work. The business that Taavi and Lev owned had been confiscated on that terrible night of the broken glass. So Lev, too, was jobless. After her sister left, Alina Margolis was miserable, but with no money to buy food and nothing to eat, there was little time to mourn the loss of her family. After their parents were gone, Alina and Gilde came to live with Lotti and Lev. Now Gilde was gone, but Alina was still living there. Lotti insisted that she stay with her and Lev. "You can't live all alone, Alina. Now is the time when you need family around you the most. And Lev and I have been like family to your family since the day Lev and I met," Lotti said.

It was true. Lotti and Lev were the Margolis' best friends. Alina's father had become very close with Lev many years before Lev and Lotti married, and the two families seemed to grow into one big family after Lev and Lotti got together.

Lotti, Lev, and Alina all searched for work because they knew it was only a matter of time before Lotti and Lev's savings ran out. Then there would be no place to live. Because good German women were expected to be housewives and never employed outside the home, it was impossible for Lotti to find work. Lev was a Jew, and non-Jews were forbidden to hire him. His fellow Jews had lost their businesses, and so they were barely surviving and had nothing to offer him, either.

Lev was forced to present his papers when applying at any of the factories, and he was immediately rejected because of his religion. He even went to see his old boss, the man he and Taavi had worked for before they opened their own carpentry business. However, their old boss was a Jew, so as Lev suspected, the shop was closed. The sign on the window said that it was to be reopened by non-Jewish owners. The same thing had happened to Taavi and Lev's store, so this news was no surprise. Jews were losing their businesses, and gentiles were not allowed by law to hire them. Alina was fortunate because she was young and pretty. The man who had been the family doctor for the Margolis family for many years took pity on her and gave her a job doing office work. Dr. Peter Millman didn't really need help, but he'd known Alina since she was a child, and when she told him about what had happened to her family, he found a place for her at his practice. Because Dr. Millman was Jewish, he was only permitted to practice on Jewish patients, many of whom often were unable to pay him. Gentiles were forbidden to go to Jewish physicians. This cut his practice by more than half. Still, he hired Alina.

Alina missed so many things, and among them was her job at the orphanage. She missed working all day with Lotti and the children. Those had been good days. That was before that terrible night when Benny was killed, and her loving father was arrested. And then her mother was gone. Her mother was her arch nemesis and her best friend at the same time. Her mother, who was her strength and her weakness. So much was unresolved between her and Michal. After that, it was Gilde. God, how she missed little Gilde. From the day Gilde was born, Alina had treated her as if she was her own child. Now Gilde was off somewhere in Britain, alone with people she didn't know. It was for the best; it had to be done, but it still hurt like hell. As each day passed without a word from her parents, she became more convinced that something terrible had befallen them. But even with all the evidence pointing towards a bitter end, Alina refused to give up hope. Two long weeks had passed since Gilde left on that morning train, and there had been no letters. Alina felt as if she were being driven to the brink of insanity. She had no address. If she and Gilde were to stay in contact, Gilde would have to write to her. She knew Gilde was angry with her, which might be why she hadn't heard from her, but Alina couldn't help but worry. She was so afraid that something terrible had happened to Gilde, too. *Keep steady, keep believing against all odds that they are all alive.*

Johan, Lotti's brother, met Alina when she and Lotti worked at the orphanage. From the first time he saw Alina, he had a strong attraction for her. Once Johan realized Alina was staying with Lotti and Lev, he visited his sister's house more often. He brought Alina books and two oranges once. They were not easy to come by, and she knew Johan had paid a pretty penny for them. *I'm being courted.* She was attracted to Johan but told herself she must not become involved with anyone. Her life was far too uncertain. She had just lost Benny, her fiancé. And although she hadn't really been madly in love with Benny, he'd been a good friend. The images of his death on the street still haunted her. And out of respect, she couldn't think of marrying anyone else, at least not now. Still, Johan came to see her often. He was a good distraction from all the pain in her life, and he was easy with jokes and conversation. Alina knew Lotti didn't approve of a romance between her and Johan. Lotti had been very clear about this.

She'd explained that her brother did not have the courage to carry on a relationship that defied the Nuremberg laws forbidding relationships between Jews and Gentiles. Johan didn't have the strength inside of him to fight against something as big and terrifying as the Nazi party, the way that Lotti did when she refused to leave Lev, no matter what the consequences. Lotti feared Alina would get hurt if she became involved with Johan. However, when he came by, Johan helped Alina to forget, if only for a few hours, how distraught she was.

Johan and Alina took long walks through the Berlin Zoo, eating ice cream cones. Alina found Johan easy to talk to, so she shared her feelings with him. She told him how much she missed her sister and how worried she was about her parents. What she did not tell him was how guilty she felt about pushing her mother's love away when her mother had reunited with her father. When she'd been so angry with Michal during her teenage years, she'd not known that one day Michal would disappear, and she could not be sure if she would ever see her mother again. If only she could just have a few minutes to tell her mother how sorry she was.

five
Michal

AFTER MICHAL HAD LOST control and, against her better judgment, had fought off the advances of the Hauptmann, she was thrown into a dirty jail cell. Cockroaches climbed the moldy walls, and a slimy concrete floor served as her bed. Even as the iron door shut behind her, she was heartsick because she knew she'd made a terrible mistake. If only she'd kept her head. Now, not only would she be unable to find Taavi, but her girls were alone at home, waiting for her return. She had no idea what was in store for them, and she wondered if she could ever return to her children. Hours passed without food or water. There were no windows, so Michal had no idea whether it was day or night. Only a single low-watt bulb hung from the ceiling, giving her just enough light to see the frightening spiders weaving intricate webs up and down the cell walls. She was being held in a single cell in the basement of the building. No other prisoners were around her, so she had no one to talk to, only the voices in her head that kept reprimanding her for her stupidity of acting rashly with the Hauptmann. The smell of damp mold filled the air and burned her eyes, bringing on fits of sneezing. There was no doubt that she was terrified of what the Nazis might do to her, but even so, her thoughts were primarily of her daughters and her husband. If she died here, what would happen to Gilde and Alina? Then she remembered Lotti and Lev and thanked God for them. They would watch over her girls. "Please, God," she whispered into the empty room. "Watch over my children." And what of Taavi? Was he dead? She couldn't help but think about the time that they had been separated from each other. How much of their precious lives had been wasted because of foolish pride? Now, all she wanted was to feel his arms around her. To even imagine that he might be dead was beyond comprehension. She felt so alone. She would have tried to scream, cry out, beg for mercy if she thought anyone would hear. But there was no one around. Perhaps the Hauptmann had locked her in here to die of thirst and starvation, alone, terrified. She put her head in her dirty hands, soiled from the dirt on the floor, and began to cry. Michal wept until her stomach ached, and her head began to pound so hard that she thought she might vomit. There was a good chance she would never see another living person again. *My children*, she thought. So, she took a deep breath, looked up at the black ceiling of the cell, and pretended she could see the heavens. *Use your imagination. It is all you have left.* Then she whispered, "God, please, watch over my children."

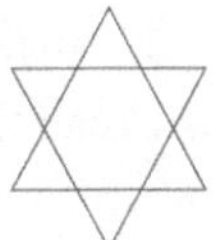

six

AFTER WHAT FELT like several days alone, feeling as if she might go out of her mind in the basement jail, Michal heard footsteps. Terror gripped her as she heard the hard shoes hitting the concrete floor, and she cowered in the corner. She had not eaten or had anything to drink since she'd been locked up, and she hoped that someone might be coming with food or water. Of course, that was the best-case scenario. It could just as easily be someone on their way to finish her off. A black spider crawled across her arm. Michal shook it off and winced.

Two female guards appeared. One opened the metal cage. The other grabbed Michal's arm. She stumbled, but the woman pulled her up from falling and brought her upstairs. It was midday, and the light burned her eyes because she'd been in the dark for so long. The guard who had led her upstairs turned to the other one. "Keep your eye on her, I'll be right back." When she returned, she gave Michal a glass of water. It wasn't cool, but it tasted like heaven. After Michal finished, the guard threw the glass into a garbage can as if it had been used by a filthy animal. Michal didn't care. She was grateful for the water. "Thank you," Michal said, but the guard didn't answer.

Next, Michal was shoved into the back of a truck filled with other women. A different female guard boarded the truck. She was carrying a gun. The guard was as big as a man, perhaps six feet tall, with short blond hair. Her eyes were alert as she watched the prisoners. Then, the truck began to move. They were on their way somewhere.

"Where are we going?" a young blond girl, a prisoner, asked.

"No talking," the guard said.

They drove for a little over an hour and then turned a corner down a country road. After a short ride through a rural area, the group arrived at a women's prison. There, they were forced into an old building. Again, Michal saw the mold on the walls and spots from water damage on the ceiling. She was led to a cell that she shared with three other women. Once all the prisoners were locked in their new homes, a tall, slender woman wearing a pressed Nazi uniform appeared. Her hair was pulled severely away from her face in a tight bun at the nape of her neck. She paced the length of the hallway between the cells as she spoke.

"I am Grupenfürher Bader. I am in charge of this section of the prison. You will find that I am fair, but you'll be working on a production line, and there is no tolerance for laziness here. This is a sewing factory. If you have never worked a machine, prepare to learn to work one quickly."

Michal realized that she was in some sort of work camp. The idea of work didn't bother her, although she had never operated a sewing machine. But she was certain she could learn. Perhaps if she followed the rules and did a good job, she would be released sooner. So, this was the punishment she was to receive for resisting that disgusting Nazi's advances. Well, at least she wasn't dead, and as long as she was alive, there was a chance she could be released and go back to her family. Her stomach grumbled, and she wondered when they would receive something to eat or drink. The woman who called herself Bader didn't seem as difficult as the man who'd put her there in the first place, at least from what she could see so far.

The women prisoners were lined up single file and ushered into a large room where roll call was taken. Then, each woman was assigned a sewing machine. Those who had never done any sewing were given instructions from a seasoned prisoner for one hour to learn their job.

A middle-aged woman with trembling hands sat beside Michal on her bench and began to show her how to work the machine. "Pay attention. I have a quota that must be filled each day, and I will still have to meet it today, even though I am taking an hour out of my work time to train you. So, you'd better learn quickly if we both want to live through this."

"Yes, I will." Michal nodded.

"I'm Hilde."

"Michal."

"That's a strange name. You're a Jew?"

"Yes."

Hilde shook her head. "The conditions are bad for all of us here, but it will be worse for you. It's much worse for Jews."

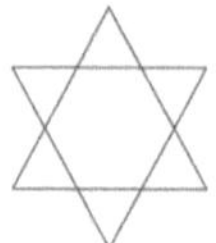

seven

Taavi

TAAVI HAD LEARNED MUCH about human nature while working as a bartender in Frieda Altendorf's cabaret. His job was to assess each customer and always be one step ahead. Through the use of this well-honed skill, he was able to prevent many of the fights that were always brewing among the customers. It proved a useful tool. Even now, Taavi watched the guards carefully. Violence towards the prisoners occurred often, usually ending with the prisoner's death. Horrible events took place right before Taavi's eyes, but he knew that he must stay cool-headed to survive. If he allowed himself to be affected, it would be his demise. There was no doubt that the guards had absolute power over the men, and how they handled that power was what Taavi carefully observed every minute of every day. He was studying, watching, and learning.

Every night, Taavi lay awake, working over the details of what he'd observed in his mind. He was going to devise a plan. Somehow, he would find a way out of this place.

The work was hard, and the food supply was minuscule. Before his arrest, he could never have imagined what it might have felt like to labor so intensely without rest for such long periods. But he quickly learned that it was enough to kill weaker men than him. He would eat whatever food was available. He would prove he could take on any job they asked of him, regardless of how challenging. And in the end, he would beat them.

Most of the guards were unapproachable. Taavi learned that quickly, but he only needed one. The right one, and he dared not make a mistake or misjudge. Even the slightest error could easily cost him his life. Better to watch and wait. He was looking for a certain type of person, a man who could easily be bought. A greedy, weak man who wasn't a patriot but was a selfish bastard willing to do anything to better his own situation. This was the man he needed. Then one afternoon, the men were working. The sun burned their skin, and their heads ached. One of the guards decided it would be fun to toy with a prisoner. So, the guard walked over and demanded that Fredrick lick the pavement. Fredrick refused. It was obvious that the young, arrogant Nazi would not back down. Taavi wished that Fredrick would have complied. It was no use fighting openly this way. Taavi knew that the enemy was armed and they would always win. But Fredrick was young, and his pride wouldn't let him give in. Taavi had held his breath and his tongue as one of the guards beat his friend Fredrick with a club. Taavi's heart was breaking, but his face was emotionless as he continued working. It took every ounce of his self-control not to lift that little Nazi and fling him against the wall.

There was no doubt in Taavi's mind that he could easily kill him. However, they were surrounded by far too many other guards with guns close enough to see what had happened. If Taavi had defended his friend, it would have meant certain death for both of them. So, he waited until the Nazi was done with Fredrick, then Taavi went to Fredrick to help him. Unlike Taavi, Fredrick was not imprisoned for being a Jew. Fredrick was a political prisoner and a well-known communist. He was young, angry, and unbending. And Taavi knew that Fredrick was just the kind of man to get himself killed in a place like this.

"Listen, I have a plan to get us the hell out of here. But you have to stop fighting with the guards. Do whatever they say for now. Give me a chance to save us," Taavi told Fredrick.

"I'm going to die here. I know it," Fredrick said.

"Not if you listen to me and keep your head down. Stop fighting, I tell you. Stop giving them reasons to notice you."

"Get away from him and get back to work." The guard poked Taavi with the same club he'd used to beat Fredrick. Taavi gave Fredrick a quick warning stare. Then he got up and went back to work.

As Taavi lay on his cot one night, he saw one of the guards, a low-ranking officer, come into the barracks.

The Nazi tapped a young prisoner on the foot with his gun. The prisoner sat up in bed. The guard nodded. Then, the prisoner followed the man out of the barracks. When he was sure they couldn't see him, Taavi jumped out of bed and followed the two of them outside. Then, as lithe as a panther, he slipped quietly behind the building next door and watched the guard lead the prisoner into the building and down a short hallway. Taavi's ears were like a deer's in the forest, alert. He crouched down and peeked into the window. Watching, waiting, learning. Taavi saw the prisoner follow the guard into a room. The guard turned the light on in the room and off in the rest of the building. Now, the building was dark. Taavi could not see into the room. There was no point in staying. All he could see was darkness. But he branded the incident into his memory to use, if at all possible, at a later date. Taavi knew that if he was caught, he would be killed on the spot. So, quietly and carefully, Taavi slipped back into his bed in the barracks.

A half-hour later, he heard someone outside gagging and throwing up. Taavi peeked out through the boards that made up the wall of his block. It was the young prisoner the guard had taken to his office earlier. The Nazi pushed the man. "Get back into your bed right now," the Nazi said. The man was still spewing vomit as he ran back into the room where Taavi lay. Then, the man climbed into his bunk.

The following day, after roll call, Taavi caught up with the young man who'd been taken to the office by the guard the night before.

Taavi had an idea of what the guard was doing, but he had to be sure before acting.

"I'm Taavi."

"Jake."

"Nice to meet you," Taavi said. The boy was a Jew; he had a yellow armband. "Jake, I want to ask you a question." Taavi hesitated, but the boy didn't speak. Jake just looked through Taavi with dark eyes, sunken in and surrounded by deep purple shadows. "What happened to you last night? Where did you go with that guard?"

"I don't want to talk about it," Jake said and walked away, leaving Taavi staring after him. Now Taavi was even more sure that he was right. He had been around enough to have a pretty good idea of what the guard had forced this young man to do. He would not ask again. Instead, he would wait for a chance to be alone with that guard. This might be his way out.

Taavi easily learned that the guard's name was Fritz Braus. He was a *Blockführer* who worked closely with the kapos, even though Braus told everyone how much he hated the sniveling tattletales. Rumors were whispered among the prisoners that Braus had a fascination with torturing teenage boys and young men.

Braus was a low-ranking officer with a *Rapportführer* overseeing him who had no respect for Braus whatsoever. Fritz Braus was a small, angry man with a potbelly and a bad case of rosacea surrounded by blackheads and pus-filled acne. Requesting an audience with Braus was dangerous business. But it was a risk Taavi had to take. Michal and his girls needed him.

"*Blockführer*, I'd like to speak to you alone, please," Taavi said to Braus.

The little man studied Taavi, and Taavi could see in Braus's eyes that Braus was jealous of him.

"Would you? And what would a cockroach like you have to talk to me about?"

"I'm sorry, but I need a private conversation with you."

Taavi saw just a hint of a twinkle in Braus's eyes and knew he'd intrigued the man. This was a good sign. Taavi had no choice but to trust it.

"Very well, go on, walk," Braus said, nudging Taavi with the butt of his gun. They arrived at the same office Taavi had seen Braus enter with Jake the previous night.

"Get inside." Taavi was led into the same room. The door was closed. This was it.

Taavi's heart pounded in his neck, making him dizzy and sick to his stomach. Within the next hour, he either would be dead or finally have found the avenue for which he'd been searching. Either way, he would be getting out. It all might go as planned, and he would be going home, or he might be about to make a fatal mistake, and Braus would end his life.

All remained to be seen.

Braus sat down behind his desk and lit a cigarette. He caught Taavi's eyes drifting over to the ashtray. "You like it? It's quite a novelty. I actually received it as a gift. Do you know what it is?"

Taavi didn't answer. He watched Braus's every move, sizing him up, praying that he'd judged him correctly and chosen the right man.

"It's the pelvis of a Jew. A woman. Quite unique, don't you think."

Already nauseated, if Taavi had a weaker stomach, he would have puked. But he couldn't show any fear or weakness right now. The future of his family depended upon it.

"You don't answer?"

Taavi shrugged. Braus laughed. "Okay, you bold Jew, you've piqued my curiosity, so what do you want to ask me?"

"I have a proposition for you."

Braus barked a laugh. "Do you now? You're even bolder than I thought. But I must say, you have guts, and you do amuse me. But remember that I have the power. So take care when you make a request. It's sort of like praying. You don't want to anger the powers that be."

Taavi nodded.

"This is rather entertaining. Go on. Tell me what you want already before I get bored and shoot you for bothering me."

Taavi cleared his throat. He tried to hide the fact that his limbs were trembling.

"There is a woman," Taavi stuttered. Braus's eyebrows went up.

"Speak already. You really are starting to tire me."

"I have a friend. A German woman. She lives in Berlin. I knew her many years ago; I worked for her." Taavi tried to keep his voice steady and to speak slowly and clearly so Braus would not know how unnerved he felt. "This woman I am talking about. She is very wealthy. If you contact her and tell her I am here, she will pay you a good sum of money for my release."

Braus took a puff of his cigarette and then bit his lower lip. "What makes you think I won't kill you here and now for even suggesting such a thing?"

"Greed? I am taking a chance that you would want enough money to retire somewhere in the country. Wouldn't the life of one meaningless Jew be worth it to you to have a better life?" This was it. He would either take the bait, or Taavi was finished.

"And what makes you think she'll pay for your release? She might just turn her back on you. She might laugh at me for even asking the question. Then I'd be very angry with you, Jew. Very angry."

"I don't think she will turn you away. I know her well. She owes me a big favor," Taavi lied. He had no idea if Frieda would come to his aid. The last time he saw her, she was furious with him. The last time they were together, he was leaving her behind, walking out on her to return to his wife. She'd been kind to him and had given him a good job tending bar at her cabaret. It was during the years that he and Michal had separated. Taavi had come to work for Frieda, and she had generously insisted that he take the apartment behind the nightclub for his own. He'd lived there rent-free for many years. During those years, she became his lover. Frieda was older than Taavi, and under her direction, he'd navigated the perverse life of a single man in Weimar Germany.

At first, it was exciting. After all, he was only a peasant from a small village in Siberia. He'd never known anyone who'd lived such an elaborate lifestyle: the excessive drink, the drugs, the sexual promiscuity. But as time passed, Taavi missed having a stable home life. And most of all, he missed his wife, his Michal. He thought of her all the time, but he didn't think she would ever want him back. Then, when he least expected it, Michal sent Lev to tell Taavi that she wanted to reconcile their marriage. He'd been ecstatic. He met with Michal that very next morning, and their love rekindled like a candle flame that was about to extinguish but had been fed just enough oxygen to reignite and become strong. The following day, he returned to the bar and explained to Frieda that he was going home. She was furious. At the time, he was sorry, but he was not sorry enough to turn around and go back to Frieda. He had never wanted to hurt Frieda's feelings. It had just happened that way. When the opportunity to go home came to him, he rejoiced. He quickly forgot the lifestyle he had shared while working for Frieda. He found joy in meeting his daughter, who was born while he and Michal were separated.

For the first time, Taavi felt settled, and he loved being a family man. Now, Taavi needed Frieda's help. There was a possibility that she was still angry and might turn on him. In fact, he couldn't blame her if she did. But she was his only hope and the only person with enough influence and money to buy his freedom. He'd pay her back every penny if she came through for him. However, he knew that she was jealous of his feelings for Michal. If she even suspected that he intended to go home, she could easily leave him to rot in this terrible place.

Braus took another long drag on his cigarette. His little mind was going like a rat on a wheel. He could use the money. Since he'd been with the party, he'd worked hard and had never been chosen to receive the promotions due to him. The party was not fair to him, so why not get a little bonus? It was true. The life of one Jew, more or less, didn't really matter in the big picture.

"Well," Braus shrugged his shoulders.

Taavi held his breath.

"Why not? Give me her name," Braus said, handing Taavi a pencil and paper. "But if you breathe a word of this to anyone, I will deny it, and you will not only be executed, but you will suffer greatly. Am I clear?"

"Yes," Taavi said.

With trembling hands, Taavi carefully wrote down Frieda's full name and the name of the nightclub she owned. Then he signed his name at the bottom of the paper and said a prayer asking God to touch Frieda's heart and influence her to help him.

eight
Blockführer Braus

FRITZ BRAUS HAD ALWAYS FELT he'd gotten a raw deal from life. When he was young, his family was very poor. His father had been wounded in the Great War, and he'd come home bitter, taking his anger out on young Fritz. They had very little money, but still, his father managed to drink to excess and beat his son and Fritz's mother often. He hated his father. In fact, he wished his father would die and leave him and his mother in peace.

Fritz was excited when he was finally eligible to join the Hitler Jugend. The uniform made him feel important, and he loved the idea of the camaraderie of joining a group of boys who enjoyed outdoor activities. He had been looking forward to when he could actually be a part of something. But he'd proven to be a terrible athlete, and to make matters worse, he began to get cystic acne. Big festering boils formed on his cheeks, chin, and nose. They were not infectious, but they were hideous to look at. Sometimes, one of his boils would be so large that it would cause one of his eyes to close, and he would not be able to see through that eye until the boil went away. His condition not only repelled the girls who had begun to take an interest in boys, but even the other fellows seemed to shy away from him, afraid that his condition was contagious.

He was so miserable that he couldn't contain the explosive anger inside himself. When the man who lived next door to Fritz yelled at him for riding a stolen bicycle on their lawn, embarrassing him in front of several other children in the neighborhood, Fritz was humiliated. A few of the other boys who were standing on the street watching laughed at Fritz. Fritz's face turned crimson, and he ran into his house to hide. But Fritz had no plans of letting this incident go. He wanted revenge. He waited until he found a time when no one was around. Then he took a bottle of rat poison out of the cellar and mixed it with a little of his father's liverwurst. Next, he checked the neighbor's backyard. The neighbor's golden retriever puppy was friendly and trusting. She was no watchdog by any means. He gave the liverwurst to the dog. Her tail was wagging, unsuspecting, as she took the gift from Fritz. Now, it was only a matter of time before Fritz would have his retribution. It came that afternoon. The little girl next door wept as her father dug a grave for her puppy in the yard. Fritz just happened to walk outside at the very moment that they laid the dog to rest. The man who'd embarrassed him glanced over to see Fritz smiling. "You did this, didn't you?" the neighbor asked. "I ought to kill you."

Fritz just shrugged his shoulders and walked back into his house. *Serves them right.*

Even after puberty, he was short in stature, shorter than many of the girls, and he had developed a weight problem. Fritz Braus was angry with the world and grew up with a chip on his shoulder.

As soon as he was old enough, he joined the Nazi Party. Then, he served time in the army, where his superiors found him to be mediocre in skills and personality. He'd never received any special honors, but he was always the first one willing to do extra work. Among the officers, Braus became known for immediately volunteering when a job needed to be done, and because he gave the party his all, he was transferred to an office job working for the SS.

His office had a cookout on a Sunday, and although he didn't have any friends, he went. It was there that he met a girl. From the first moment he saw her, he thought she was the most beautiful girl he'd ever seen. Her hair was the color of onyx, and her eyes were bluer than sapphires. When she laughed, it sounded like the ringing of tiny bells. He'd tried to sit next to her, but she had already gathered a crowd of male admirers, all more attractive than Fritz. Still, Fritz tried to talk to her. She was nice enough, but when he asked if she would go out with him that Friday night, she'd gently refused. What had he expected? All he had to do was look in the mirror to know why.

Fritz wanted to get married. His male hormones were raging, and he needed sexual release. So, he'd settled for a girl who lived down the street from him. He knew she would accept his advances because she was plain and shy. None of the other boys had any interest in her. It wasn't much of a romance. They got married three months later. Then he'd been out drinking one night when he'd seen a friend he'd met in the army. His friend had offered him this filthy job as a guard at a camp. It paid better than his low-grade office job, and since Fritz needed the money, he accepted. He'd worked very hard but never received recognition. Now, at the height of his career, he was still only a low-ranking officer. It would have been wonderful to rise in the party, but he had no skills and wasn't smart enough to figure out a way to make himself useful to any of the party leaders. He'd heard rumors about Himmler's occult castle and wished he could be invited there. He had no idea what kind of magical rituals they performed. But he allowed his fantasies of the place to consume him. Perhaps if he could just get an invitation to the castle, he could learn to cast spells to make himself handsome and successful. Of course, he never received an invitation. He was never even officially told anything about it. However, what he did have and enjoyed through this job was power over the prisoners. All of his life, Fritz had been treated like an inferior. And although his superiors still shunned him, here at the camp, he had power. A man like Margolis might be strong and handsome, but it did him little good in a concentration camp. At the end of the day, Fritz decided which prisoners would live and which would die. Fritz had the power to play God in this little corner of the world. Here, he was a superior man.

Now, a man like Taavi, with his muscular body and good looks that still remained intact despite the terrible conditions he was living in, angered Fritz beyond comprehension. Fritz would have liked to smash Taavi like an insect, and he had the power to do just that. In fact, he could shoot Taavi at any time, and there would be no repercussions. However, he had learned something over the years. Destroying what you hate is not nearly as satisfying as profiting from it. And that was precisely what Fritz Braus planned to do. He planned to profit.

nine

Alina

AGAINST LOTTI'S WISHES, Alina and Johan began to spend a lot of time together. Something was blossoming between them. Alina would not have called it love. But she was very lonely with her parents and sisters gone and needed to feel close to someone other than Lotti and Lev. The sweet, tender, innocent relationship with Johan made her feel cared for. Johan would drop subtle hints that his feelings for her were growing into something more than friendship, but Alina wasn't sure what she felt, so she said nothing. Often, Johan would come over, and he and Alina would take long walks and talk for hours. She shared her dreams with him, such as how she longed to go to university and study to become a teacher. "It was difficult enough when women were discouraged from getting an education because they were women. But now, because I am Jewish, I'm not allowed to go to the university at all. I feel like the Nazis are strangling the life out of me and my family. They are taking everything away from us. Even our dreams," Alina said.

"No one can ever take your dreams, Alina," Johan said, gently caressing her face with his palm.

She told him how she'd mothered her little sister and how she'd enjoyed working at the orphanage. "I feel that teaching is such an important job. A teacher helps to mold a child. Sometimes even more than their parents. At the orphanage, since none of the children had parents, I felt like I was their mother. Does that make sense to you?" she asked.

"Everything you say and do makes sense to me, Alina. I think you would make a wonderful teacher and an even more wonderful mother," Johan said as he took Alina's hand. She blushed and looked away.

Since he was a young boy, Johan loved working with his hands. He'd been a tinkerer, a handyman of sorts, so he believed he could move anywhere and scrounge at least a meager living. "Which university do you want to attend?" he asked Alina one sunny afternoon.

"If I had my choice, I'd love to go to Munich. I've heard it is so beautiful there. Like a picturesque city out of a fairy tale."

"I have an idea." He smiled. "Let's go to Munich together. I can always find work. I can fix almost anything, and I can paint a house, too. I'll support you while you attend classes. If you want to study in Munich, let's go together. What do you say?" They sat under a tree in the back of the building where Alina lived with Lev and Lotti.

"If we move far away where no one knows us, you could pose as my sister. We could say that you have been living in Poland. That way, you can register for university using my last name. No one would know that you were Jewish."

"I don't know, Johan. You and me living together? Is that something that you think is proper?"

"Of course," He smiled. His voice cracked. He hesitated. "We could marry if you are willing. It would have to be done secretly because of the laws. Then it would be proper, wouldn't it?"

"How? Who would marry us? It wouldn't be legal. No one would take that kind of risk."

"Alina, I believe that things are going to get worse in Germany. All the signs point to it, and I think it will be dangerous for you here in Berlin. You grew up here. People know you. They know your family is Jewish. In Munich, nobody knows you. Nobody knew your family. Even though the Nazis have a strong hold on Munich, if no one knows you're Jewish, it should be safe for you there."

"So, we would be married, but not legally."

"Yes, I'm afraid so. I don't know what else we can do. It is not as if I wouldn't marry you legally. I can't. You know that."

"Johan. Living as man and wife without papers…"

"It's shameful for you. I know. But it is all I have to offer."

"More than shameful, it's dangerous. It's against the law. Whether we are married or not. I am a Jew, and you are an Aryan. Our being together is illegal."

"Yes, it is. We would have to change your name and have papers drawn up so that there would be no record of your being Jewish."

"Illegal papers, Johan. If we get caught, we will be in serious trouble."

"You don't realize it, Alina. Jews are already in trouble. I want to help you. Can't you see that?"

"Oh, I don't know. My family, my parents, they will be returning here to Berlin."

"And when they do, Lotti will contact us. I've given this a great deal of thought, and I truly feel that this is the safest thing for us, Alina."

"I'm afraid, Johan."

"I know." He was afraid. It was not like him to take risks, but the more he knew this strange, quiet girl, the better he liked her. Johan knew he was asking a lot of her. But their relationship would put him in just as much danger as it put her. And for some reason, he was willing to take the risk. Perhaps he was falling in love. So far, they had only shared a few kisses, and now he was suggesting that they move in together in a city a long way from her home. But what other choice was left to them? Until Johan had gotten to know Alina, he wasn't sure he ever wanted to marry anyone. But now, he felt differently. This girl was special. She was refined and gentle, but he sensed a strength beneath the surface that made her wildly intriguing. Her being Jewish put an air of mystery around her. Her full, wavy dark hair and eyes as black as a panther set his heart on fire and filled his body with a passion he'd never felt for another woman.

Would he, the man who had always been determined to stay a

bachelor without commitments and responsibilities, have married her if it was legal? It was hard to say because it was forbidden, and he didn't know what he would do if things were different. After spending his early life caring for his parents, the thought of being tied to anything or anyone repelled him. He knew what it felt like to be smothered and unable to break free. Johan's relationship with Alina was different than any he had with the Aryan girls he'd dated. It seemed to him that the others were always pushing him for a wedding ring. Not so with Alina. He wasn't sure if it was because a marriage between them would be illegal. Regardless of the reason, because she had never pressured him to make a commitment, he found he could relax when he was with her. This made him enjoy her company even more. It was nice not being put in the position to decide whether to marry or not. His relationship with Alina was dangerous. It was true. But, for Johan, it was easier than it would have been if he had to surrender his freedom unconditionally to an Aryan woman. He just wasn't sure he would be able to agree to promise himself to some girl for the rest of his life. But he knew for sure that if he were ever to consider pledging his heart to any woman, it would be Alina.

When Johan and Alina presented their plan for the future to Lotti and Lev, Lotti was angry with Alina. She told Alina that she felt responsible for her and that Alina's parents would never approve of her moving in with Johan. However, Alina insisted that she wanted to attend the university, and it would have been impossible without Johan's help. That night, after Johan went home, Lotti went to Alina's room to talk to her.

"You surprise me," Lotti said, shaking her head. "Your parents will be so angry with me if I don't try to stop you from moving in with my brother. They will want to know how I could allow you to go so far away from here to live with a man who isn't your husband. What are you thinking, Alina?"

"I'm thinking that I am a Jew. Jews are not allowed to go to the University of Munich. I want to attend university, so what are my options?"

"And, Johan? You and Johan? I assume you would be lovers, living in sin? I am not a child, Alina. A man and woman cannot live together for long without that sort of thing happening. And I see how he looks at you. It is only a matter of time, and that is if it has not already happened."

"Nothing like that has happened between us. I promise you, Lotti. And the truth is that we would marry if we could. We've discussed it. But the laws forbid us from getting married. There is nothing left for us to do."

"So, you will live as husband and wife?"

"Yes. We will get married secretly. I know it won't be legal in the eyes of the law. But I don't know what to do. I care for Johan. He cares for me. I want to get an education. We cannot marry. What do you suggest?"

Lotti's shoulders slumped. "I wish you would have listened to me and not gotten involved with him. He's weak, Alina. He can't stand up to the Nazis. I know him better than you do."

"So you have told me."

"And? Why didn't you listen to me?"

"Because I want a future. I can't go to a university here in Berlin, so I am going to study in Munich."

"I don't know what I am going to tell your parents when they return."

"If they return," Alina said, her voice deep but hollow, sounding like an echo inside a cave.

Lotti shrugged her shoulders and shook her head. She had no answer.

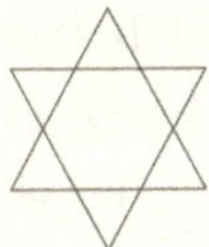

ten
Michal

1939

ON A BEAUTIFUL DAY IN JUNE, when the sun was shining and everything looked alive and green, Michal and the other prisoners were transferred to a camp outside of Berlin. It was a new structure that had just been built a month earlier. This was to be an all-women prison called Ravensbrück.

Michal had never been so horrified or humiliated as she was on the day when she first arrived at Ravensbrück. She was told to strip naked, and all the hair on her body was to be shaved... a delousing, they said. Michal's eyes grew wide; she could not bear to think of these people invading her private parts. When she looked around, the other prisoners had the same horrified looks on their faces. One of the women prisoners resisted. She refused to take off all of her clothes. A guard shot her in the face. Michal watched as the woman fell. Blood pooled around her, and her face was no longer recognizable. It was a mass of bloody tissue. Michal trembled at the sight, and then she took off her clothes. Most of the guards were women, many of them terribly mean. They were shouting, *"Schnell, Schnell." Just close off your mind,* Michal told herself. *Pretend you are not here.* But she could not help but look at the guards. When she did, she saw several male guards standing around and watching. Michal felt exposed and violated.

She stood in a line waiting to receive a white uniform with blue stripes, a white kerchief to wear over her head, and a fabric gold star with a black background that she was told to sew onto the left sleeve of her uniform. She dressed quickly. Then Michal was ushered into another line where she was given a small cube of soap, a bowl, a spoon, and a washcloth. One of the guards instructed the prisoners as to where they were to keep their belongings. They were taken over to a well-organized shelf, where each prisoner was allocated a space. Michal did as she was told, but bursts of anxiety kept her heart pumping, and she felt as if she might have a meltdown at any given moment. Before she was transferred to Ravensbrück prison, she deluded herself into believing that there was a chance she might be released. Her every thought was of her daughters and her sweet, tender Taavi. She prayed constantly, no matter what she was doing. A voice in her head was in constant conversation with God. She was pleading for the safety of her loved ones and for the day when she would be reunited with them. But now, here in this dungeon for forgotten souls, she began to doubt that she would ever see her family again. She knew she had to fight the feelings of being trapped and helpless, or she would go mad and start screaming, and then, for sure, she would be shot immediately.

The other prisoners were not all Jews. There were political prisoners, social outcasts like prostitutes and madams, gypsies, and homeless women. Then there were the Jehovah's Witnesses, who refused to be silenced. These Jehovah's Witnesses were a strong bunch. Even at the risk of death, they openly declared that Hitler was the anti-Christ. They refused to do any work that would help the Nazis in the war effort, and it broke Michal's heart to see how they were punished severely with the hardest work details. Still, they would not bend. Again and again, the guards gave them the opportunity to renounce their religion and swear allegiance to the Nazi Party, but they refused. Michal admired their strength. In the face of terrible beatings, they still remained faithful to their religion. Michal had to admit that if she had been given the opportunity to escape and go home, she would have said anything they wanted her to say.

Each prisoner was given a patch to wear on the sleeve of her uniform. The color of the patch was determined by the crime the Nazis had convicted her of. Jews wore the yellow Star of David; the gypsies and prostitutes wore black triangles; the political prisoners, red; Jehovah's Witness, purple; homosexuals, pink; and so on.

All Jews were separated from the other prisoners, and even if a Jewish woman was convicted of another crime, for instance, political treason, her Jewish heritage was always considered the most heinous of her crimes. And the most punishable.

Then, there were those who were known as the rabbits. These were poor young women in their twenties who were tortured and used for medical experimentation. Michal was not aware of them when she first arrived, but she would later learn of the horrors and inhumanity that these young girls suffered at the hands of Hitler's Third Reich doctors.

Michal was assigned to a bunk covered in wood chips, where she was surrounded by other women on either side. All wore the Gold Star, and all were Jews. Even the other prisoners in the camp, as bad as the Nazis thought they were, were not terrible enough to be subjected to sleep beside Jews.

eleven
Lotti and Lev

LOTTI'S generous heart and willingness to help others always seemed to result in gifts of gratitude from friends and neighbors. On a bright fall morning, an old woman who lived in the apartment above Lotti and Lev had been fortunate enough to acquire six eggs. Six eggs, a coveted fortune in Nazi Germany in 1939. She could have selfishly saved them for her husband and herself, but she remembered how Lotti had taken her on the bus all the way across town to see a doctor one afternoon when she was afraid she was not strong enough to go alone. It was over eight months earlier. The poor old woman had told Lotti of her condition. Someone had said that a doctor across town could help, but she was weak and ill and afraid to go so far on her own. Lotti had listened; she'd been kind and understanding. In fact, it had taken a full day of her time to take the woman, but Lotti had never complained. And so, on this autumn day, just a week after Britain and France had declared war on Germany, the old woman who lived upstairs knocked at Lotti's door. Lotti opened the door, and the woman handed her a small basket with a towel that covered two beautiful, clean white eggs. At first, Lotti tried to refuse. She didn't want to take the old woman's rations.

"You were so kind to me, Lotti. It gives me pleasure to share this with you. You must take it, for my sake," the old woman said.

Lotti hugged her and carefully placed the basket on the counter.

It certainly was a treasure.

Lotti had very little butter left from her rations. She managed to find enough to grease the pan as she prepared a surprise of scrambled eggs for Lev. He had been out looking for work again, as he did every day, against all possible odds. He had promised that he would be home before noon because he was building a chest of drawers for an old customer and wanted to finish it by the end of the day. It wasn't much work, so he hadn't charged much money. However, the little money he earned would certainly help. And they were both grateful for any job he was able to secure, regardless of how little it paid. Lotti could hardly contain the excitement she felt at being able to serve him such a rare treat for lunch. It had been long since she'd tasted eggs, and she would have loved to take a single bite. But she resisted. Instead, she saved them both for Lev.

It had been difficult for Lotti after the children from the orphanage left for England. Then Alina did the unthinkable by moving to Munich and moving in with her brother. As angry as she was at Alina, Lotti forgave her almost immediately. She loved her friend too much to hold any grudge.

Lev walked in just before noon, as he'd promised. He'd never broken a single promise in all the years that she and Lev had been married. She smiled when she thought of that. He kissed Lotti, then sat down at the kitchen table. Food had become so hard to come by because there was so little money. And with Lev not working, they had begun to trade their own furniture and anything else they had of value for anything edible. When Lev was able to find any wood, he'd create something that could be bartered and, once in a while, like today, sold. Lotti loved him. In his eyes, she saw the kindness of the man she had come to love. He was a few years older than she. And she knew that he had always wanted to give her a better life. At the beginning of their marriage and for a while after, he'd been able to do that. But now, things were hard.

"I have a surprise for you," she said, smiling.

"Oh? You know how much I love surprises." He winked at her. "So, tell me already," he said. He was always the optimist.

She carefully dished the eggs onto a plate and then added a heel of hard bread to the platter. Lotti poured Lev a cup of coffee made from acorns and served him the food.

"Where did you ever get eggs?" he asked.

"A present from Mrs. Slienberg upstairs."

"Very nice. Where did she get them?"

"I have no idea. I never asked. She probably got them on the black market somehow. Who knows. I don't like to pry," Lotti said.

"Nu, where is yours?" he asked.

"I ate mine already. I ate with Mrs. Slienberg. She wanted me to eat with her. I hope you're not angry?" Lotti lied. She knew he would never eat the eggs unless he thought she had already had some. If he knew the truth, he would have insisted she eat them.

"She brought enough for the two of you, and this for me too?" Lev said as one of his eyebrows lifted slightly

"Yes, she did." Lotti smiled at him.

"You're sure you ate?" he asked again.

"Lev, have I ever lied to you?" She had never lied unless the lie was something like this. "I told you that I had some earlier. I promise. Now, please eat before it gets cold."

Lotti watched as he savored every bite, and she got more joy from watching him savor the food than she would have gotten from eating. Instead of asking him about his job search, she decided to just sit quietly and take pleasure in his company.

Just as Lev finished his food, a loud knock came at the door.

"Gestapo, open the door," a harsh voice hollered.

Lotti felt her heart plummet. She looked at Lev. He dropped the fork that was dangling in his hand.

"Open the door!" the voice boomed again from outside.

"Hide!" Lotti said.

"Where?"

"I don't know. In the closet. Hurry."

He did what she said, but it was no use. They found him within minutes. "Glassman, you dirty Jewish pig! Is this your wife? A clean Aryan woman. You soiled her. You should know this is against the law!"

Lev didn't speak; he was more worried about Lotti than he was about himself. The man kicked him in the calf with the toe of his black leather boot. A sharp pain shot through Lev's leg and down through his foot, but he grabbed onto the wall and remained standing.

"And you, you're an Aryan." The Gestapo agent shook his head and glared at Lotti. "You should be ashamed of yourself. Did you lie with this Jew? Tell me you didn't. Tell me he forced you, and I will take him away and arrest him for rape."

"She didn't. I forced her. It's not her fault. Nothing is her fault," Lev said. The Gestapo agent hit Lev across the face, and blood spurted on the agent's black leather coat. Lotti gasped and ran to her husband.

"Stay away from him. You've done enough damage to yourself." The agent turned to the other Gestapo agents who'd come with him and said, "Take him!"

The two men in long black leather coats grabbed Lev's arms and pushed him down the stairs. Lotti ran to the window. She saw the Nazis push her husband into the back of a black automobile. He hit his head. Lotti felt the pain that Lev must have felt shoot through her. A small scream that no one heard escaped her lips. "Oh, Mein Gott," she cried. Lotti was shaking. As she ran through the kitchen, she looked down at the half-eaten plate of eggs and felt a gut-wrenching sadness. Tears rolled down her cheeks. Her heart was racing with fear. She couldn't feel the danger to herself as an Aryan woman who had broken the law. All she could feel was that she was losing Lev. Lotti tripped and fell, skinning her knee as she ran down the wooden stairs of the apartment building. She was crying out loudly so he could hear. "Lev, Lev, I am here waiting for you. I love you. Please come back. Lev…" She got to her feet and rushed outside. The Nazis were getting into the car. She was just in time to see Lev turn his head to look at her. It was just a brief moment. Lev's eyes caught Lotti's.

He tried to muster a smile as if to say he was alright. She knew he was trying to protect her. But he couldn't. The car began to pull away. Lev blew her a single kiss, and then he was gone. Lotti fell to her knees on the side of the road and leaned against a tree. Then she wept.

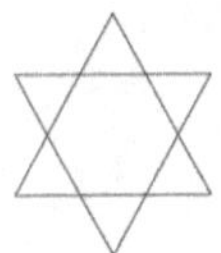

twelve
Lev

LEV WAS TAKEN to the local police station. His crime was considered especially vile. He'd dared to spoil an Aryan woman by marrying her. The men surrounding him at the station were young, strong, and armed. Lev was over forty, thin, and had not eaten well in a long time. He knew they planned to hurt him, and all the way to the station, he'd been afraid. But now, as they circled him like a pack of hyenas coming in for the kill, he was no longer afraid. A light went on inside of him, and he felt the presence of God. The Nazis were yelling at him, damning him, but he could not hear what they were saying. All he could hear was a voice that told him he would be all right. "Take care of my Lotti," Lev told the voice. Someone struck him. The pain rushed through him like a lightning bolt. Then the voice in his head returned. "I'll watch over Lotti," it said, and the pain disappeared. Again, they struck him. He heard himself cry out. Then, the tender voice was once again in his mind. It said, "Lotti will be all right. Surrender to them, Lev, you cannot fight this. Fighting will only prolong the pain. Lotti will be with you soon enough." The voice in his mind was clear, and it drowned out the voices of the Nazis. Lev saw the Gestapo agent point the gun at his head. He gasped. "Hold my hand," the voice of spirit said, and Lev felt the warmth of God beside him.

He never heard or felt the bullet enter his brain.

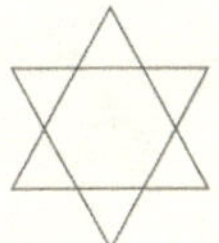

thirteen

Alina

JOHAN HELPED Alina move her things into the small apartment that he rented. It was within walking distance of the University of Munich. He'd made sure that out of respect, Alina would have her own bedroom, as did he, but they shared a kitchen and a bathroom with the rest of the students who lived in the building. Alina registered at the university with false papers that Johan had paid someone with his late mother's pearl ring to prepare. The papers said that she was a Christian, and she and Johan were siblings. Alina had protested at first when Johan told her that he was planning to sell the piece of jewelry, and he'd promised that he wouldn't. But he hadn't kept the promise. Instead, he'd given her the papers upon her arrival and insisted she use them. Alina's new name was Adelheid Strombeck. "You shouldn't have sold that ring, Johan. It was your mother's," she said.

"Yes, but you will need papers to survive. It was necessary, and besides, I have other things of my mother's to keep as memories. So, please don't even think about it."

"Adelheid?"

Johan laughed. "Yes."

"Oh, Johan, I don't know what to say. I feel like I owe you so much.

Why did you do all of this? Why did you sell your things and put yourself in danger for me?"

"Because I knew you wanted to go to university. You couldn't go as Alina Margolis, could you? Now you don't have to wear the yellow star on your sleeve or live in fear anymore."

"Johan, Johan…" She hesitated, choked up. "And you did this for me?" she said, shaking her head.

"Of course."

"Johan…" she whispered his name again.

He smiled. "I wanted to give you the opportunity to fulfill your dreams, Alina. But now that we are at war, I am very concerned about the future, even here in Munich. You see, I was sent away for a time when I was twenty-three. I don't know if you were aware of the RAD, the Reich's Labour Service."

"I heard something about it, but I really don't know much."

"It was terrible. Hitler wanted to put everybody to work, but it was backbreaking work. The government sent me off to various farms to dig ditches. In exchange, I received a little money to spend, some food, and a place to sleep. I had to go away for six months of training. And then I had to live in a military camp and wear a uniform."

"Was it the army?"

"It was a sort of prelude. I served six months and came home to find my parents both very ill."

"That had to be terrible. I mean, to come home and see them both sick."

"Yes, it was. They needed care. I felt responsible. In fact, it was in many ways like a weight that I carried around with me all the time."

"Were you planning to join the army?"

"Me, no." He smiled. "I'm not that brave, I guess. So, the answer is no. I would not voluntarily join the army. But, now that the country is at war, I am afraid I may be called up."

"And you would have to go?"

"Yes, probably I would."

She looked at him. "I know where this conversation is going. You think we should get out of Germany?"

He scratched his head. "Well, actually, that is what I wanted to talk to you about. I know you want to further your education, and I want that for you, too. In fact, I had every intention of finding work while you attended classes. But Germany is a dangerous place for both of us right now, and it seems to be getting worse every day. I worry for you because if, for some reason, the man who forged your papers is ever caught, I have no doubt he will give you up. After all, forging papers is punishable by death. I know him well, that is why he was willing to take the risk for me. But if he were tortured, I am sure he would turn us in."

"I am sure he is your friend, but the ring didn't hurt," she said.

"Yes, that is true. The ring and even a little cash helped to convince him. But I understand how much he had to risk. Still, he is not the kind of man who would keep a secret to protect his integrity. And, truth be told, how could I blame him? So, even though you have the papers, every day you spend here in Germany is unsafe. And as a man, for me, the war changes everything. I could be called up to fight at any time. If I were taken away and you were all alone here, I don't know if you would be safe. There is so much to consider. I realize this may sound cowardly to you, but yes, I think we should try to get out of Germany. Would you go with me? I mean, if I can find a way for us to get out? You have papers now. If God willing, the papers pass, and we are out of Germany, we will be free of Hitler…"

"My family, Johan? I can't even contact my sister anymore. I sent her letters, but they came back unopened. Germany is at war with Britain. Of course, no mail can get through. Still, I try. Once we leave, how will we stay in touch with Lotti and Lev? When my parents return, they will go to Lotti and Lev before anyone else. That is how I will find them again. My sister, too. As soon as she can come back, she will go to them. We can't lose touch with Lotti and Lev. What do you suggest we do?"

"Letters. We will stay in touch with my sister through letters. Perhaps we will have a code so that when the Nazis censor our mail, they will not know what we are asking. I mean, we will have double meanings for everything that we write, meanings that only Lotti and Lev will understand. What do you think?"

"Oh, Johan, my life is a disaster. I don't want to play spy. I just want my family back. I feel that I've lost everyone and everything I know and love."

"You haven't lost me."

"No."

"But you don't love me," he said.

"I don't know. I have so many mixed emotions. Part of me is terrified of love. After all, our lives are so fragile right now. It's hard enough just to stay alive."

"Yes, you're right. They are very fragile, and that is why love is so important. But on a more practical note, if we want to stay alive, then we should get the hell out of Germany. I suppose my sister told you I am a coward. She was right. I don't like to fight. In fact, when I was a boy, and someone would pick a fight with me, I would run away. I am not proud of it. I was picked on and bullied, but Alina—Adelheid, I suppose I should get used to calling you Adelheid—I hate pain, I hate violence, and I am not a hero. But I care for you and want to protect you if I can. But I can't do that here in Germany. I can't face the Nazi Party and fight them the way Lotti and Lev are trying to do. And yes, you have papers now, which makes things a little better. But sometimes, I lie in bed and think that when we wake up in the morning, we will not know if someone has betrayed us. Every day, we walk a tightrope. Every minute of every day, I live with the fear that we might both be murdered or arrested. Or I will be drafted and sent to fight. I can't bear the uncertainty. I am ashamed. But I am not the man I wish I was."

"Johan," she whispered his name. His eyes were glassed over with unshed tears. "It's alright. You have already proven to me that you are a hero. You risked your life to have these papers made for me. You are living with a Jewish woman. That takes courage."

He kissed her gently. "I wish I could marry you and make you love me. I know that if things were different in the world, I could do it. I could love you enough to make you love me back," he said, and he was beginning to believe it was true.

If he had the chance, maybe he would give up his freedom for this woman with a background so different from his.

"Oh, Johan. I can't say that I won't ever return your love or even that I don't love you now. All I can say is that I am so lost and confused. I am far too confused to know my own true feelings. Do you understand? Can you understand?"

"Of course. Of course, I understand."

"Johan, where would we go? If we can get out, where would we go?"

"I don't know yet. I will look into it. I want to get as far away from here as we can."

"Oh Johan, my family…"

He took her hand and led her to the sofa. "Sit down. There is something you should know."

She sat beside him, wrinkling the skirt of her dress in her fist as she listened. "Go on, please, tell me."

"I didn't want to tell you this. I didn't know if I should. I wanted to whisk you away without telling you anything bad. But I suppose I have to. It's only right."

"Johan? What is it? Is it my parents?"

"Lev has been arrested. Lotti called last night. She was in hysterics. She is planning to join some crazy group of Gentile women who are married to Jewish men. They are going to protest and try to get their husbands released. She'll probably get herself killed. And, God knows what will happen to Lev."

"I have to go to her. Lotti is my best friend. She needs me. Lev has been like a brother to me. I can't go anywhere except back to Berlin right now."

Johan took her small shoulders in his hands and turned her so he could look deeply into her eyes. "You can't go anywhere near Lotti. You shouldn't even call her. Who knows, the Gestapo might be tracing calls. Lotti is putting herself in the spotlight. I told her she was making a big mistake, but she won't listen. Plenty of Gentiles are being arrested. She is not safe. Even though she says she doesn't care, the truth is that she is risking her life. She said she would fight for Lev no matter what. If they arrest or kill her, then so be it, she says. Lotti said she would not stop until they released her husband. You are Jewish. Yes, you have papers, which is a good thing, but some people in Berlin still know who you are. There is a reward for reporting Jews who are involved in relationships with Gentiles. No one is safe. Your old friends and neighbors can no longer be trusted. Believe me, if we went back to Berlin to see Lotti, someone would turn you in, and the Gestapo would pick you up in a matter of hours. You might go to prison or even be murdered on the spot. I care too much for you, Alina. Just do as I say. We need to get out of Germany as quickly as possible."

Her hands were cold and shaking. Johan took them in his, then held the palms up to his lips and kissed them. "Please, Alina."

"Johan, you might as well tell me. I am sure you have somewhere in mind for us to go, or you wouldn't have brought this up. Please just tell me what you have in mind."

"You know me so well. Yes, I do have somewhere in mind. It's far, Alina, very far. And that's another thing I wanted to talk to you about."

"Go on…"

He cleared his throat. "I have found a sponsor, someone who will sponsor us to get into America."

"What?" Her voice was shrill. "That's the other side of the world. My family is here. Lotti and Lev are here. When Lev is free, he will go back home to Lotti."

"Yes, that is if he is ever freed. My sister is a fighter. Who knows where that will lead her? I can't say. For her sake, I hope it doesn't get her killed. But I know Lotti, and I can't stop her. She's always been headstrong. She'll take on the entire Nazi Party regardless of the consequences."

"How can we go away and leave everyone and everything we know? America, for God's sake? We don't know the language. Johan? Besides, it will cost a lot of money to live in America."

Johan pursed his lips. "We'll manage. We have to. This is dire, Alina. If we stay in Germany, we might not live through this. Besides, I have the money," he said, his voice soft.

Alina cocked her head and looked at him, a question in her eyes. "You do? Where did you get it?"

"There are things you don't know about me, Alina. Things that even Lotti doesn't know."

"And do you plan to tell me?"

"Not now. It will only complicate things. I will tell you when we get to America."

"Johan, that's not fair. You want me to leave my home, the only home I have ever known, and you are going to keep secrets from me? I have so many questions, Johan. Who is our sponsor? How did you find a sponsor to get us into the United States? And where did you get all of this money? If you don't tell me, I won't go."

"Alina, please, just this once, don't ask questions, just do as I ask. I'll tell you everything when we get out of Germany. For right now, just please trust me. The less you know, the better."

She wrapped her arms around her chest and shook her head. "I don't know what to do. What if Gilde needs me? It would be hard enough to get to Britain from here."

"You wouldn't be able to get to Gilde anyway. You can't get into Britain. We are at war with them. Do you think that they are just going to let you in? Don't be a fool, Alina. Besides, if you did have to get to Britain, you'd have a far better chance of getting there from America than from Germany. Come with me. We'll come back here to Germany after the war. It can't last long. Once it's over, it will be safe for us to be here. Then we can find your sister, my sister, Lev, and your parents. Right now, the best thing to do is to get the hell out of Germany while we can. We are very lucky to have this opportunity to leave. Many people would give everything they own to get out."

"But what if Gilde needs me? What if she writes to me asking for my help? I won't be able to help her. What about my mother and father? What will happen when they come back and I am not there?

They won't know what to do or where to find me." Alina felt her shoulders slump; she knew he was right. All of her questions and concerns were meaningless. The truth was that she and Johan were powerless, caught in the winds of a tornado that was growing larger every day. There was nothing they could do for their loved ones, and every moment they stayed in Germany, they risked their own lives. If she had any hope of survival or any dreams of living long enough to go to a university, she must get out of Germany.

He walked over to her and put his arms around her. Johan didn't want to share his thoughts with Alina because he didn't want to scare her. But he wasn't sure Alina's family would ever return safely. For all they both knew, her entire family might already have perished. He was sure that deep in her heart, Alina had wondered the same thing. But she wanted to believe they would all be fine and someday reunited by some miracle, and he didn't want to strip that hope away from her. Yet, he knew without question that there was no time to lose. As soon as they were able, they must leave Germany. Gently, he patted her back, trying to soothe her. "Alina, come with me. Please," he said.

▭

She shook her head as if she could somehow shake out the confusion. "This is madness. Moving in with you was difficult enough. I can't believe this is really happening to me. I can't make sense of it. It feels like a nightmare, and I can't wake up. I don't know where my parents are. My sister is growing up without me. And now I am living with a man who is not my husband. All of this was hard enough to swallow, but now you want me to go with you to America? To America, Johan. I don't know how I will get along in that foreign country. I don't speak English. It is English that they speak, isn't it?"

"Yes, it is. I want to take you with me to safety. We'll learn the language together. I'll work hard, and we'll be safe. We'll get married. Legally. I'll make you happy. And we'll only stay there until after the war is over. Then we'll come home. Please, Alina."

"We'll come home if Hitler is defeated. If not?"

"If not, we will thank God we're not here in Germany."

"I don't know. I don't know what to do."

"Alina, there is no choice. You are not safe here. That's all there is to it. Now, look at me. Look into my eyes." She did as he asked. "I love you." His voice was hoarse. "This is the only way. You have to believe me."

His eyes were wet with tears, and she knew he was right.

"As soon as you say the word, I will make all the arrangements. I want to get this thing started because we will have to wait until our visas come through. It will take time. And, the sooner we can go, the better."

"Are we going to tell Lev and Lotti?"

"We can't tell anyone. Not yet. It's too dangerous. Just tell me that you will go with me? I need a promise from you now so I can take care of the details."

Alina shrugged her shoulders and shook her head. "I don't know what to do."

"Alina, my sweet, innocent Alina, I wish I had some magic to make all this disappear, but I don't. And all I can say is this might be the only way that we can survive this madness." He took her in his arms and gently kissed her. "I wish I could tell you to take your time, think it over, and decide, but we don't have much time. I need to know by morning."

She felt tears well up in her eyes. If she went with Johan, she would leave Germany and all her connections to everyone she loved. But, if she stayed, Johan would be drafted, and then she'd be alone. All alone, praying every day that her true identity would not be discovered in Munich. That by some random act of chance, she might not be recognized. Because lying and hiding her Jewish background would mean certain death.

Johan gently brushed the hair from her eyes and ran his fingers softly down her cheek. "I love you, Alina. That's not something I would say to just anyone. In fact, I've never said it before in my life. I promise you that I will do everything I can to take care of you. Come with me to America," he said, and every time he realized that he meant it, the realization shocked him. Johan was in love.

Her shoulders dropped, and she felt herself surrendering to his arms. He kissed her again and then led her to his bedroom.

She was trembling so hard that she felt she might fall down. Johan helped her to sit down on the bed. "I would marry you right now if I could. If the law would allow us to marry."

"I know," she said. Her voice was small. She was confused. She liked Johan well enough but hadn't had time to know if she truly loved him. There was no doubt that she was dependent upon him. Without him, she was a Jew alone in a hostile country.

"I want to make love to you," he said. "Do you want me to?"

She looked directly at him. "I think so."

Johan believed that if he could seduce her, he might be able to make her fall in love with him.

"Johan…"

"Yes, my love?"

Alina cleared her throat. "I'm a virgin."

"I know," he said. "I will never lose respect for you. And I swear you will be my wife as soon as we are in America. Do you believe me?"

She nodded, but her eyes stung with the tears she was holding back. This was not the way her first time was supposed to be.

"Do you trust me?" he asked.

"Yes, Johan. I do."

She was shy as Johan removed her clothing. But he was gentle and considerate, and once it was over, she felt close enough to him to do what she knew she must do. Leave the country.

Her voice was barely above a whisper in the darkness as she lay naked in his arms. "I'll go with you," she said.

"And will you marry me as soon as we get to America?"

"Yes."

After Alina fell asleep, Johan got out of bed and poured himself a glass of water. He gazed out the window and thought about all the secrets he kept from everyone, even Alina. But what could he do? He had no other choice. Things were going downhill fast in Germany. If he stayed, he'd be sucked into the army, and only God knows what would happen to Alina. Given the circumstances, he was doing the best thing for them both.

fourteen

Taavi

WHEN TAAVI MARRIED MICHAL, he'd been the kind of man who kept to himself. He'd adored her from the first time he saw her, but opening up and understanding her had been a slow process. And as Taavi came to know and trust his wife, he'd opened his heart and almost all the secrets inside to her. Almost. The only secret he'd kept to himself was the one that shamed him the most. He'd never told her the whole truth about his parents. His father had sworn him to secrecy as a boy. He'd made Taavi promise never to tell anyone about his mother's illness. "If anyone finds out about your mother, they will look at you as if you, too, have the same problem. You will never be accepted. You will spend your life on the outskirts of society. People will say that if your mother was insane, then you must have some of her insanity in your blood," his father would tell him. And Taavi believed.

As a child, Taavi was sometimes afraid of his mother. She would descend into fits of madness; sometimes, she would throw things or scream and cry. Other times, she would lie in bed, refusing to eat or speak to anyone for several days. When Taavi was just a child, he would watch her through the door of her room, wishing he could crawl into her bed, lie beside her, and make things better. But his father warned him that when he was at work, Taavi was to stay away from his mother. "She cannot be trusted, Tavala," his father said, calling him by his pet name. "She would not hurt you on purpose. But sometimes, she doesn't know what she's doing. It's best to stay in your room when I am not home," Taavi's father said. Then, when Taavi got a little older and could understand, his father told him that his mother had lost her mind following a miscarriage a year after Taavi was born. His father explained that she'd had a miscarriage and lost a baby in the eighth month of her pregnancy, right on the kitchen floor. The child was another boy. He was born dead. His mother blamed herself because the night before the miscarriage, she and Taavi's father had been arguing. During the argument, she'd said that she was sick and tired of being pregnant and uncomfortable. She'd blamed Taavi's father for not only her discomfort but for ruining her figure. She'd been an undeniable beauty in her youth, sought after by many men. Taavi's father had gone to see his mother's father to offer a proposal.

Without her father's approval, the marriage would not have taken place. It was an intense moment for Taavi's father. But then his future father-in-law agreed. And Taavi's father had been elated. He'd married the prettiest girl in the village. But with her beauty came selfishness and vanity. After giving birth to Taavi, she'd declared she didn't want any more children. And so when she got pregnant again, she was depressed and angry. The fight ensued, followed by the miscarriage. Taavi's mother was sure she had brought the wrath of God upon herself for being so ungrateful for his blessing.

She'd bled profusely and almost died. But it wasn't until Taavi was much older and his father was very ill and knew he was dying that his father finally told him what had caused his mother's insanity.

"I knew the day would come when I would have to tell you the truth," his father said. "You deserve to know. She was your mother, after all." His father had been coughing up blood and grew more tired every day. "I am dying, Taavi. Before I go, I must tell you."

He explained that his mother had been having an affair with a young farmhand who lived about a mile from their house. "I knew it. Believe me, in a village as small as ours, news travels. People told me.

You know how people can be. They are always ready to stick their nose where it doesn't belong. Yes, I knew. But I loved her, and you were so young. I didn't want to leave her. I didn't want to break up our family. I felt that a child your age needed his mother. So I looked the other way. The baby she lost could have been his, her lover's child, I mean. But she blamed me. I know this because when she was unconscious as she was recovering, she would awaken sometimes and be delirious. She cried out in anger, cursing me sometimes. Other times, she begged God to forgive her for her sins.

"After she miscarried, I thought it best to move to another village, someplace where no one knew us. Believe me, that was not easy. I had land that had to be sold, and I didn't get what it was worth because people knew why we were leaving. Still, I did it for you. I wanted you to have a chance to live without the stigma of your mother's madness."

Taavi could still remember his mother. After the miscarriage, as the years passed, Taavi's mother got worse. She would rage and strike Taavi or strike out at his father. Her behavior became dangerously unpredictable. When Taavi was eight, his father took him as an apprentice. He was too young to learn carpentry. But his father decided it was best for Taavi for two reasons: he enjoyed his son's company and wanted to keep the boy away from his mother. However, being alone in the small cottage didn't help his mother's condition; in fact, it only worsened. One evening, Taavi and his father came home from work to find that she'd destroyed all of their clothing. Another time, she had severely burned both of her arms, crying out that she'd done so to drive the devil out of her. The burns blistered, and the blisters turned red and oozed pus. Taavi's father had gently cleaned and covered the open wounds with bandages. He told Taavi that he feared they would become infected, but they didn't. If they had, she would have died. And, perhaps, it would have been best. However, she healed.

When Taavi was fourteen, he was already a full and capable carpenter. His father had taught him well, and he'd become even better at the trade than his father. Taavi was an artist; his work quickly became known throughout the village. His relationship with his father was close, but his mother was like a strange animal to him.

One evening, when father and son returned from work, his mother was in the kitchen. Her eyes were wild with madness as she cried out, pointing at Taavi, "I know who you are. You are a dybbuk," and she came at him with a large kitchen knife. Sweat trickled down his forehead. How was he ever going to take the knife away from her? With wild, uncombed hair and darting eyes, she came at him. The knife in her hand caught his arm, and he felt the blade slice through his flesh. He backed up, terrified, as the blood spilled on the floor. Just then, his father walked in and saw the situation. There was little time. His father charged his mother, who was very strong when she was under the control of her disease. She cut him across the cheek. His father grabbed for the knife. Things happened so fast. Taavi knew his father never meant to hurt her. He was only trying to take the knife away, but somehow, it ended up piercing his mother's neck. She gasped, choking on blood as Taavi's father ran to find help. But when the doctor arrived, it was too late.

Taavi's father could not speak. There was no doubt in Taavi's mind that his father had loved his mother. For three days, Taavi's father did not leave his bedroom. Taavi asked through the door if he could get him anything. But his father always said no. If they were to keep their clientele, the business must remain open. So, Taavi went to work to complete their jobs, and when he returned home on the fourth night and asked his father if he could get him anything, his father came out of the room. He looked like he'd aged twenty years. He was never the same and only lived a few months more before he passed away. When Taavi's father died, Taavi was heavy with grief. He would miss his father greatly. However, although he was still just a boy, Taavi was self-sufficient. He kept the business open and managed the house by himself. All was well for many years until he'd fallen head over heels so deeply in love with Michal that he couldn't see straight. The first time he saw her, Taavi was looking out the window of his shop, and she was walking down the street doing her shopping. Michal was on her way to one of the other stores. Their eyes had met, and for the first time, Taavi understood how love could obsess a person. He thought about Michal day and night. Watched for her through the window of his shop. When he saw her, he felt electrified. Then, as was the custom, her parents chose a husband for her, and she married Avram. The whole village knew about the wedding. So, of course, his customers told him the gossip. Taavi was heartbroken. At that point in time, he resigned himself to a life of solitude. But then, an unexpected turn of events had brought him the woman of his heart. It had been a tragedy for the village but a godsend for Taavi.

Early one winter morning, the Cossacks had come. They were wild men on horseback galloping through the small Jewish settlement. They attacked the little village, raping, pillaging, and killing so many of the Jews. During the assault, Avram, Michal's husband, had been murdered. Taavi saw it happen. He would have helped Avram even though he had never stopped loving Michal. But it all happened so fast that all he could do was grab Michal's arm and pull her along with him until they were deep into the forest. They stayed there with an old wise woman for a while, and his love for Michal grew. Finally, she agreed to become his wife. He'd been euphoric. But their marriage had been hard because of all she'd been through. Taavi didn't know how to communicate with women. He had very little experience, and his mother had not given him much of a role model. It took him time. In the beginning, he was young and prideful but clumsy and awkward. So, he and Michal had their problems. After numerous fights, a painful separation, and a great deal of suffering, they found their way back to each other. And for several years after they reunited, their lives had been joyous. The happiest of days for Taavi. He worked hard, and his business flourished. He had his wonderful wife and two beautiful daughters. Then came the terrible night of the broken glass, and everything changed when the Nazis had taken him prisoner.

Because Taavi had never had a real family before he'd married Michal, and they'd had their two girls, he treasured his family even more than he could have ever dreamed he would. Now, stuck in this Nazi concentration camp, all he could think about was his wife and children. They needed him. That was why he'd called on Frieda. He'd

worked for her as the bartender in her cabaret before the rise of the
Third Reich. During that time, he and Michal were having problems,
and they'd been separated. Those were the years of Taavi's life when
he'd lost all sense of morals and lived an existence of pure debauchery.
Frieda had seduced him, and the two became lovers. Once the bar
closed, he and Frieda spent hours experimenting with all aspects of
depravity, from sexual perversity to drugs. When Taavi reflected on
his years with Frieda, he forgave his wild explorations by telling
himself it was just a sign of the times. And it was. Weimar Berlin was
exploding in every way. The arts and sciences had flourished, but so
had sexual exploration, drugs, and excessive use of alcohol, and Taavi
had been swept up into it like so many others. Frieda's cabaret was a
hot spot, giving her access to friendships with all sorts of people.
Before the war, their regulars consisted of artists, scientists, writers,
and leaders of all different political factions.

But since the Nazis came into power, Taavi assumed that the
people who patronized the club were different. Now, he thought the
club was probably a popular hangout for the upper echelon of the
Nazi Party. Because of the club, Taavi thought she probably still had
influential friends, and if she could find it in her heart to forgive him,
she might have the power to help him. The question was not if she
could but if she would. He'd walked out the door, leaving her angry
and rejected. Now, she was his only hope. Taavi took a deep breath.
What could he do? He'd made the proposal to Braus. It was in God's
hands now. Several weeks had passed since he'd made the proposition, and so far, he'd heard nothing. He couldn't even be sure that
Braus had sent word to Frieda, but he was counting on Braus's greed.
If Frieda came through, he had promised Braus that she would reward
him generously. He hoped he was right because if he wasn't, Taavi had
no doubt that Braus would kill him. *Dear God*, he thought. *I have
sinned many times. But for the sake of my wife and children, I am begging
for your forgiveness.*

More time passed, and Braus still had not sent for Taavi. Most
days, when Taavi returned hot and exhausted from the brickworks, he
would see Braus sitting in his office. Sometimes, Braus would look

out the window, and their eyes would meet. Then Braus's face slowly descends into a sinister smile, and Taavi feels a terrible tingling, like tiny spiders crawling up the back of his neck.

One afternoon, while the prisoners were out on work duty, Fredrick whispered something to one of the other prisoners. A guard saw him and felt he was talking instead of working. Then, as punishment, the guard beat Fredrick severely. The beating was so bad this time that Taavi was afraid his friend would die. Fredrick could hardly stand. Even though Taavi had worked hard for sixteen hours that day, he had little appetite. The possible loss of his only friend weighed on him. He could bear the hard work and the lack of food, but he was devastated by the very idea that he had no power to help Fredrick. None.

The men lined up for their dinner. Taavi followed the rest of the men into the food line. He received his ladle of what passed for soup and the moldy bread and sat down to eat. His head ached from the strenuous work in the scorching sun without enough water to drink. Now, he gulped the soup down, not paying much attention to the insects that floated alongside the quarter of soggy potato. Poor Fredrick. He was young and such an idealist. Taavi had once been young and believed he could change the world single-handedly. He'd not been political, but he believed he could build a decent life for his family by working hard. Now he realized that being a Jew, his chances of overcoming the dangers of anti-Semitism and living a comfortable life were nearly impossible. After all, he'd been a fairly successful businessman. It had taken him years of saving and then hard work to build that carpentry shop. However, when the Nazis decided to wage their pogrom on his people, they destroyed his entire world in one night. And even though he'd been a respected member of society, at the end of the day, they would always see him as just another Jew. They broke him down, beat him, and threw him into this dreadful hell hole. They had no respect for him as a contributing citizen of Berlin. To them, like to the Cossacks and the White Russians that he'd lived amongst in his youth, Taavi was nothing but a Jew. And Jews had no rights. Taavi knew that Jews would always be second-class citizens;

no matter what, they were always at the mercy of the rest of the world.

Even though Taavi was worried about Fredrick, he was so exhausted that he fell asleep instantly as soon as he lay down that night. The work was so strenuous that as soon as he relaxed, he could not stay awake even if he wanted to.

In the middle of the night, someone pulled on his foot. Taavi opened his eyes. It was Braus.

"Come with me," Braus whispered.

Taavi got up and followed.

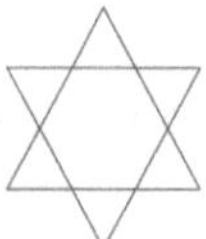

fifteen
Michal

MICHAL DID as she was told, but a vacant look was in her eyes as if a part of her was not there anymore. There was a constant lump in her throat, and she began to believe that she would never see her family again. The guards at Ravensbrück were women, but they were relentless in their brutality. To the non-Jewish prisoners, they were harsh and mean, but to the Jews, they were evil spirits who walked the earth. Michal was no stranger to anti-Semitism, but she had a hard time believing that women could be so hard and uncaring to other women. Some of the guards were mothers. How could a mother, who had borne a child and known the love that only a mother can feel, be so heartless? The female prisoners were tortured sometimes just to the point of death. Other times, they were brutally murdered outright. At one point, Michal had a glimmer of hope. Two of the Jewish prisoners were released. But then, the following day, as Michal was standing in roll call, she witnessed a guard murder a young girl who had been unable to make her bed to the standards that had been set at Ravensbrück.

Michal was no stranger to horror. She'd witnessed the brutality in the Cossacks and the Nazis, but they were men. Women had the gift from God to bear children, and Michal had always believed that having that gift made them kinder and more sensitive. That was before she met the guards at Ravensbrück. Most of these women were heartless; they could easily overlook the pain and suffering of others. In fact, Michal believed that some of them even enjoyed the power. It made her sick to see women act like beasts. The guards lived in quarters away from the camp. Michal had not been there, but some of the other prisoners had been sent to the guards' house to do the cleaning, and they returned, telling the others that the guards lived in lovely surroundings. The prisoners who'd worked at the guards' living quarters said that when the guards were home away from the camp, the women were just like other women. They discussed the men in their lives, husbands, boyfriends, and dates, talked about fashion, and shared recipes. Yet as soon as these same women walked through the gates of Ravensbrück, they turned into monsters. It was unfathomable.

There was always discussion of ways and plans for escape between the prisoners. They would whisper about plans as they lay on their bunks in their block at night. But the truth was that the camp was surrounded by barbed wire. Escape was nearly impossible.

The guards found a new pastime that winter. For their entertainment, they sent some of the women outside and then sprayed the poor souls with water. The women were underdressed as it was, and the water froze the thin uniforms to their shivering bodies. From the warmth of the building, the guards watched as the women froze to death.

And at night, there was no heat where the prisoners slept. The women found warmth only from curling up against the cold.

Some women were not strong enough to endure the physical labor that the guards demanded of them daily. Those women were shot immediately. The Jews worked seven days every week. Other prisoners had Sundays off, but not Michal. It was a brutal winter that year, and all she had were open clogs for shoes. Every night, her feet bled from the exposure to the harsh elements, and she lost two toes from frostbite.

Food was scarce. Sometimes, prisoners, driven by the madness of hunger, would try to steal a bit of bread. If they were caught, they were tortured and made an example for the rest of the prisoners lest anyone think they could get away with such a crime. Most days, the women only received a hunk of bread and water in the morning. Occasionally, on very good days, they got a bowl of watery soup after they finished work.

Michal began to feel weak and defeated. Between the hunger, the cold, the beatings, and the hard work, she lost her will to live and began to pray for death. Then, one afternoon, a rain fell that turned to ice as it hit the ground. Michal was attempting to shovel sand off of a prisoner who had been buried during a cruel game one of the guards was playing to entertain herself. Michal was a small, slender woman, and it was difficult for her to move the sand. She was almost in tears from the effort when a woman she had never noticed before came to help her. Her name, she said, was Heida. She was a tall, strong woman with an athletic build that had thinned out from lack of food. Still, her height gave her an arresting appearance. If someone else had come to help Michal dig the prisoner out, the helper probably would have been punished. But Heida's height and confidence seemed to intimidate the guard, and for that moment, the guard left her alone.

"Let me help you." Heida smiled. She grabbed a shovel, and what had been nearly impossible for Michal seemed easy for Heida. She moved the shovel quickly to reach the prisoner before the poor woman suffocated. When the prisoner's head was unburied, the poor woman began coughing fiercely. It was such a haggard cough that Michal thought it sounded like the sand had gotten into her lungs.

Another guard, a woman as tall as Heida but much heavier, walked over from the other side of the yard. She was carrying a club, which she used to smack Heida on the shoulder.

"Come on, get back to work."

Michal heard the loud thud that the club had made when it found its mark on Heida's body, and she cringed at the pain that must have caused, but Heida just smiled and winked at Michal. Then she turned and went back to the other side of the yard to her own work. It looked to Michal like Heida was mocking the guard. Michal was astonished at Heida's fearlessness. And when Michal glanced at the guard's face, she saw a hint of admiration.

Michal was amazed. She was sure from the crack the club had made that the guard had broken a bone, but Heida seemed fine. How was that possible? Michal decided Heida was probably in pain, but Heida wouldn't give the guard the satisfaction of knowing she'd injured her.

Heida wore a pink triangle on the arm of her uniform, and from that, Michal knew Heida was a lesbian. She didn't want to lead Heida on. So she decided to tell Heida right away that she was a mother with a husband somewhere outside of this pit in hell.

Later that night, Michal found Heida.

"Thank you for helping me today."

Heida nodded.

"How is your shoulder?"

"It hurts."

"Do you think any bones are broken?"

"I don't think so."

"That was very brave of you."

"Brave? We all have to help each other. Otherwise, none of us will survive this. You want to know who's brave? Look at that young blond girl over there. She can't be more than four foot eleven, and I'd say she weighs about eighty pounds. Wouldn't you say?"

"Yes, I think you're right." Michal looked at the girl. She'd grown accustomed to looking at the felt patch on the arms of the other women so that she knew if they were Jewish or had been accused of some other imaginary crime. This one's patch was light purple.

"She's a Jehovah's Witness," Heida said as if she'd read Michal's mind. "That's another religion that Hitler has decided to persecute, but not nearly as badly as the Jews. It's amazing just how much hate these Nazis can have, huh? Have you seen how they treat the Polish women? What amazes me is that some of the guards are such young girls. Where did they find the anger inside of them to be so heartless? It boggles the mind. No? But never mind about them. Anyway, back to what I was telling you about that little girl over there, the Jehovah's

Witness. She's so young and delicate. She is barely a woman, but she has the courage of ten men. You know what I saw?"

"What?"

"One of the guards told her that if she would denounce her religion and accept Hitler as God, she would be released from this pit."

"Really?"

"Yes, and you know what? She refused. She said that Hitler was the anti-Christ. She had the courage to say that to the guard. I was stunned. I was sure the guard would kill her. But surprisingly, she didn't."

"I'm Jewish. I don't know what that means. The anti-Christ…"

"It's a long story, but in essence, it means that Hitler's no God, he's pure evil, the devil."

"That's for sure. Nobody here could argue that fact. Did the guard hit her?"

"Of course. But she still refused to accept Hitler as her God. Do you know who the guard was? It was Dorothea, the monster. I'm sure you know her."

"Yes," Michal said. "I know her. I wish I didn't."

"Well, this Dorothea is some bitch. She did more than hit the kid. She beat the hell out of her. From what I understand, Dorothea is supposed to be some great beauty. There is gossip that she is very popular with the male SS. They all want her. It's amazing that she is so pretty on the outside, but her heart is like a rotting tomato full of worms. She's a true sadist. The things I have seen her do would just make you want to vomit. But, anyway, you must give that little Jehovah's Witness girl credit," Heida said, shaking her head and smiling. "She's a tough little thing. I don't know if she'll survive this place, I doubt it, but she earned my admiration that day."

"I don't want to hurt your feelings, and I want you to know that I appreciate your help, but I, well, I have something that I have to tell you. Now, before our friendship becomes too deep, and maybe you'll be expecting something from me that I can't give you," Michal said.

"You are not a homosexual?" Heida said, and she laughed. "I didn't think so. I am not looking for a lover, although sometimes I feel that the comfort of love in this place would be a Godsend. Although love does make you very vulnerable. That's for sure. But, believe me, I am not looking for anything like that with you. You needed help. I knew I could help. No strings attached. Just friends. We both need a friend."

Michal smiled. She liked Heida. She liked her a lot. The woman had character integrity. In this dungeon, Michal watched as so many women lost their humanity. They turned on their friends for many things, for bits of bread that were used as rewards or to avoid a beating. How could she blame them? They were starving, and not many of them were brave. They were just average women, alone, hungry, and terrified. In fact, except for the political prisoners who had strong convictions, many of them were just mothers. Some of the women even had their children with them at the camp. Those were the most vulnerable because they would rather die or sacrifice anyone to protect their child. Michal couldn't blame them. She thanked God every day that Alina and Gilde were not in this terrible place with her. Although she missed them every day and worried about them constantly, Michal would have done anything, anything at all, to keep her daughters from harm, even if it meant being separated from them. But she was concerned about them even more because she had no way of knowing if they were safe. Strangely, the exhausting work was so taxing that it was the only thing that kept her from going completely insane.

Because at the very few moments when she slowed down, like during a meal, she immediately felt bolts of fear shoot through her. The bolts were as piercing as any bullet. She was terrified of what might have happened to her husband and daughters while she was locked up and could not help them. It seemed like when she was working and sweating and struggling to stay alive, even though she would have welcomed death, there was something inside of her that made her take that next breath. But at least during those moments of unbelievable labor, she was so immersed in the pain of the moment that she temporarily forgot to feel the terror. And any physical agony was far better than the insane horror of constant worry. The continuous not knowing, the maddening questions that could not be answered. The truth was that she had no idea whether those she loved were alive or dead.

From the first day they met, Heida befriended Michal. Michal assumed that Heida could see how weak she was and probably pitied her. Michal didn't care. She could accept the pity if it meant she had a friend, someone she could trust and talk to. Michal knew Heida was different than anyone. Often, she was fearless and reckless. She sometimes stole food from the kitchen and usually stood up to the guards, enduring beatings without even wincing. Michal assumed that the guards had not killed Heida because they were fascinated by her spirit. Not only was Heida a fighter, but she was also generous with the food she stole. She forced Michal to accept extra food and warned her not to give up on living.

"If you don't keep believing that you will get out of here someday, you will die here for sure. Every day, you must remind yourself that the time will come when you will be free again," Heida said.

"I can't believe that. I feel as if I am spiraling down a dark hole, and in the end, it is only death," Michal said.

"Self-pity is dangerous. It will swallow you up, and you will drown in it. I am telling you this because I've seen it happen to many people."

Michal shook her head. "I know you're right."

"Look at the people in here who are in worse shape than you are. Some of them are sick. Others have children to protect. You know, there is a very young woman in the other block who is in serious trouble. She looks to me to be about eighteen years old. She's a political prisoner, and she is nine months pregnant. Because she's been starving, her stomach is small, but if the guards find out she's going to have a baby, God only knows what they'll do. She'll have the baby any day now, and there is no one here to help her. She'll have to somehow manage on her own. Then, if she doesn't die in childbirth, how will she care for a baby in this place? Babies cry, especially if you leave them alone all day. And it would be impossible for her to take the child to work with her. So, you see, Michal, you may think you have it bad. Someone else always has it worse. Try to remember that."

Michal looked up at Heida. "I can help her."

"Help who?"

"The girl. The young girl who is about to give birth. I worked as a midwife. I can help with the delivery."

Heida's eyes lit up. "You can help? That's wonderful. I never suspected that you were a midwife."

"Yes, I can help. But how will I get over to her to examine her?"

"Later tonight, I will come and take you to her. This is dangerous for you. Are you sure you want to do it?"

"Yes," Michal said. "I'm sure. I need something to make living feel worthwhile. At least this will give me a purpose. Right now, I want to give up. I am afraid I will never see my husband or my children again. If I can help this poor girl, I will feel I have a reason to go on."

"Stop that right now. Stop thinking about dying, Michal. Once the Nazis conquer your spirit, you are as good as dead. If you let this happen, it will only be a matter of time before you are dead. I know how hard it is, but you must keep believing that someday you will be free."

Michal nodded. "I hope so. The Nazis have imprisoned us here without cause, so it's hard to believe that they will ever release us. The only reason we are in this jail is because they hate us. If we were accused of real crimes, I might believe that someday, if we were found innocent, we would be released. But the only crime I have committed is being born a Jew. And for that, I believe they will never release me."

Heida pulled at her sleeve and indicated the pink triangle sewn on it.

"I am not ashamed that I am a lesbian. Somewhere out in the world is a woman who is very dear to me. I pray every day that she is safe and far away from a place like this. But I don't know. The most terrible part of being here is not knowing if those you love are safe."

Michal looked down at the ground. "Yes, I know. I worry about my family every day."

"People don't understand the love I have for my friend. But believe me, it is no different than the love you share with your husband. We are like an old married couple." Heida smiled a sad smile. "I miss her every day. Still, even though I would give up my life to see her even one more time. I pray that she is far away from here, even if it means I will never see her again."

"Are you afraid of dying?" Michal asked. Then, in a small voice, she added, "Sometimes I am. And then other times, I wish I could just die and leave this nightmare behind me."

"Afraid? Yes, only because none of us knows what happens when we die. But I am even more afraid of losing my will to fight. I hate Hitler. I hate everything the Nazi Party stands for.

"And I hope I can endure whatever these bastards put us through and somehow survive to tell the story of what happened here."

"You are so strong. I am not."

"You're stronger than you think," Heida said, looking around. It was perilous to be caught loitering. "We should go before we are caught here talking. I will come and get you later tonight so that you can see what you can do to help that poor young pregnant girl."

Heida started to walk away.

"Heida," Michal said. Heida turned around, and their eyes met. "Thank you."

"For what?"

"For giving me strength."

Heida nodded and turned the corner at the end of the building.

Michal stood alone for a minute. She knew that any second, the bell would ring for roll call. But the words Heida had spoken sparked a tiny flicker of light, a flicker of hope inside of her, and she began to let herself believe that by some miracle, she might get out of Ravensbrück alive.

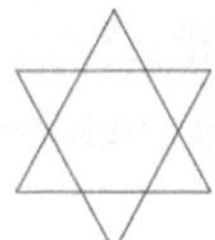

sixteen
Alina

1941

THE LARGE SHIP Alina and Johan boarded had a logo with 'Red Line' written across its side. They knew their voyage was not to be a luxury trip by any means. Immigration to America had slowed considerably over the last several years; in fact, it had almost come to a halt. The passengers on board this ship were lucky to be getting into the United States. Johan and Alina were directed deep into the belly of the boat in the area known as third class or steerage. The hot, stale air hung heavy over the crowded main room filled with poor and wretched souls. Souls who'd sacrificed everything they had to escape from Europe. The sanitation facilities weren't equipped for the many passengers on the boat, so they didn't work well. This lack of proper sanitation left the ship filthy with sewage and urine. Some of the passengers were ill, and they coughed loud, wet, wrenching coughs all night long. It was the middle of summer before Johan and Alina left Germany. The heat and the smell onboard the ship were overwhelming. The winds kicked up as the vessel left the harbor in Bremen, and the ocean liner rocked and teetered on mountains of white-capped waves. The motion of the water, mingled with the foul odors of the ship, made Alina ill. She gagged and vomited into a bucket. As she did, the smell of the contents of the refuse in the bucket wafted up, slapping her in the face and causing her to retch uncontrollably. Johan held her as she threw up bile.

"Shhh. Calm down. It's going to be all right. Here, lie down," he said once he'd found an open room with a bunk bed. Johan led Alina into the room, but he hadn't had a chance to close the door before a young girl walked by.

"Someone told me that bed that you're lying on over there is full of lice," the pretty young redheaded girl said, pointing to the cot just as Alina was about to lie down. "Come on over here," the girl said. She helped Alina and Johan find another cabin.

Alina plopped down on a bunk that was more like a hard piece of wood than a bed and held her face in her hands.

Johan sat down beside her. He felt so helpless. What could he do? They could have stayed in second class if he had more money. That would probably have been better. But he'd spent everything he had on the visas, the papers to get in, and the passage. But most of all, he'd compromised everything he believed. He'd done something for Alina that he swore he would never do. He contacted the only man he knew in America, Trevor Powell. Johan begged him. And then Johan threatened him, which forced Trevor to finally agree to act as a sponsor for Johan and Alina. Powell was a man he hated, who he'd kept buried like a bitter secret since he'd found out about him. Trevor Powell was his birth father. Johan had believed that the man who raised him was his father for years. Then, on her deathbed, his mother had cleared her conscience and told him the truth. She told Johan that he was born out of wedlock, the son of an American who abandoned them. Johan had no desire to make contact with his birth father when he got to America. The letter he'd received from his father was enough. Even now, that letter was burning like acid in his pocket. No, he would not ever contact his birth father. Once they got to America, he would do whatever he had to do to take care of Alina without Powell's help. He'd work sixteen-hour days if need be, but he would never go to that man.

"Lie down, my love. Try to rest," Johan said.

He was right, Alina thought. She felt a little better lying down. Her stomach was still sick, and the weaving of the ship didn't help, but at least she didn't have to worry about falling over as the boat tossed her way through the perilous seas.

Alina overheard two passengers talking in one of the other bunks in her room as she lay there. They were saying that this boat was not nearly as crowded as the boats were in the early part of the century. America had all but closed its doors to immigrants due to the country being in the throes of a depression. A depression. The very word struck fear in Alina. Laying on a cot as hard as a concrete floor, Alina's mind drifted back to her past. She vaguely remembered a time when she was young, and she and her mother were separated from her father during a depression in Germany. She only remembered some details, not all. But she remembered that things got hard after her mother lost her job as a nanny for a wealthy family. Her mother had taken her to eat at soup kitchens. Even now, Alina remembered they were horrible places with bad smells and dejected and often sick people. She only remembered bits and pieces, but she knew that the dire circumstances had been a big part of the reason her mother had gone to see her father, even though they were separated. It had turned out to be the best thing that could have happened to the family. Her parents had reunited, and together, they'd built a family.

A good family, a family she longed for now and missed terribly. Her sister, Gilde, had been born, and although she should have been jealous of her sibling, Alina had felt just the opposite. She'd adored Gilde from the moment that Gilde was born. In fact, as soon as Alina had a sister, she no longer cared for her dolls. Everything in her world was about mothering Gilde. God, she missed her sister. Alina said a silent prayer that conditions would not be as bad in America as she remembered them as being in Germany during that depression. She held fast to Johan's arm. Every day, her life became more and more uncertain. Johan was all she had left from her life in Germany. Alina nuzzled her head into his shoulder. And finally, exhaustion overtook her, and she drifted off to sleep.

seventeen

Alina

WHEN SHE WOKE UP, Alina found Johan still asleep beside her. Two male passengers in the main room were arguing loudly about theft. One of the men was accusing the other of taking his shoes.

It had been a rough day at sea. The evening meal was being served very late. It was close to nine p.m., and everyone was gathered in the shabby steerage class lounge. Johan felt Alina's movement in the bed beside him and stirred awake. He stretched for a moment. Then whispered, "Come on, sweetheart." Johan was groggy, but logic kicked in quickly. "If we don't hurry, there might not be any food left."

Alina rose from the cot. Her back ached, and she had no appetite; in fact, she was having a hard time keeping her stomach steady. As they searched for a place at the table, the two men who had been and still were arguing began fist-fighting. Everyone tried to get out of their way, but the room was crowded. They pushed each other into tables, turning them over. Johan pulled Alina close to him to get her out of harm's way and instinctively put his hand over the back of her head to protect her. She was shaky from the waves of the boat, and she almost fell. Johan quickly maneuvered Alina around the side of him, holding her up and putting himself between Alina and the two men fighting. There were too many people crowded into the small dining area for Alina and Johan to get out. They were boxed in by the crowd. Johan was trying to push Alina through the crowd to the back of the room and away from the fighters. Just then, one of the men pulled a knife out of the belt of his pants, where he had been hiding it beneath his worn cotton jacket. At first, everything was happening so fast that it seemed unreal. It was so surreal that instead of being afraid, Alina wondered how the man who was fighting could bear to be wearing a jacket. The third-class area of the boat was so dreadfully hot.

"Come on, you son of a bitch. I am going to teach you a good lesson today," the man with the knife said. He was a massive mountain of a man with hair the color of fire and a long, thick beard to match. The exploding volcano of his voice brought Alina back to reality, and she jumped. Johan held her close to him. The red-haired man's opponent was a small, dark, rat-like little fellow who moved as fluidly and quickly as a black mamba. The men were moving all over the room in a circle. Their eyes were glued to each other. The crowd did what they could to get out of the way. Some of the women screamed when the fighters got too close to them. Johan tried to put himself between Alina and the fighters.

Some of the other male passengers had begun to take sides. They were waging bets with each other and egging the two men on. Over the last ten minutes, the storm that the boat had been battling all day kicked up, and the ship rocked even more violently in the waves. Johan had now put both arms out to the sides, giving Alina even more protection in case one of the fighters tripped or fell. She tried to stay on her feet, but the ship was unsteady, so she curled into Johan's body like a child.

"You'll be all right," Johan whispered to Alina, never taking his eyes from the fighters. He knew that a good many of the passengers had been drinking. And from the way the man with the red beard was swaying, Johan had a feeling that the man was drunk.

The red-haired man with the knife ran at his opponent, but the rat-like fellow was too quick.

"Stop this right now!" A woman with a thick waist and blond wavy hair bounded up to the flame-haired man. "I have had it with you. Stop this before someone gets hurt."

"Shut up, and keep out of the way. This doesn't concern you."

"I am your wife. And as long as you are my husband, it does concern me." The woman grabbed onto his sleeve. He flung her off of him just as the ship hit a wave, and she fell, sliding across the ship floor into the crowd of passengers. When she hit them, several people fell down like bowling pins.

Now, in the chaos, someone had handed the rat-faced man a knife to even up the odds, and the rat was slithering in a macabre dance as the steel of the blade glittered in the small overhead light.

Again, the big man rushed his opponent, and again, the other escaped just as the heavyset man thrust his knife forward. The boat hit another heaving wave that sent the mountain man falling backward. Johan was standing right behind him. It was too late to get out of the way. Besides, there were people on all sides of Johan. But at least Alina was behind him. As the big, bearded fighter tried to regain his balance, his knife sliced Johan's arm. It was just deep enough to cut through Johan's shirt and break the skin of his upper arm. The blood seeped through slowly. But nobody noticed because as soon as the large man lost his balance, the rat was upon him, thrusting his knife into the big man's neck. Blood spurted from the red-haired man's wound. Women screamed. The man's wife raced to his side. Blood was oozing from his lips. Alina felt like she might faint, so she looked away. The big, bearded man was on the floor, his life pouring out all around him. Alina touched Johan's arm, and it was then that she realized he was bleeding.

"You're hurt," she said. She'd been so absorbed in the terror of the fight that she hadn't realized what had happened to Johan.

"I'm all right," he said. "It's just a small cut."

"Roll up your sleeve, and let me take a look at it."

Johan did as Alina asked. It was not a deep cut; it didn't need to be stitched. But Alina needed help. There were far more men on the boat than women, and until now, Alina had tried to keep a low profile. She was young and pretty, and she knew that the less attention she had attracted to herself, the better. But right now, she ignored her safety and walked over to one of the men sitting at the table in the corner, not paying much attention to the commotion. He was drinking something from a bottle in a brown paper bag. Alina assumed it was alcohol.

"Where are you going? What are you doing?" Johan said, shocked, but Alina didn't turn around. Instead, she pulled all of her inner strength and walked over to the man.

"Excuse me," she said with as much courage as she could muster. "Excuse me, but my husband has been hurt. Please." She cleared her throat. "Please, is that alcohol?"

"Certainly is. It's whisky."

"Can I have just enough to wet this piece of cloth?" Alina said, taking the sleeve of her blouse between her teeth and ripping it. She handed him the fabric. "Please?"

A smile crept over his face. "You are a pretty one, all right," he said. "I suppose I could do that for you," he added, wetting the white piece of cotton from Alina's shirt.

Alina smelled the alcohol as she took the torn piece off her sleeve. "Thank you so much," she said.

He smiled and nodded and then winked. Alina ignored the wink. She tried to pretend she didn't see the brazen act of flirtation. Instead, she just turned and walked back to Johan.

"You shouldn't talk to strange men, Alina. I thought I told you that before we got on board," Johan said.

"Yes, I know, but for right now, just let me clean this wound," she said gently, wiping the blood that was still oozing from the cut.

"Ahh, that burns," he said, grimacing.

She gently blew on the open wound.

He smiled at her. "You know, you're unlike any woman I've ever known. Sometimes, I am so surprised at how strong you are. And I love you."

She smiled back at him. Then she ripped the sleeve on the other side of her blouse and wrapped it around his cut, making a bandage.

"You amaze me. Do you know that?" Johan asked.

"I amaze myself." Alina laughed. "I've always been squeamish at the sight of blood. Even when I worked for a doctor years ago, I'd feel a little lightheaded when I saw a lot of blood."

"Thank you," he said and touched her face. Then he gently kissed her.

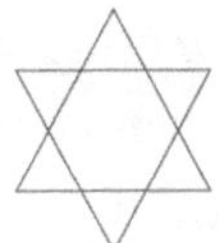

eighteen

Taavi

"GET IN HERE, MARGOLIS." Braus pushed Taavi in the back with his gun. Taavi would have liked to have turned around and taken that gun away from Braus. He had no doubt that he was strong enough to overpower the small guard, who was nothing without his gun. It would be easy to take the weapon away and turn it on him. How much would Taavi enjoy the look on the Nazi idiot's face right before he shot him? But he couldn't, for two reasons. One, he knew that if a shot was fired, more guards with guns would arrive, and he would eventually be overpowered. But the second was even more important. Braus's greed could very well be his ticket out of this miserable place. Taavi gritted his teeth to control his anger. Then he walked quickly as Braus continued to nudge him with the gun into his small office.

Braus closed the door, keeping his eyes and weapon fixed on Taavi. When Taavi looked closely at Braus, he thought he detected just a hint of fear in the Nazi's eyes. Taavi decided that Braus was well aware that, at any moment, Taavi could kill him. That was why Braus never kept his finger far from the trigger of his firearm. Now, the *Block-führer* sat down and placed the gun in front of him on the desk. He still had it pointed at Taavi. With a wicked smile, he leaned back in his chair, his finger playing with the trigger of the gun. Taavi felt a bead of sweat form at his brow, and he hoped Braus didn't see it. The bastard had something to tell him. But what? This meeting could go well, or it could be a catastrophe. Either way, Taavi was fairly sure there was news about Frieda. If she refused to help him, Braus, the sadistic bastard, was probably toying with him and would kill him when he got tired of the game. Taavi studied Braus's eyes, waiting for him to speak. But Braus was enjoying watching Taavi squirm. Taavi wouldn't give him the satisfaction. He held his head up and his eyes straight forward, looking directly at Braus until the guard had to turn away.

Taavi began to think that maybe this wasn't about Frieda. It could be about Fredrick. Poor Fredrick. The harder that poor man fought back, the more pleasure the guards found in torturing him. And Braus knew that Fredrick was Taavi's friend. It would be just like this son of a bitch to get him out of his bed just to tell him that they'd done something terrible to Fredrick. Braus would have gotten such pleasure from seeing the agony it caused Taavi to see his friend hurt. If Fredrick was dead, it would come as no surprise. Taavi knew that they would eventually kill Fredrick, but for now, they had fun looking for new ways to make every hour of Fredrick's life a living hell. Still, the silence continued. Somewhere outside, the leaves on a tree rustled, but Braus did not speak. It was all Taavi could do not to attack him and tear him to pieces. The waiting was pure agony.

Taavi tried to read Braus's face. Should he even allow himself to believe that after the way he'd left Frieda high and dry, she would still find enough compassion in her heart to help him? Braus's face told him that Braus was happy with what he was about to say. The *Block-führer* lit a cigarette and cleared his throat. Then he hesitated, smiling, his jowls jiggling as he pulled a long puff of smoke deep into his lungs. It was obvious that he was enjoying the power he held over Taavi. Taavi tried to stay disconnected and in control of himself, but his hands trembled, and his legs shook. The words that this guard spoke within the next half hour could very well determine whether he would see his beloved wife and children again.

Several minutes that felt like hours passed before Braus finally opened his mouth and spoke.

"You were right, Margolis. I can extort money from your friend, Frieda Altendorf. She still owns a thriving nightclub. I sent someone to talk to her, to tell her where you are. Believe it or not, she is foolish enough to be willing to pay for your freedom. Why? Who knows, women are such fools, so easily manipulated. But, I must say I was surprised that such a successful woman would be willing to help a Jew. Now, this is a stupid woman. But it makes no difference to me. In fact, I must admit, I am quite pleased with the outcome of the meeting with this Altendorf woman. She was willing to pay a hefty price to keep you safe, Margolis. It looks like you're worth more to me alive than dead. Who would have thought anyone would care about the life of one Jew? Anyway, I told her that I would deliver you to her. She was quite pleased. She knows she will have to keep paying me monthly to keep me from coming back and arresting you again. And, if she is unhappy with you for some reason and she stops paying, you can be sure you will find yourself right back here. Maybe if that happens, I will make sure that things will get even worse for you. So, you'd better behave like the dog you are for this woman. Once this Frieda Altendorf gets your ass out of here, she owns you."

Taavi couldn't believe his good luck. Frieda, God bless Frieda. As difficult and hard as she was, her underbelly was soft, and there was a kindness in her that he would repay. He would be grateful to her for the rest of his life.

"Go back to your bunk. Tomorrow night, I will come and take you out of here with my auto. Get out now. You're stinking up my office. Why are you Jews so damned filthy? You all stink!"

Taavi walked to the door of his block. He turned to see that Braus was standing in the doorway of his office building watching him, the gun pointed at Taavi. Did that stupid guard think that Taavi would run now? Now that freedom was so close? Did Braus really think Taavi would risk death to escape?

Taavi lay down on his bunk. Soon, he would hold his wife in his arms. If he closed his eyes, he could feel the softness of her skin and smell the freshness of her hair. Michal. It would be a matter of days before he would hear the joy in Gilde's laughter that he'd missed so much or look into Alina's eyes and hear her soft voice telling him all about her day at work. Taavi thought about having a drink with his dear old friend and business partner, Lev. It had probably been hard for Lev to run the business alone for over a year. Well, he would make that right. As soon as he got back, he would give Lev some time off to spend with his wife, Lotti, just relaxing. Yes, he would do that. And Frieda? What could he do for Frieda? He knew that she loved him. He was sorry that he'd hurt her when he left; he was even sorrier now. Taavi had never wanted to hurt Frieda; things had just happened that way. How was he going to make them right? Taavi took a deep breath. He would figure it out once he was free of the confines of this prison. For now, he preferred to bask in thinking about the joy that awaited him just outside the barbed wire.

Finally, exhaustion overcame him, and even in excitement, Taavi fell asleep. The morning roll call sounded, and he rushed outside. He must lie low and do nothing that might alter his good fortune. All day, he worked at the brickworks, working even harder than usual so as not to attract the attention of the guards. In his mind, a nagging voice kept saying, "Be careful; don't let yourself hope too much. You know how the Nazis love to give the prisoners hope and then take it away. It's more painful that way. Try to keep a level head." But as much as he reminded himself of the possibility that all of this was just another hoax, that Braus was only toying with him, he couldn't help but feel almost giddy. If he dared to believe that this miracle could actually be true. If Frieda really had agreed to pay for his freedom, this nightmare was almost over. He knew he had one more difficult hurdle to jump. He had to explain everything to Frieda. The pride of his youth was no longer an issue. To make Frieda understand his gratitude, he would get down on his knees and thank her. If only she would accept that alone. But he was afraid that she would not. In exchange for his freedom, she might want things back as they were when she was his lover. And he wasn't sure how he was going to make her understand. Once he was given over to Frieda, she held his life in her hands. He longed to believe she loved him enough to let him go home to his family. But did she? Did she really? *Dear God, help me. I am so close to the time when I can finally return home and hold Michal in my arms.* He knew better than to dream. Dreams were dangerous in a concentration camp. But he couldn't help himself. What if Frieda had done this out of pure kindness? What if, by some miracle, she decided to just let him go? Just like that? What if he could make her understand? She had a big heart sometimes. He remembered how she gave food to the homeless. Taavi would never forget this kindness, and somehow, he would find a way to pay back all the money it cost her. These things he promised to God as he prayed for his freedom. *Dear God, please send me back to my wife and children.* Taavi prayed silently over and over that entire day. How good it would feel to be home. And this small glimmer of hope was enough to make the bricks at the brickworks lighter, to make the hunger in his belly subside, to transform him from a walking dead man into a man who thanked God every few minutes for the wonderful blessing of life.

nineteen

FRIEDA WAS SITTING at the bar in the empty cabaret smoking a cigarette when Taavi was brought in to her by a Nazi in uniform. It was past closing time, and all the customers and employees had left. She'd kept the room dark. The only light was from the moon, the streetlights outside, and the tip of her cigarette. This was the agreement she had made with Braus. Night was more private than day. Taavi was to be delivered in the dark of night. In the past, when Taavi had worked at her club, she was known to have a style. She always wore men's suits in the Marlene Dietrich fashion, but today, she wore a long black gown. It had been years since she'd last seen Taavi, but her feelings for him, a mixture of love and hate, were still as strong. And she wanted to look stunning when he saw her again. There was no doubt in her mind that Taavi had managed her club better than anyone she'd ever hired before or since, and possibly even better than she herself had. But more than that, he'd kept her intrigued. In fact, she'd never stopped wanting him. Even as he had walked out on her all those years ago, she'd longed to run after him and throw herself into his arms. But when that stubborn Jew made up his mind, there was no talking to him. Taavi. He was a jerk, a cad, an ingrate, and sadly, he was desperately in love with his wife. But he was the most intense, incredible lover Frieda had ever had, and there had been many, both men and women.

"Here he is." The guard pushed Taavi with the butt of his rifle towards Frieda. She nodded and handed the Nazi an envelope filled with money as she agreed upon with Braus.

Then the Nazi guard left, and Frieda and Taavi were alone. For a few minutes, there was an awkward silence.

"You look terrible," she said. "So skinny and dirty, and I hate to say it, but you smell."

"Yes, I know. And you know I was in a prison camp."

"So I hear. And you had your guard; what was his name, *Block-führer* Braus? Wasn't that his name? You had him get in contact with me, didn't you?"

Taavi nodded, wishing he had never been forced to take this action. He could see that Frieda was gloating. How could he blame her? He didn't care that she was happy to have gotten the upper hand. But he just hoped that somehow he could convince her to let him go home. Quite honestly, he'd treated her badly and was willing to admit to it and beg for forgiveness if only she'd release him. She'd trusted him, given him a job, good pay, and a nice place to live, but as soon as Michal had come to him wanting him to come home, he'd left Frieda behind without a thought. Now, he needed her, and she knew it.

"Yes, Frieda. I had him contact you. You were the only person I knew with enough money and influence to help me."

"You were right. I have plenty of money and friends, too. The club has built quite a large clientele that is influential in the party. They like me. I buy them drinks." She put her cigarette out in a crystal ashtray. Then, she smiled at him. "Why don't you sit down? You look as if you might fall over."

He sat. "Thank you. Thank you for everything, Frieda," he said, clearing his throat. "I want you to know that I am sorry. I am sorry for everything I did. I should have at least given you some notice that I was leaving." He wished they could go into the back where he'd had an apartment when he worked for Frieda. Being in the front of the club, he was afraid. Someone might look through the window and see him.

He was so close to being free. But he dared not suggest it, or she might think he wanted to make love to her. She might misunderstand.

"At least, Taavi. At least some notice would have been nice. Besides treating me like shit, you had no respect for my business either."

His shoulders slumped. "I'm sorry, so sorry, Frieda," he said. What else could he say? Still, he didn't want to get back into the decadent life he'd once shared with Frieda. All he wanted was to go home to his wife and daughters. But how could he tell her that? How, after all she'd done for him. The words would not come. Taavi looked into Frieda's eyes, and he was certain that she wanted him back. He could no longer work for her as an employee because he was a Jew and would have to remain hidden, but he knew she wanted him to be her lover.

"I am trying to have papers drawn up for you that declare you to be a non-Jew. That way, you can work for me here at the club again," she said. It was as if she'd read his mind. "However, it could take time. It's very dangerous and very expensive," she said. He was right. She wanted everything back the way it was.

"And as for you and me, Taavi. I don't want you as a lover unless it is what you want. If I have to force you, then we have nothing." She stopped speaking, looked down at the table, and took another cigarette from her jeweled case. Next, she handed the matches to Taavi so he could light it for her. He did. She smiled. "If you don't want me, then I have nothing else to say."

What could he say? What could he do? He liked Frieda as a good friend. But he'd never loved her. His heart had always belonged to Michal. From the first time he'd seen Michal in Siberia, he'd known she was the one for him. Frieda was staring into his eyes, and he could feel her desperation. If he dared to tell her the truth, he was afraid she might feel scorned again and have him sent back to the camp.

"So, Taavi? So what's your answer?"

"I've missed you," he lied.

"Do you want me?"

"Give me time..." Taavi could hear the pleading in his voice, and the sound disgusted him.

"Time for what?" She glared, and he caught the look immediately. He had to be very careful.

"Time to heal. I am sick, Frieda. I am weak. I need food and a bath. I need rest."

"Of course. I didn't mean tonight. I meant, do you want me? Do you care for me? Are you coming back to me? Are you mine again?"

He felt his stomach turn over. "Yes," he lied again. "Yes."

"Then kiss me."

"As dirty as I am?" He was wearing old clothes given to him by one of Braus's men before he left. Braus didn't want him leaving in his uniform. It would have been too easy to spot him that way. He had not washed his face or body or brushed his teeth in months.

"Yes. I want you to kiss me."

"Are you sure?"

She nodded. Then she got up and walked over to Taavi. Frieda bent down so that she could be even with the chair where Taavi was sitting, and she kissed him full on the lips. Afterward, she took his chin in her hand and smiled. "You're quite right. You desperately need a bath."

twenty

AS HE LAY in the bathtub, Taavi felt the warm water caress his aching body. He'd spent so long ignoring the pain in his joints that now that the water had soothed his body, he realized how much he'd endured. Since there was no hurry, he languished in the warmth for a long time, lathering his hair and body with the clean fragrance of soap. Even as he scrubbed, the smell of the camp still lingered in his nose. He wondered if it would ever leave him or haunt him forever. Once the water had cooled beyond warmth, Taavi reluctantly rose to leave the bath. He looked at the pile of dirty clothes he'd thrown on the floor and was loath to put them back on his body. But he was afraid that if he left the bathroom wearing only a towel, Frieda would interpret that to mean that he wanted to make love to her. That was the last thing he wanted right now. It would be a betrayal to Michal, and it would also confuse Frieda so that when she learned the truth about his feelings towards her, she would be even more angry. Besides that, he didn't think his body was strong enough to perform. He picked up the dirty clothes from the floor. The odor in his nose grew stronger. If he could, he would burn those clothes and with them the horrible memories of his days in hell. For just a moment, he thought of Fredrick. His heart sank with pity, but there was nothing he could do for his friend. He was barely able to help himself. So, he put it out of his mind and got dressed.

When he came out, Frieda was waiting for him. She had some cold sausage and bread, even a sliced-up apple. And a large mug of dark beer.

"I'll have to go out and get you some clothes tomorrow. These absolutely stink. My God, Taavi. The smell is horrendous," she said. "Oh well. For now, sit down and eat. When you're finished, you'll get some rest."

He gobbled the food. It was impossible to eat slowly; he'd been so hungry for so long. At first, the food tasted wonderful. His taste buds exploded, and he felt almost ecstatic. But then his stomach lurched, and he ran to the bathroom and vomited.

"You ate too fast," she said from outside the bathroom. "That's all right. It's all right. Just relax, and you can try to eat again in a little while. I didn't realize how bad of a shape you were in. Next time, you'll eat a little more slowly. Yes?"

He didn't answer. He was ashamed. Taavi leaned his head against the cool tile of the bathroom wall. Frieda loved him. He had not understood just how much before. He knew it, but he had not realized the depth of her feelings until tonight. Or maybe he just didn't want to believe that she really loved him. He had chosen to think that all she felt towards him was lust and a broken ego. But seeing her tonight, how she had been so kind and sympathetic even as he stunk and vomited like a filthy animal, told him her feelings for him were more than her just wanting to win. She loved him. A terrible wave of guilt came over him because he knew he would leave her again, and he hated himself for being so callous. He was using her. He'd been forced to do it, but he was using her, nonetheless. Frieda was a good person. She had a good heart, and she didn't deserve this. He liked her, admired her too. But she was not the woman he loved. Taavi Margolis loved his wife.

"I'll let you rest," she said. "You've been through hell, from what I can see."

"Yes, it's been hell."

"I am not sure why you were arrested, but I won't question you tonight. I am glad you're here, Taavi. Get some sleep. Tomorrow, when you are stronger, we can talk more."

She had been sitting on the sofa, her arm spread across the top. Frieda stretched her back and got up to go. Taavi took a moment to really look at her. Although her features were too strong to be beautiful, she was a handsome woman. Her jaw was square and prominent, and her cheekbones were high and defined.

"When the fellow from the Gestapo approached me and told me that they had arrested you and put you into a concentration camp, I have to admit I was worried. I hated you for what you did to me, but I'll be damned if I wanted to see you die in some Nazi prison."

"Thank you, Frieda."

She nodded. "Taavi, you're a little skinny, but you're still one handsome devil. And, by the way, you're welcome." She gave a slight laugh and winked at him. There was sadness in her eyes. He could see that she felt bad for all of his suffering. Then she left quietly, closing the door behind her.

It had been a long time since Taavi had slept in a real bed. The pillow was so soft that he felt like he was drifting on a cloud. How strange it was. Once upon a time, many years ago, it seemed like a lifetime ago, he'd lived right here in this room. Then Taavi had taken this very bed and these same pillows for granted. *How strange.* Being in that camp had changed him. He was sure the change would last forever. There, in that manmade hell, the worth of his life had been reduced to less than that of an insect. And he had witnessed and endured the utmost suffering. Because of this, his appreciation of even the smallest things of beauty or comfort was so intense that they brought tears to his eyes.

He lay there for a few minutes, just taking in the pleasure of feeling a clean sheet under his bruised body. The warmth of a soft blanket covered his sore and calloused feet. His hands embraced the feather pillow that cradled his head. A tear of gratitude to God dripped down his cheek. Then he closed his eyes, and his thoughts drifted. He saw Michal's face in his mind as he fell into a deep, dreamless slumber.

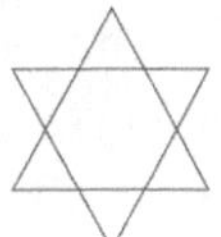

twenty-one

TAAVI WAS NOT sure how long he'd slept. It felt like minutes, but Frieda assured him it had been three days. She'd only awakened him, she said, because she was afraid he would starve to death.

He laughed softly. She had no idea how close he'd already come to starvation. Unless one had been subjected to the lack of food and water, it was hard to explain how little the human body needed to sustain life. For a moment, he wondered what her reaction would be if he told her he'd eaten insects. He decided not to tell her.

"It's good to have you back with me, Taavi. I don't like to admit it, but I have truly missed you."

He bit his lower lip. How would he ever make her understand that he cared for her deeply, but only as a friend? Frieda reached out and gently stroked his face with the tips of her fingers.

"You are a mess, my Taavi. But it's nothing that some good food and a little rest won't fix."

He nodded. "I don't know what to say, Frieda. I can't express the gratitude I feel towards you. You saved my life."

"As if I would not have come to your aid. Come on, Taavi. You must know that I had to remember what we shared. I couldn't leave you there. Tell me the truth. Did you ever doubt I would come through for you? Did you really doubt it? You had to know that no matter how angry I was with you, as soon as I found out what was going on, I would find a way to get you out of there."

"And you did, Frieda."

"Of course I did."

He took a deep breath. She deserved better than what he was about to give her. But how could he go on lying? And even worse, he would not escape at night and leave her without an explanation, like a coward. "Frieda," Taavi said, "you are my dear friend, and you've helped me get on my feet more than once. I owe you. I know that. But..."

"But? You don't owe me anything, Taavi. Just having you here is enough."

"Frieda." He got up and stretched his legs. Every bone and muscle in his body seemed to ache even more than when he'd first arrived. Or maybe the comfort had made him more aware of the pain. "I am so sorry, but I must go home to my family."

"Taavi? But you had the Nazis contact me. I thought you wanted to come back to me?"

"Oh God. What can I tell you? I never wanted to hurt you or to use you. But, you were my only chance for freedom. You were the only one who gave me even the slightest hope of getting out alive. I knew you had friends, influence, and money."

"Oh, Taavi." She rose and walked to the window, crossing her arms over her chest. They stood on opposite sides of the room, neither looking at the other.

"You could send me back to the camp if you wanted to. I know that. But I won't lie to you and make false promises. I care too much about you. You've been too good of a friend."

Her eyes flashed at him in anger. She glared at him for several moments. Then, her shoulders slumped. "Taavi, Taavi, Taavi, you did use me, I suppose. But, how can I blame you, eh? Yes, I still have feelings for you, like a fool. And this hurts me. But I believe you when you say you don't mean to hurt me. And I won't turn you in. I'll keep paying the blackmail to keep you safe. Go, go home to your wife. Stay hidden, Taavi. They think you're here with me. If they find you and your wife, who knows what will happen. Yeah?"

He nodded. "Thank you, Frieda. You have a big heart."

"Eh, I am getting soft in my old age. Get dressed and get out of here tonight as soon as it gets dark. And for God's sake, Taavi, be careful."

She allowed her eyes to cover him from head to toe as if she were memorizing every inch of his face and body. Then, in a very soft voice filled with pain and regret for a love and life that might have been, she whispered, "Goodbye, Taavi."

He nodded. "Goodbye, Frieda. I will never forget you."

"Wait," she said. Then she left the room but returned with a suit and a pair of shoes. "Take these. One of my lovers left them here. I saw them this morning. I guess he figured he might need them for the next time he stayed the night. I'll tell him they were stolen. He'll believe me. Anyway, change your clothes. There is no doubt you would be very conspicuous in those filthy clothes. There's a razor in the bathroom. Shave clean so you look like a businessman instead of an escaped prisoner."

Taavi looked at her.

"Well, you can't go wandering around the city looking like some kind of derelict, can you. The Gestapo would pick you up for that alone, right?"

He shook his head. "Oh, Frieda. You are a good person."

Frieda opened her mouth as if she wanted to say something, but instead, she shook her head, then turned and walked out, closing the door to the small apartment behind her nightclub and leaving Taavi alone.

twenty-two
Michal

IT HAD BEEN years since Michal had delivered a baby. Years. She'd learned to be a midwife from the old wise woman, Bepa, when she and Taavi hid in Bepa's small cottage deep in the forest after the Cossacks invaded her village. Taavi knew Bepa, and he brought her to the cottage. He told her that this was the only place that seemed remotely safe. And now, as Michal remembered her time in the woods, the fragrant smell of clean air, and the song of birds when spring arrived, it seemed like she and Taavi had been living in a haven. Especially compared to Ravensbrück.

Heida came to Michal's block that night. She put her finger to her lips and whispered, "Shhh," so Michal would not speak and awaken the others. Then Heida took Michal's hand and led her to where the young pregnant girl was waiting. Several times, Heida's eagle eye would spot a guard, and she'd pull Michal into a dark doorway. But finally, they arrived at their destination.

It was so dark that it was almost impossible to see. The guards had already turned off all the lights on the block, and it was a moonless night. It took several seconds for Michal's eyes to adjust, but when they did, she saw a young girl sitting quietly on a cot, waiting.

"Light a candle," Heida commanded to the crowd of women gathered around to see what was happening. The women all scrounged around until one brought out a tiny piece of a candle and lit it. Candles were hard to come by, and this small piece was a treasure. "Thank you," Heida said to the prisoner who'd shared her candle.

The woman nodded back.

"I'm Michal," Michal whispered to the pregnant girl, trying to make her voice as soft and comforting as possible. She knew how personal and embarrassing the exam she was about to perform would be, and she was trying to put the poor girl at ease.

"I'm Miriam."

"You are a Jew?" Michal asked.

The girl nodded. "The Nazis don't know it. Somehow, they just don't know. I'm here for being a communist. I suppose I'm lucky. It's worse if you're a Jew."

"I am a Jew," Michal said, gently touching the girl's hand. Miriam reminded Michal so much of her daughter, Alina, that she wanted to cry. "I am going to examine you. All right?"

The girl nodded.

Heida turned to the other prisoners and said, "Why don't we all go away and give them some privacy. Yes?"

One of the other prisoners said, "If she thinks she is going to keep a baby in here, she's crazy. It would bring trouble to the whole block. We'd all suffer because of her. I say we turn her in."

"We can't do that, that's inhumane. You know they'll kill her," another prisoner said.

It was hard to determine who was speaking in the darkness. Michal only heard the whispered arguments.

"I'm not going to put my own life at risk for a stranger, a girl who means nothing to me. Not only will we be punished if she's caught giving birth in here. But then what happens after that? Then what?"

"What do you mean, then what?"

The voices were all different. The prisoners were discussing Miriam and the dangers her predicament was bringing to all of them.

"Then there will be a baby in this block. The baby will cry, the guards will find it, and we'll all be punished for not turning her in.

The last thing we need is a screaming infant in here. Aren't things bad enough?"

"Oh, please don't say that, Marta, you're a mother too. How can you feel that way?"

"Shut up. We are all trying to survive. Things are not the same here as they were before. Now it is every person for themselves."

The women's voices grew louder as they became engrossed in the argument. Heida gave one of them a shove, then she said, "All of you. Be quiet. We aren't going to turn anyone in. You're all better than that. You aren't Nazis; don't act like them. Get out of the way so Michal can help this poor girl."

The others followed Heida as she herded them like a flock of sheep to sit on the other side of the block. All except for the one holding the single candle.

"Lie down," Michal told Miriam.

The girl did as Michal asked, and Michal began the examination. Miriam was built like a ten-year-old boy. She was small and slender, and even though she was almost ready to give birth, her breasts had hardly swelled. Michal had never done a delivery without Bepa's help. She whispered a silent prayer that Miriam went into labor at night because if she went into hard labor during the day, the guards would probably shoot her on the spot. Michal bit her lower lip. Miriam's hips were so small, and she wondered if the girl would be able to deliver naturally. And if not, would Michal be able to cut her to take the baby out? And then the chances were very slim that the mother would survive.

What would Michal and Heida do with an infant in their predicament? Michal felt nauseated and dizzy as she examined Miriam. The girl was about to deliver, but the baby had not yet turned. Could she reach in and turn the child if it did not do so on its own? "Bepa." She whispered the old woman's name in her mind as she felt herself gag slightly. *God, Bepa, I wish you were here.* There was so much that could go wrong, and Michal was inexperienced. And then, God willing, if Miriam went into labor at night, she must not scream from the pain. This poor child must endure childbirth in silence, or the guards would come, and they would all be punished. It was hard to see by the light of only one candle. But that was all she had, and she must be quick because she would need to use what was left of the candle on the day Miriam went into labor. *Oh, dear God. Can I do this?*

She didn't want to alarm Miriam with her lack of confidence, so Michal smiled and said, "Everything looks good."

"What are we going to do with the baby here in the camp once it's born?" Miriam said, her face lined with fear and pain.

"We'll figure it all out together…" Michal touched the young girl's cheek, and her heart ached for her own children. *Where were they? Were they safe? Oh God, watch over my children. Dear God, please, I beg you to take anything from me, even my life. But, please watch over my children.* Then Michal turned back to the young girl trembling on the dirty cot. "Right now, all I want you to do is not worry. Can you do that for me, please?"

Miriam nodded.

Michal smiled. "I'll come and check on you. But you should be going into labor very soon. If you feel any pain, have Heida or one of the others come to get me."

"What if it happens during the day when I am at work? What then?"

"You try to be as inconspicuous as possible. You don't want them to know. You must do your very best. With God's help, you will go into labor during the night."

That was all Michal could tell Miriam. Then she left and began to sneak back to her bunk. On her way back, Michal came just inches from being caught by a guard. The blood pounded in her throat as she held her breath until the blond woman pacing the camp carrying a black club turned the opposite way. Then, as quiet and graceful as a deer, Michal ran back to her block. As she squeezed between the other women into the tiny spot where she slept, she began to weep softly. In her mind, she saw Taavi's eyes, his strong arms, and how safe and protected he had made her feel. Taavi. If only she could reach out and touch him. She pictured Alina reading at the kitchen table, so quiet and studious. Then she thought of Gilde, laughing, singing, always singing. What a lovely voice and what a lovely child.

Sweet little Gilde. Her baby, Gilde, would be fourteen years old now, almost a woman. Michal sighed. *I wasn't there when she got her first period, as I was with Alina. I hope someone, Alina or Lotti, helped her and explained things to her. Dear God, please help me to be able to deliver Miriam's baby. Give me the knowledge as only you can. Give me the strength. Guide my hands. Help me to do the right things at the right time. And please help us to know how to hide the child once it's born. I am lost and unsure of what to do. And, somehow, please hide this poor child's pregnancy from these terrible Nazi guards. Never in my life would I have believed that women could be so cruel, so sadistic, but they are here at Ravensbrück. How did Hitler ever find so many terrible women? God, you are the only protection we have, the only place we can turn.*

Michal tried, but she did not sleep at all that night.

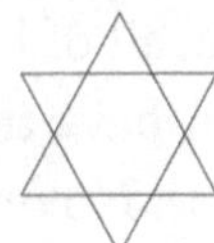

twenty-three

Taavi

AFTER THE NIGHTCLUB CLOSED, Taavi stayed in his apartment for two hours, listening to every movement to make sure that no one was left in the club. He decided it was safe to go when he heard nothing but the sounds of the night, the distant hoot of an owl, and the rustle of the trees in the yard. Taavi opened the door. It had been a long time since he'd been a free man. As he left the apartment behind Frieda's nightclub, his stomach was in knots. And his soul was filled with both joy and fear. Taavi was so close to his home, family, and all he'd yearned for. But being this close, he was even more afraid of being caught and having his dreams thwarted than he was when he had no hope at all. He huddled in alleyways and moved quietly as an invisible man through the night. He took a long walk home on trembling legs, but Taavi kept going. He had to get home. Then, once he reached his destination, his heart sank. He and Michal had lived above the store he'd owned. There it was, his carpentry shop. But his sign, the sign outside that said 'Margolis Fine Furniture,' was gone, and in its place was a new sign: 'Kertmer Hand Made Furniture.' Taavi didn't know anyone by the name of Kertmer. But what he did know was that somehow Lev had lost the business. He would talk to Lev in the morning. Together, they would fix the problem and figure something out, Taavi assured himself. At least the building was still standing. And, right now, it was the middle of the night, and he wanted to feel the familiar warmth of his wife's arms, to lounge like a sleepy bear going into hibernation in the softness of the bed they shared. When he'd been arrested, they'd taken everything he'd had on him, all of his jewelry, his money. They'd kept everything. He didn't even have the key to his own home, so he knocked on the door to his house. No one answered. Taavi knocked again a little harder. *Michal and the girls are asleep,* he assumed. Finally, the door opened just an inch. A pert young woman with her blond hair in pin curls peered out cautiously.

"Who are you?" Taavi asked the woman. "Where is my family?"

"What are you talking about? Are you insane? I don't know you, and it's the middle of the night. Who are you? You must be drunk."

"This is my home. Where are my wife and children?" Taavi's voice was raised, and he knew he sounded hysterical, but he couldn't control his fear.

"I don't know what you're talking about, but if you don't leave this minute, I will call the police."

Taavi knew trying to explain everything to this girl would do no good. She would not help him. He had to get away before he was captured and sent back to jail. He had to be very careful. He turned and began to run. He was stunned with disbelief that his family was gone. What had happened during the time he was imprisoned? Where was Michal, and the girls? His nerves were on edge as he slipped through the dark streets on his way to Lev's home. Lev would have the answers. *Oh God, I pray that Lev is still there...*

When he arrived, Taavi paid no attention to the fact that it was the middle of the night. He pounded his fist on the door. He had no idea what awaited him, and the anticipation made him twitch with anxiety. He was breathing hard and felt a tightening in his chest, which began moving slowly down his left arm. After finding a new family living in his home and a new owner's name on his business, Taavi feared what unimaginable things he might find here at Lev's house. It took several minutes, which seemed like hours, before the door opened slowly.

"Taavi? Is it you? Is it really you?" Lotti looked much older than he remembered. If he calculated correctly, she was only thirty, but her hair that had once been full, curly, and blond was now thin, limp, and sprinkled with a brassy yellow-gray.

"Get in here, hurry," she said as she grabbed Taavi's sleeve and pulled him through the door.

She grabbed him and hugged him. Tears ran freely down her face. "Taavi, my God, Taavi..."

"Lotti..." he said. "What's happened here? I went to my home, and my family is no longer living in our apartment. The business has a new name? I need to talk to Lev right away. Can you wake him?"

Lotti's hand squeezed Taavi's shoulder. Then she took her sleeve and wiped the tears from her cheeks. "Sit down, Taavi. I have a lot to tell you."

He studied her, but he did as she asked.

"I don't know where you have been or how much you know about what is happening here in Germany. But Germany is at war."

"I've been in prison. I didn't know."

"Yes, the air raids go off constantly. I'm not sure what will become of any of us. Anyway, Taavi, it warms my heart to see you again. How did you get out?"

"It's a long story. A complicated story. But for now, at least, I am free. Germany is at war? At war with who?"

"The country went to war when Hitler, that son of a bitch, attacked France. As it turns out, Germany is now at war with France, Britain, Australia, and New Zealand. And since Hitler broke his treaty with Stalin, the Nazis are fighting Russia too."

Taavi nodded. "Is Lev in the army?"

"No, Jews are being arrested, left and right, for no reason at all. Taavi. If you stay here in Berlin, I have no doubt that you will be arrested, too."

"I was in prison already. Arrested for nothing. Has Lev been arrested? Is he in prison?"

Lotti closed her eyes and shook her head.

"Where is Lev?"

"He's gone. Gone…"

"What do you mean gone?"

"Well…" She took a deep breath. "Do you mind if I smoke?" she asked.

"I never knew you smoked. No, I don't mind. Go ahead."

"I didn't smoke before. I do now." Taavi saw Lotti's hand tremble as she lit the cigarette.

"The Gestapo rounded up all the Jewish men and took them in a big truck. Arrested them. I tried to find out what I could, but all the police would say was that he was being detained. Weeks turned into months. Then I met a woman. She was a Gentile like me who had married a Jewish man. She introduced me to an organization of Gentile women who were openly protesting. They were trying to get their husbands released. Some of their men were released, and I was so encouraged." Tears began to flow again. "So encouraged. I thought that somehow I would be able to find a way to bring Lev back to me. I went to the police, and I begged. I told them a list of the names of all of the other men. These were men that I knew they'd already released. Why not Lev? I asked. Why not? I think the police chief might have felt sorry for me. Who cares what he felt? The son of a bitch should only rot in hell. Anyway, the officer checked through his records. Then he apologized to me and said that Lev was dead. I asked him why? Why? He said Lev caused trouble and was uncontrollable. So, they'd done what they had to do."

"Lev? Dead?" Taavi had seen death at the camp. He'd seen plenty of death. Why was he so surprised? "Oh God, Lotti. I am so sorry." Lev had always been like a brother to Taavi, and the loss felt like a dull knife had been plunged into his gut.

She nodded. "I wish I had died too. If I weren't such a coward, I would have taken my own life."

A few minutes passed in heavy silence. Lotti smoked. Taavi looked at the floor.

"Michal? Where is she?" Taavi was afraid to ask. He had to know.

"I don't know, Taavi. All I can tell you is that Michal is gone. I don't know what happened to her. The day after you were arrested, she went to the police station to find you, but she never returned. After a few days, I went to the police station and asked about her. No one would give me any information."

Taavi felt the color drain from his face. He was chilled and shivering. "Michal? My Michal?" Taavi felt his chest constrict. The pain down his arm was more intense now, and he could hardly breathe.

"Yes, I am sorry."

"The girls? My daughters? My children?"

"Gilde is in England. An organization arranged for Jewish children to live with families in Britain until the war ended. It was a good opportunity for her Taavi. Alina and I wanted to do what we could to get her out of Germany. In fact, I even tried to talk the group into taking Alina, too, but she was too old. Since Gilde has been gone, I've tried to write to her in Britain, but I get no answer. I don't know. Maybe the Nazis will not allow the letters to go through because we are at war with Britain." Lotti took another puff from her cigarette and smashed it in the ashtray.

"And Alina?" Taavi felt his throat constrict.

"Alina went to stay with my brother in Munich so that she could go to the university. He had papers made for her. So she could pose as a Gentile, like his sister. But I have been trying to contact them, and I cannot find either of them. Neither Alina nor my brother Johan. When I tried to call them, the number was disconnected. All of my letters to them have been returned unopened." Lotti shrugged. "I am sorry, Taavi. It seems we've both lost everything."

The news was so stunning that Taavi found it hard to believe. But he knew in his heart that everything Lotti had just told him was true. He felt sick, not sure where to turn. He was the father and the man of the house; it was his responsibility to provide for and protect his family. Taavi felt like he'd failed them, and now they were gone. Would he ever find them again? Dear God, the thought that he'd lost them all forever was weighing heavily on him. Then he looked at Lotti. She was desperate, too. His heart ached for her.

"How are you getting by?" Taavi asked. Not that he had any money or anything to give her. But he felt like he should.

"I am lucky, I suppose. I have a job working for a hotel. I earn enough to stay alive. But that is all I am doing, just staying alive and not living. And worse than that, I am ashamed to admit that I have gone back to using my maiden name. I live as a non-Jew. The Nazis leave me alone. Oh, Taavi, forgive me for being so weak. I couldn't fight anymore once I knew Lev was gone. There was no point, and I am tired. I am alone and afraid..." She buried her face in her hands.

"Shhh, it's all right, Lotti. I understand. Anyone would understand. I think you did the right thing. Use your maiden name, do whatever you can to stay alive. With God's help, they will leave you alone now, and your non-Jewish background will keep you safe. Trying to fight against them will get you killed."

"Do you think Lev would understand?"

"Yes, Lotti, I do. He loved you. He would not want you to suffer."

"Thank you, Taavi," she said. "I will carry this shame for the rest of my life. But I guess I always thought my brother was a coward, but it turns out he wasn't. It was me. I am the coward."

"No one knows what they will do in a situation like this. There is no shame in what you have done, Lotti. Lev would have wanted this."

"I miss him so much. I miss Alina and the orphanage. I miss our lives before."

"What happened to the orphanage?"

"It's gone. All of the children went on the transport with Gilde to England. I am alone."

"They took all of the children?"

"Yes, it was a blessing the British took all of them. They were the first transport out of Germany. There have been more since. I've even heard rumors of a little-known organization trying to arrange a Kindertransport to America. It's horrible here. Any child that can get out must get out."

Taavi was trying to process all that he was hearing. "How can I find Michal? Where can I look? I have no idea where or how to begin to find any of my family."

"Do you have papers that say you are a Gentile?"

"I don't have any papers at all. And no money to have them made."

"I know, Taavi. I know. It's very expensive to have papers drawn up. Anyone who makes illegal papers will be killed if they are caught, so they want a hefty price for the risk they are taking. And worse yet, it's not safe for you to stay here at my house. I am being watched all the time because I was married to a Jew. If I thought you would be safe, I would hide you. But, as soon as the Jewish men were arrested, all of my neighbors turned on me. People who were once my friends, or so I thought. Especially the children in the Hitler Youth. They are so convinced that what the Third Reich is doing is good for Germany that they have no loyalties to anyone or anything but Hitler. The Nazis insist that it is their duty to turn on their friends and family if they even suspect that their loved ones are hiding Jews. Would you believe that they have even trained the young children to turn on their own parents? If anyone even had the slightest suspicion that you were here, we would both be arrested or shot on the spot. It's best for you to go. Hide in the country. Get out of the city, Taavi, or they will surely find you. Lay low. If I had the money to make papers for you, I would do it. I don't have the money. I am barely surviving. I keep telling myself that this war can't last. It can't. Once it's over, I'll help you find Michal and the girls. Come back here then, and we'll try together. I wish I had more to give you."

What could he do? He knew she was right. He had no idea what to do, so he decided that until he could come up with a plan, he would try to get out of the city.

"Taavi." She took both hands in hers and then looked into his eyes. It was as if she had read his mind. "Taavi, stay alive. That is all you can do. If you are dead, you will never be able to help your family."

He nodded. "I'll get out of Berlin tonight."

"Go on foot, Taavi. Don't try to take a train. They will check you for your papers."

"I don't have money for a train anyway."

Lotti got up and took a few reichsmarks from a glass-covered cookie jar she kept above the stove. "Take this. It's all I have. You'll need it."

"I can't."

"You must," Lotti said, forcing the bills into his hand.

"Now go, and God be with you."

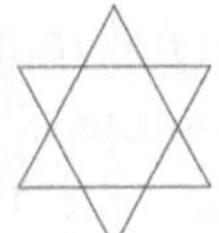

twenty-four
Blockführer Braus

BRAUS HAD EXPECTED that there would be trouble when Taavi did not show up at the roll call. He knew that there was hell to pay for an escaped prisoner. This was not good for the morale of the other prisoners. It gave them hope. But as long as nobody could point a finger at Braus, all would be well. Braus had already planned for the investigation that he knew would come, and he had devised a way to blame Taavi's escape on another guard he'd never liked anyway.

Braus' accusation was so convincing that the guard was transferred and demoted. Braus smiled secretly when he'd heard that his coworker had lost his rank. It all worked out well, Braus thought. He had killed two birds with a single stone. He'd rid himself of an enemy and created a secret income from the money he would receive from that Frieda bitch. Now, he could finally enjoy some of the finer things in life. And who knew, maybe later he would increase the payments to keep that Jew safe. He might even demand sex from that bitch. She was old but not bad-looking. Why not?

Braus was amazed at how easy it was to make a little extra cash on the side. He arrived at the nightclub on the first of every month to collect his payment. Frieda let him in just before sunrise once everyone had cleared out. Then she counted out his money and handed it to him. He never had to say a word. He just put the cash in his pocket and left.

Frieda met Braus's demands with a heavy heart. She never told him that Taavi was not with her. Months passed, and Braus never suspected that Taavi had been gone the entire time.

As far as Braus knew, Frieda had hidden the Jew somewhere under a floor like the rat that he was, but Braus wasn't complaining. She continued paying him, and he enjoyed the padding on his income. He hadn't mentioned sex to her yet, but he was considering it. If it wasn't so profitable for him to let that woman keep the Jew alive, it would have given him great pleasure to report that handsome Jew to the Gestapo. Braus was jealous of Taavi, and so the very idea of Taavi suffering to pay the price for his escape had become a sweet daydream for Braus. But Braus had to admit that turning Taavi in was far too self-defeating for him to indulge his fantasy. The extra cash made his life a lot easier. He was able to purchase better food and beer. And if the party wasn't going to promote him, he would find a way to promote himself.

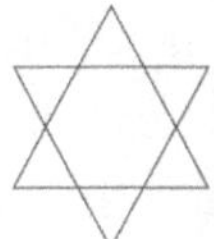

twenty-five

Taavi

BEING ALONE in the forest for several months without human contact gave Taavi much time to think. He rehashed his life and the mistakes he'd made. All the wasted time he'd spent away from Michal, and all out of pride. It was true that he'd been raised without a mother's love, so when he and Michal first got married, he did not know how to love her. He'd been insecure and afraid to show his true feelings. In their early days together, Taavi had been far too quick to anger. When Michal had rejected him physically because she was still traumatized by the day she'd been raped by the Cossack, he'd tried to understand, but it was almost impossible for him. He was young then, and they were newly married. Taavi had waited until they were wed, and once they were, he'd wanted to make love to her so badly. Every time she pushed him away, his anger grew like a volcano until he exploded and left. What a fool he'd been. If only he could retrieve those lost years that he and Michal spent apart, he would have been more patient and loving. Now, she was lost to him, and he had no idea what to do to find her. Lotti had recommended that he stay hidden. But how could he do that without doing what he could to help his family? He could not hide like a child to save himself. There had to be something he could do.

Taavi walked through the woods. The sweet fragrance of nature filled his nostrils. Because he'd endured the noxious odors of the camp, the clean air was even sweeter and very precious to him. If he lived a thousand years, he would never forget the smells of that camp. Finally, one afternoon, he was deep in the woods. Sitting with his back against a tree, he thought once again of the only person he knew who could help him find his family, Frieda. But hadn't she done enough for him already? How could he expect her to help him find his wife when he knew Frieda was in love with him? To find Michal, Frieda would have to put herself in grave danger. Taavi put his head in his hands. He cared for Frieda. She was a good friend, and he was grateful for all she'd done for him. But right at that very moment, Michal might be suffering in some prison camp the way he had been. Just the thought of that possibility was unbearable to him. It made him want to panic, to do something, anything, quickly. *Think, Taavi.* He knew he could not ask Frieda to take such a terrible risk without giving her something in return. But what did he have to give? He was a penniless Jew, hiding like a frightened animal. All he had was himself, and although he could never give her his heart, and although the very idea made him uncomfortable, he would give her his body. All he could hope for was that it would be enough. He cringed with shame when he remembered the perversions they had engaged in during their affair.

It had been a time in his life he would have gladly put behind him. A box filled with sins he would have gladly sealed forever and buried in the recesses of his mind. But now, this was all he could offer... all he could offer. And he would give anything, even his own life, to save his family.

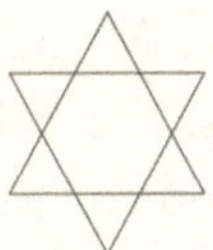

twenty-six

Michal

IT WAS while the prisoners were eating that Miriam went into labor. Michal heard a low moan, and something inside of her told her to look for Miriam. The sound was familiar to her. Michal had heard many women in labor moan the very same way. She'd hoped that it would happen at night, but it came as no surprise. She'd been expecting this. She glanced to her left and did not see Miriam. Then she looked right and saw Miriam sitting on a rock, doubled over in pain. Michal's eyes darted through the crowd until she found Heida. She stared at Heida until Heida turned to look at her. Michal was sure Heida felt the weight of Michal's eyes upon her and looked up. Then Michal motioned with her head for Heida to look at Miriam. Heida nodded, and Michal knew she had acknowledged what Michal was trying to tell her.

The prisoners were not given much time to consume their meals. Michal choked down her food. They had a full day's work ahead of them. How would Miriam ever get through the grueling workday while she was in labor? Michal knew that no matter what, the guards would have no sympathy for the young Jewish girl. And Michal knew that if the baby decided to come, it would come no matter where Miriam was or what she was doing. Michal bit her lower lip. How was she ever going to pull this off? Even if Miriam could, by some miracle, wait until nightfall, and even if everything went perfectly with the birth and the mother and child were healthy, how would they keep a baby a secret from the guards? Babies cried, and the guards would hear the cries like wolves waiting to kill a little lamb. Just thinking about what they might do to the child and the mother gave Michal a chill. She'd heard horror stories that had spread amongst the prisoners of the cruelty of the guards towards pregnant women. And from what she'd experienced and seen since she'd arrived at Ravensbrück, she didn't doubt a word. Michal let her eyes dart quickly to the two guards talking while they kept an eye on the prisoners. Then Michal said a silent prayer for the pregnant girl.

At least it was autumn and not winter. If it had been winter, Michal had no doubt that Miriam would die. The conditions in winter in the camp were so brutal.

When she was younger, before she'd ever known of Nazis and concentration camps, Michal had loved fall. She'd loved the crisp air. Winters had been hard in Russia. It was bitter cold, even colder than Germany, making everything that had to be done more difficult. But nothing Michal had ever experienced could compare to the misery of winter in Ravensbrück. The guards made sure of it. Even now, as she felt the brisk autumn wind, instead of feeling alive, all she could think of was that this was the beginning of another winter in hell.

A few days earlier, one of the women that Michal did not know but had seen around the camp had gone into some kind of fit during roll call. She fell and began rolling around on the ground. A flash of fear came over the guard's face. "Get up," the guard yelled at the prisoner, sounding very stern. But the woman continued to shake on the ground. "Get up, I said."

Michal watched the guard and realized how scared she was that she was losing control of the woman in front of the others.

Another prisoner tried to help the woman get up, but the guard told her to get back in line. Still, the prisoner writhed on the ground, twisting and turning in all directions and making terrible choking sounds. The guard pulled her gun and shot the woman. The sound of the gunshot pierced the morning, and Michal felt dizzy as if she might faint. But she dared not. *Breathe deeply. Keep breathing, and for God's sake, don't look at the dead woman or the massive pool of blood around her.*

Then, as if none of this had happened, the inmates were lined up at gunpoint and marched to their sewing machines. Michal stole occasional glances at Miriam, who seemed to be holding up, but barely. Her face was lined with pain, and she held her small, rounded belly, but she marched with the others. From what Michal could determine by watching Miriam, she decided that the labor pains were about thirty minutes apart. She would have done something to lighten Miriam's load, at least for the day, but there was no way to protect the young girl. The worst of it was that the woman who had been made the *Blockova* for the Jewish women (a prisoner who was given special treatment for keeping the other prisoners in line) was put into Ravensbrück for committing illegal abortions. Her name was Marianne, and because she'd had so much experience with female reproduction, Michal was afraid that Marianne would recognize the symptoms and know that Miriam was pregnant and that she had gone into labor. If it hadn't been for the lack of food, which kept Miriam from growing a larger belly, Michal was sure that Marianne would have seen the evidence of pregnancy long before today. But, because Miriam was so slight of build and starving, she showed no visible signs.

Michal watched Miriam and shuddered. She knew of women who'd come to the camp pregnant and had given birth. These poor mothers were forced to abandon their children at the Kinderzimmer, where the tiny infants were left to die of starvation or be eaten by rats. She couldn't help but think of the days her daughters had been born. She'd been so happy. How would she have survived leaving Alina or Gilde to die in the Kinderzimmer? "Oh God, help this girl, please in your mercy, find a way to prevent her from suffering a fate worse than death. Please, I beg you, don't let her be forced to watch her baby die." Michal said. Then she whispered a Hebrew prayer under her breath.

Today, like many days when they were not sewing, the women were told to shovel heavy loads of sand. Michal's arms and legs ached and swelled as they did every day, but even in pain, she kept a watch on Miriam. There were no clocks. The only way to determine the time of day was to watch the sun. From what Michal gathered by looking at the sky, it was about four o'clock in the afternoon when Miriam's water broke. She didn't know if anyone else saw the trickle of liquid run down Miriam's leg. And since many times the prisoners urinated on themselves rather than risk angering a guard by asking to be allowed to step away from the crowd to relieve themselves, Miriam could have urinated. It was possible. After all, being very pregnant and ready to give birth, the baby would be lying on her bladder. But still, Michal thought that Miriam's water had probably broken. A dry birth made matters even worse. From where she stood, Michal could not see the color of the water running down Miriam's leg. The color would tell her if the baby had a bowel movement. If it had while it was still in the womb, then the child was in distress. Michal felt helpless. She wished that she could step out of line and go to Miriam. But, of course, that was impossible. All she could do was watch in horror as the situation unfolded right before her eyes.

As time passed, there was no denying that Miriam needed help. She began to double over, unable to stand up. Finally, she crumbled down into a sitting position, her hand cradling her belly.

When the guards weren't looking, one of the other women pulled Miriam to her feet. "Don't let them see you sitting," the woman said. But Miriam was so thin, weak, and in pain that she fell back down again.

The guard turned just in time to see the prisoner helping Miriam. "What's going on over there? Get back to work, both of you. This minute. I won't tolerate your laziness."

The prisoner who'd been trying to help Miriam did as the guard demanded and left Miriam's side. As she walked back into the shoveling line, her eyes were cast down on the ground.

Miriam forced herself to stand, holding on to a rock to pull herself up. Her legs wobbled, and it seemed they would no longer have the strength to hold her at any minute. Michal watched, but she could do nothing to help. Nothing at all without risking her own life. And she couldn't find the courage to do that. Tears came to her eyes. Michal knew this situation could not have a good ending.

"Work, I said. What's the matter with you?" The guard was clearly angry at being defied. She was standing very close to Miriam and yelling in Miriam's face.

Miriam gagged and began to dry heave. Michal watched. From where she stood, it looked like Miriam was unable to stop. She leaned over and kept gagging. Then she vomited, but only bile spewed onto the sand. Michal felt herself gagging, too. *Please spare this child.* She prayed silently, thinking about Alina all the time.

"She's sick," the guard said. The other women gathered around, and it was plain to see that the guard felt she was losing control of the prisoners. Michal knew that the Nazis always got meaner when they feared that they looked weak. The guard was clearly agitated, trying desperately to show her dominance over the prisoners. "Get back to work right now, all of you, or I swear I will shoot every single one of you." The guard pulled her gun and shot into the air. The sound shook the women back to reality, and they hurried to lift their shovels. There was a look of fear on the guard's face. It seemed that it was the first time the guard realized that the shovels in the prisoners' hands could be used as weapons and that there were more prisoners than guards. Any possible drop of compassion the guard might have shown towards Miriam was gone. She believed it would be easy for these women to interpret compassion as weakness. Any show of fear or sympathy and the inmates would close in for the kill. She had to stay in command no matter what happened, and there could easily be an uprising. Inside, she did feel a bit sorry for the girl, who looked so young, sick, and vulnerable. But not sorry enough to let the rest of them think she was a pushover. That must never happen.

From where she stood, Michal could see the Nazi's hand was trembling as she pointed the gun at Miriam and pulled the trigger.

Miriam was still standing with a look of shock on her face as she raised her upper arm where the bullet had entered.

The sound had been deafening in the quiet afternoon. Michal gasped. Then the guard shot Miriam again, this time in the belly. Miriam tumbled soundlessly to the ground in a heap like a rag doll. Miriam's eyes were wide open, and from where Michal stood, she could see the horror and disbelief reflecting back at her. From that day on, she often had dreams of Miriam's eyes. Dreams where she was glued to the ground, and although she tried to move to help Miriam, she was paralyzed. Sometimes, Miriam's face would change in her nightmares, and she would become Alina or Gilde. On those terrible nights, Michal would awaken sobbing. The women who slept beside her on the long wooden boards that served as beds were so close that she could smell their breath. She tried to stifle her crying so as not to wake them up, but it wouldn't have mattered. They'd all grown used to hearing each other's snoring, coughing, and sobbing during the night.

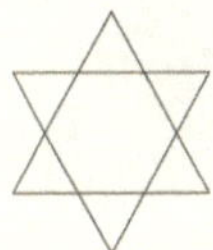

twenty-seven
Michal

THANK GOD FOR HEIDA. Heida's unbelievable strength pulled Michal out of the depths of her depression once again. Miriam's death had pushed Michal to the edge of a breakdown. Still, whenever they had a moment to talk, Heida offered comfort and words of wisdom.

"Miriam is better off. It's cruel to say such a thing, but how terrible would it have been if the guards had killed her child in front of her? She is dead now. She doesn't suffer anymore. If you want to survive, you must put these things out of your mind. Believe me, Michal, this war will end. And the time will come when you will see your family again. But that can only happen if you live. In order to live through this, you can't look at what is happening around you. You have to find a way not to see it. Instead, try to think about the good times you had before the Nazis came to power. Be very careful not to let yourself wallow in the horror of what you saw happen to Miriam or any of the other terrible things surrounding us. If you do, you will lose the will to live, and when that happens, you're finished."

"She is better off, Heida. I know you are right. But I can't help but think that she was just a child."

Heida nodded. "Better to die than to suffer such a terrible thing as having to witness the death of her child. And if she lived, the baby would have made her so vulnerable. They would have hurt the baby, and that would have been worse for her than death."

"You are a lesbian, no?"

"Yes," Heida said.

"So you have no children; how do you know this is how it is to be a mother?"

"Because I did have a child. Once, long ago."

Michal touched Heida's shoulder. "What happened?"

"He was kidnapped and murdered. His body was found. But the criminal was never caught. My husband blamed me. I wasn't watching him. I allowed him to go and play at one of his friends' houses. He never returned."

"Oh, Heida. You always seem so strong. I had no idea you'd been through so much."

"Yes, well, haven't we all suffered?" Heida patted Michal's arm.

twenty-eight
Alina

THE WOUND that had begun as a small cut in the flesh of Johan's arm now swelled and festered with pus. It threw off a strong odor of infection that made Alina feel both terrified for Johan and sick to her stomach. She had no medical background. She'd done paperwork for the doctor she'd worked for, and occasionally, she'd assisted him by bringing him this or that, but she had no formal training. Then she remembered her father saying that alcohol was good for cleaning an infected wound. Plenty of the passengers had brought bottles with them, and they drank, but after she'd asked for the man to wet her cloth with whiskey when Johan was injured, she hadn't had the nerve to ask anyone again. Finally, when she was beside herself with worry, she went to a man who she noticed had a bottle of vodka that he'd been nursing for several days. Alina walked over to the man, and in the sweetest voice she could muster, she begged him to pour just a small smidgen of the liquid on a piece of cloth so she could use it to clean Johan's wound. The passenger was reluctant to share his vodka at first. But when he saw the tears in Alina's eyes, he gave in and did as she asked. He wet the cloth and wished her luck with Johan. She had grown into a soft, dark, delicate beauty, much like her mother.

To strong and confident men, Alina seemed fragile, like a newborn kitten they wanted to protect and nurture. This stranger was exactly that type of male. He was a tall, robust man who didn't seem weakened by seasickness or fear of leaving home and going to a foreign land. She addressed him in German, and he answered her in German with a Russian accent. Alina recognized that accent because it sounded just like her father. Alina had noticed that the other men on board had eyed this Russian's bottle of vodka, but none had dared to steal it. Alina had seen him many times during the voyage. He was always alone. She decided that he was a loner. From what she gathered, he'd boarded the ship by himself without any friends or family, and he'd made no attempt to make any friends during the trip.

Alina remembered early on in the voyage that there had been an incident where one of the others, a boy of about eighteen, had called this Russian a dirty Jew. He'd ignored the insult. But it turned out that the younger man was the ringleader of three other boys who felt powerful enough in a gang of four against one to try to intimidate the big man into sharing his liquor. The bullies kept at him like a child who continued to pick at the scab on a sore until the Russian had finally had enough. Alina remembered watching as the Russian slowly got up from his bunk and took on all four of the boys with his bare fists until they all lay on the ground, bleeding from their faces. Then he sat back down and began drinking again. From that day on, no one talked to or bothered the Russian again. And Alina would not have ever gone near him if she were not so scared that if she didn't clean and dress Johan's wound, he might die.

Alina went back to the bench on which Johan was sitting and gently wiped his cut with the wet fabric.

To Alina's surprise, the Russian came over to her bunk the following day to find out how Johan was doing.

"Let me pour a little more vodka on that cloth," he said.

He certainly was handsome. She watched him as he wet the torn piece of Alina's blouse. Then he bent to look at Johan's arm. Johan looked at him skeptically.

"It's alright. I'm only trying to help," the Russian said. "My name is

Ugo Blok, but my papers say I am Oliver Block." He smiled at them both.

"My name is Adelheid Strombeck," Alina said, remembering the name on her papers. "And this is Johan Strombeck."

"Nice to meet you both. Your arm looks pretty bad."

Johan nodded. "I'm really not feeling well at all."

"You're flushed. You probably have a fever, too. Here." Ugo handed the bottle to Johan. "Take a drink. It'll make you feel better."

"Thank you for your kindness," Alina said.

He smiled. His smile was genuine, and for the first time since Johan had been hurt, Alina felt safe on the ship.

"You're not German?" Johan asked.

"I'm from Russia."

"I thought so," Alina said. "My father was from Russia. He had the same accent."

"You speak German pretty well," Johan said.

"Yes, my father taught me. He did a lot of trading with other countries and spoke several languages. I helped him in his business, so I had to learn them, too."

"Are you Jewish?" Alina asked.

Johan gave Alina a questioning look as if to say, why would you ever bring that up? "Excuse her, please. She talks out of turn sometimes," Johan said.

"It's just that my parents are Russian. You have the same accent as they do. And well, I remembered how you fought those boys so gallantly when they called you a Jew. That's why I thought you might be Jewish," Alina said.

"No, I am not Jewish. But I don't like to see anyone persecuted. I am going to America to get away from all of the persecution in Russia. I want to go to a land where everyone has equal opportunity."

"That's quite noble of you," Johan said, mustering a half smile. "Adelheid isn't Jewish either, but we feel the same way about persecution." Johan gave Alina a threatening look.

"Yes, that's right," she said, shaking her head.

"Well, if you need any more vodka, just come over and ask," Ugo said. Then he got up, took his bottle, and left.

"Thank you," Alina said, loudly enough for him to hear as he walked down the hallway.

Ugo turned back. He looked at her, then he nodded and continued on his way.

Alina covered the open sore on Johan's arm as gently as possible with another piece of cloth that she tore from the bottom of her skirt. Johan winced in pain. Looking at him closely, she saw that his face had turned dark red and was hot to the touch, but his feet and hands were like ice.

"Johan, the vodka should help."

"Alina, you must be careful what you say to people like that man. You don't know who he is or how he feels about Jews. Don't ever give anyone the vaguest idea that you might be Jewish. I don't know how people are going to treat Jews in America. But there is no need for you to bring attention to yourself. You might not get into America if they suspect you are Jewish. You might be sent back to Germany. Please, be more cautious of what you say."

"I didn't tell him I was Jewish."

"Don't even mention the word Jewish. Do you understand me? Please?"

"Yes, Johan. I am sorry. You're right. You went through so much trouble getting me these papers and getting us out of Germany. I'll be more careful of what I say from now on."

Johan smiled at Alina. He reached up and touched her face. But she could see how their conversation had tired him out, and she knew he was weak and very ill. "I'll let you get some sleep," she said, getting up and walking away. "I'll just be sitting by the table right over there." She pointed a few feet away.

"No. I have to talk to you while I still have the strength, Alina."

"You need to rest. You'll feel better when you get up. We can talk then."

"Alina, we have to talk now. I'm getting weaker every day. Please sit down and listen. I don't have the energy to argue."

She sat back down on the bed beside him and took his hand. "Yes, Johan, go on. I'm listening."

"We have to face facts, Alina. I think I might be dying."

"No, no, you're going to get better. The alcohol will kill the infection, you'll see. You'll be fine. We'll get married just like we planned. You can't die, Johan. You can't leave me all alone in America, Johan."

"Shhh, Alina, listen. This is important. There are things you don't know about me, and now I must tell you before I no longer can tell you." He took a labored breath, and she could see how hard it was for him to speak, but he continued. "Listen closely. This is important. My mother was married in Germany and had two children, Lotti and me. But neither Lotti nor my father knew the truth about me. The man who raised us was not my real father. My biological father was an American. I didn't even know this about myself until my mother was dying. God forgive me. I put her into a home. I couldn't take care of her anymore. Her illness was taking the very life out of me. I wonder if maybe this cut happened to me as a punishment for abandoning her when she was old and needed my help. It was wrong, Alina. I knew it then but couldn't bear to care for her anymore. I am ashamed, but I just wasn't strong enough. I still went to see her every day at the home. But at least I was able to work. I couldn't leave her for even an hour when she was at home. Oh God, forgive me for what I did to her. But at least I was there with her when she was dying. That was when I learned the truth about who I am."

His eyes were glassy, and he was rambling. Alina didn't know what to say or do, so she just sat and squeezed his hand, letting him know she was listening. "Oh, Alina, it was terrible. She was a skeleton. Half the woman she was when I was a child. As she lay there dying in that home, she grabbed onto my arm. Her eyes were so bright when she told me the truth. She said that she'd had an affair with an American who was married to a woman in America. He'd gone home to his wife, and she was left behind pregnant with me. She was married to the man who raised me, and he had no idea that I was not his son. But she contacted my real father by mail and threatened to come to America if he didn't send her money. He sent her money for years, and she put it all away for me. She saved it for me, Alina, and look at how I treated her. I deserve everything that is happening to me. Right before she died, she told me where to find the money, where she had buried it in the house, and along with it, she'd left my father's address. She'd left it in a small wooden cigar box. I kept the box with me, but I kept it closed. You see, I never planned to use the money. The thought of using it made me sick because of what I did to her. But then, when we needed a sponsor to get us into the United States, I could see no other way out of Germany. So, I contacted my father. It took him a while to answer. I thought he might ignore my letter. Finally, I got mail from him, and he agreed to sponsor us as long as I never contacted him or anyone in his family when we got to America. He also made me promise to leave him alone and stop expecting money from him. I agreed. That is how we got our sponsor. I used most of the money that my mother left me to pay for your papers, our visas, and our passage. What is left is in the bottom of my left shoe. Take it, and use it when you need it, but there isn't much, and it won't last, so try to find work. My father's address is there with the money, but I doubt he will help you, so I don't recommend you go to him unless you are so desperate that you can see no other way. I pray that does not happen."

"But, Johan, you can't die. Please don't die. I am terrified to be all alone in a strange country. I don't even speak the language." Her stomach was turning, and she felt sick. Tears began welling up in her eyes.

"I know. Dear God, I know. I am sorry. I never meant for it to be like this. Never..."

She could no longer hold the tears back. She turned away so that Johan would not see them streaming down her cheeks. She wiped her face with her sleeve and then looked back at Johan.

"Try to rest," she said. She no longer wanted to sit up alone. She wanted to be as close to Johan as she could for as long as possible. Alina wanted to spend Johan's last hours in his arms. Somehow, she knew that he was right. Their time together was coming to an end. Alina lay down beside Johan and curled her body into his. The warmth of his arms around her gave her momentary comfort, and by some miracle, she drifted off to sleep. Alina was not sure how long she slept, but the next thing she knew, everyone was yelling with excitement. "Look, look, there it is! the Statue of Liberty." They were able to see it through a small porthole in the ship. Alina hated to leave Johan, but she had to see the New York harbor. "I'll be back in a minute." She whispered and kissed his cheek. Then she stood up and pushed through the crowd to the window. The torch the lady of liberty held in her hand gleamed like a golden fire in the sun. Alina felt afraid of what lay ahead and excited at the same time.

She went back to her place in bed and cuddled back into Johan.

"Johan," she whispered. "We're here." Alina gently shook his sleeve, but he didn't move. Then fear rumbled in her stomach. She knew this was coming, yet she was still horrified to know it had happened. Gently, with the tips of her fingers, she touched his face. His skin was cool. "Johan…" She shook him harder this time as if she somehow might change things. But she knew he was dead. She laid her head on his chest and softly wept.

The boat eased into the harbor. Everyone in steerage was gathering their belongings, holding tightly to their children. The noise level was deafening to Alina, who wanted to lie beside Johan and stay safe in his arms, pretending he was only sleeping. Everyone started to get off the ship. Alina called out for help, but no one came. The ship's staff were all busy. She got up and began pushing through the crowds, trying to find help. Finally, she found one of the crew. He was busy directing people and trying to keep them from pushing and shoving. Alina tugged on his sleeve.

He was a tall man, and he looked down at her.

"My husband died. I have to take his body on shore and have it buried."

The crew member looked and shook his head. "Sorry, Ma'am. You can't take a dead body into the United States. You'll have to leave him behind."

"I can't. How can I just leave him?" Alina said.

"You can because you have to. There is no other choice. There is nothing you can do." Then he looked at her, and she saw that his eyes had become sympathetic. "Alright. Listen. I promise you that he'll have a proper burial. You go on now. Follow the others and get off the ship."

She knew he was lying to her. There would be no real burial. Johan's body would be thrown into the ocean. The thought of it made her feel like collapsing on the floor. But she knew that she couldn't. She walked back to the cot where Johan's body lay lifeless. Her heart ached. But Alina knew the time had come to leave Johan and walk into her uncertain future. She leaned over and kissed him on the lips. Even as she did, she could feel that the life force was gone from him like a flame extinguished on a candle. Still, she leaned close to his ear and whispered, "Goodbye, Johan. I will miss you. God, how I will miss you. And now I can tell you what I was planning to tell you after we were settled in America. I am pregnant, Johan. I am going to have our child. I'll name the baby for you."

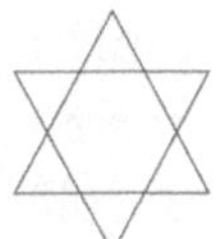

twenty-nine

ALINA HAD BEEN through a lot in her young life. But she had never been as afraid as she was now. She was alone, all alone. Her family was gone, and now Johan was dead. And here she was in the harbor of a strange country in a city called New York without a friend in the world. With all the turmoil in Germany, she doubted that any letter she wrote would ever reach Lotti, and the last time she'd written to Gilde, her letter had been returned. Her parents? Where were they? Were they still alive? Even if she could find anyone, how could she ever keep in contact with them when she had no return address to send with a letter? Where was she going to live? *God, help me,* she thought. A small voice in her head whispered: "Don't forget to take the money." With trembling hands, she removed Johan's shoe and retrieved the small roll of bills. They were in a currency she'd never seen before. But knowing how Johan always planned ahead, she realized she should have known that he would have already converted them to American dollars.

Adelheid Strombeck. She repeated the name softly. *I am no longer Alina Margolis. I am Adelheid Strombeck.* The name sounded so foreign to her. *Oh, Johan.* Over time, she knew him, and he became a good friend. She couldn't say she was madly in love with him.

But she loved him as one loves family. And there was no doubt that she would miss him terribly. After all, he was the last link she had to Germany and the life she'd once known. The ship was almost empty. It was time to go. There was no point in carrying Johan's cardboard suitcase with her. He would never need those clothes. Just thinking about his things and remembering how he'd packed them carefully made her want to lay on top of him and weep forever. But there was no time. No time left for weeping. Alina squared her small shoulders and picked up her suitcase, which contained everything she had in the world. She found a ship staff member and told him that Johan had died. He reassured her that the crew would dispose of the body. There was nothing more she could do for Johan. Then, without any idea what to do next, she got off the ship at Ellis Island. At that moment, Alina Margolis legally became Adelheid Strombeck. Although she would always go back and forth between both names.

The line for inspection was long and moved very slowly. Sweat beaded on her brow and in the armpits of her dress. It trickled down her back as the sun baked the top of her head until it ached. People stood in line for inspection, holding babies and possessions. There were whispers among the immigrants. They had heard that if a person looked sick, that person would be sent to the hospital and not be allowed to enter the United States of America. Alina saw the fear in the eyes of the other passengers. She knew that America had slowed her immigration down to almost nothing. It would be very easy for them to return her to Germany, especially if they thought she was unhealthy or Jewish. A woman in line had pricked her finger with a pin and was smearing the blood on her child's cheeks to make them look rosy. Alina could see that the child was pale and coughing, too.

What were the chances that the mother and child would be sent back? Alina felt sorry for the mother. But she couldn't help her; she was alone and frightened herself. Alina's eyes darted through the crowd until she found the only friend she'd made on the boat. Ugo. He was standing silently, not talking to the others. Alina didn't really even know him. But she was trembling with fear; after all, he was a man, and a woman needed a man to take care of her. With Johan gone, she was a vulnerable target for any man with bad intentions. *I must be crazy. This man will think I am insane.* But the fear in her stomach made her feel she needed to cling to someone or something. She was so desperate. What else could she do? She walked over to Ugo.

"Hello," she said. "How are you?" Alina suddenly felt foolish and awkward for going over to him.

"How is your husband?" he asked.

"He passed away." She must have looked so needy. He probably thought of her as pathetic. She should never have gone up to him. What was she thinking? He must have thought she was soliciting herself. She was no common tramp.

"I'm sorry," he said.

"Thank you." Now, there was nothing left to say. She stood there feeling ridiculous with her black suitcase on the ground beside her. Then he smiled; his smile was so genuine that she thought she might cry.

"Adelheid Strombeck isn't your real name, is it?"

She shook her head. Tears were welling up behind her eyes, but she wouldn't cry.

"I didn't think so."

"My real name is Alina Margolis. But I have papers that say I am Adelheid Strombeck. And they say that I am a Christian. But I am not. I'm a Jew." She must have been crazy to tell this man the truth. Johan would have been so angry. What was she thinking? Only that she wanted a friend, a real friend who she could tell the truth.

He smiled again. If he saw her eyes glazing over like she might weep, he was too much of a gentleman to mention it. "It's probably a good thing for you to use those papers."

She nodded.

"Is your sponsor going to meet you here?" he asked. Alina was amazed at how well he spoke German.

She shook her head. "No."

The sun was bearing down on her shoulders. She cleared her throat and tried to sound like she was making a casual conversation when, in reality, she wanted to say, "Please help me. Please protect me.

I am all by myself here in this strange country. I hardly speak English. I don't know what is going to happen to me." But she just stood there, trying to muster a smile.

"Is your sponsor going to meet you here?" she asked.

"Yes, my brother-in-law sponsored me. My wife came to America first. She's been here for about a year now. I kept working until I could get a visa. Now, I will join her and the rest of our family."

He was married. She felt a lump forming in her throat. She wanted to run away. What a fool she was making of herself. Of course, he was married. What had she expected, that some strange man she'd met on the *Red Liner* would take her in and care for her? *Pull yourself together, Alina.* Her voice came out hoarse, but she tried to sound casual. "Oh well, that must be wonderful for you. You will finally be reunited with your family."

"Yes, I am excited. My wife and I only married a few months ago when her brother offered to sponsor us. We both thought that it was a good idea to come to America, but we hardly had any time together before she left. Still, I am glad we did it this way. There is an opportunity for a better life here."

"So they say." Alina smiled and then looked away from him at the water where the boat was docked. Johan's body was still on that ship. *God help me.* Then she thought of Johan. And she quickly wiped a tear from her cheek with the back of her hand.

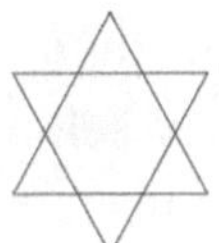

thirty

Alina

AFTER ADELHEID PASSED through Ellis Island, she found herself walking through a crowded park filled with people reuniting with their loved ones. They were laughing and crying and hugging all at the same time. No one awaited Alina.

Adelheid Strombeck. *I am going to have a difficult time getting used to this new name.* She continued to walk, trying not to let her fear get the best of her. Alina saw Ugo across the walkway. He was waving to a man who looked strong but aged. The man ran over to greet him. Then, a young woman came walking over to Ugo. She was pretty and slender with striking wavy red hair. Her dress was fitted and modern, making Alina feel frumpy in her old-fashioned, dirty traveling dress. Alina was lost and sick to her stomach, just looking at the redheaded woman as she embraced Ugo. *She must be his wife.*

The line for inspection had been long, and it had been hours since Alina had sat down. She was exhausted and hungry, starving. She had nowhere to go. No one to meet. When she'd taken the money, she'd also taken Johan's father's address, but how could she appear at his door? She wasn't even Johan's wife. And worse yet, Johan had made it clear that his father didn't want to see either of them. What was she going to do? Finally, she saw a bench. She plopped down and set her small suitcase beside her. There was a big sign with black lettering, but because her English was so limited, she could only read the word "Park."

So I've come all the way to America to sit on a bench in the park. As she thought sadly, she noticed that there were other people around her. People who seemed to be living in the park. They were mostly men, but a few were women and children. Some had piles of dirty belongings that they were using as pillows. Some of them walked up to her and asked her something. Through their gestures, it appeared to Alina that they were begging for money. But since she didn't speak English, she wasn't sure that she even had enough to share. She had to hold on to every penny. The men living in the park looked rough, and she wondered how safe she would be once night fell. Would one of these desperate people rob her in the darkness, or worse?

Alina wiped the sweat from her brow. Groups of immigrants who had come in from the harbor rushed by her with their suitcases. Perhaps she should just use the address Johan had given her for his father. He might throw her out. It was very possible, but what else was she to do? The sun was low in the sky, and soon it would be night. She was a young woman alone in a park, surrounded by what appeared to be hungry, homeless people. Alina sucked in a ragged breath. *Don't cry. It won't help you.* Then she squared her shoulders, got up, took a moment to stretch her back, and began following the rest of the crowd of immigrants out of the park and into the city.

If she thought Berlin was bustling with people, then New York was jam-packed. Everywhere, she heard voices and conversations in what seemed like a million different languages, none of which she recognized. *Keep walking. Maybe you will hear someone speak Yiddish or German, and you can ask him or her how to get to the address of Johan's father.* There was no place else to go. What else could she do? Alina walked for several blocks until her feet ached, and she was exhausted. It had been a traumatic day, and she still had no place to go. She passed couples, women with babies in buggies and men in suits until she finally heard two young girls speaking German. The dialect was a little different from hers, but at least she understood them. Her heart skipped a beat. She ran up to the girls, perhaps a little too quickly because one of them stepped back and stared at her suspiciously.

"I am Adelheid Strombeck. I don't speak English," Alina said in German. "I am sorry to bother you. But I heard you speaking German, and I am lost. I am looking for this address." Alina had been holding the paper with Johan's father's address written on it so tightly that the sweat from her hand had blurred the text. But it was still readable. One of the girls took the paper.

"You can take the subway," she told Alina in German. "Here, let me explain. You take the A train for three stops, then get off and transfer to the B train…"

Suddenly, it all seemed too much to Alina. She was overwhelmed, and hearing her native language in this foreign country touched her so deeply that she started crying. There was so much to remember. The A train, the B train… How was she ever to find these trains when she didn't speak, let alone read, English? Then, if by some miracle she stumbles into Johan's father's neighborhood, how would she find the address? Her eyes burned, and her head ached from the heat, the voyage, the stress, and the grief of losing Johan. "I'm sorry," Alina said. "Please, forgive me for this emotional outburst." She tried to smile. Then she cleared her throat and said, "Explain again. I didn't catch all of the directions."

The girl, who had been suspicious of Alina from the first moment, shook her head, but the other one had kind eyes. "Here," she said as she handed Alina a cotton handkerchief.

"Thank you," Alina said in German. The girl smiled. She was pretty, Alina thought.

"Are you going to see a relative?" the kind girl asked.

"I don't know if he is a relative," Alina said. "I just got into America. My husband died on the boat on the way over here from Europe. I am all alone, and the man who lives at the address written on this paper is his father. But he doesn't even know me, and I doubt he will welcome me into his home." Alina looked into the girl's eyes. They were warm. In a way, they reminded her of Lotti. Why did everything always bring back some painful memory from her past? Maybe because she wanted to see Lotti in this girl the same way she wanted to see her father in Ugo. It was a way to hold on, to grasp, even for a moment, all that she'd lost.

"Do you need a job?" the girl asked.

"Yes," Alina said. "But I don't know what I could do. I have no real skills, and the language…"

"I am Wilma, and this is Simone. You said your name is Adelheid?"

"Yes, Adelheid Strombeck," Alina said. Would she ever get used to being Adelheid Strombeck?

"Well, come with us, Adelheid. Maybe we can help you."

Alina nodded and began to follow the two girls, but she felt a lump forming in her throat. Her mind was racing. Alina didn't even know these two young women and had no idea where they were leading her. Doubt clouded her thoughts. Would she have been better off staying in Germany with Lotti? Yes, Germany was a treacherous place, especially for a Jew. But, at least she knew someone. She was not so alone. Everything around here in America was a reminder of how foreign she was, from the signs on the street to the people. Lotti had warned her not to go and live with Johan. But she'd wanted to go to university. Now, here she was in a strange country without any family. For the first time in her young life, Alina Margolis was all alone.

If she ever found a safe place to live, she would write to Lotti and tell her about Johan. Just thinking about communicating with Lotti made her feel a little better. After all, Lotti was his sister and Alina's best friend, and she deserved to know about Johan's passing. She missed those days of working at the orphanage with Lotti, but she decided that even though she loved Lotti, she would keep Johan's secret. She wouldn't tell Lotti about Johan being her half-brother by another father. If Johan had wanted her to know that, he would have told her. She would not betray him in death.

Alina hurried along, pushing through the crowds on the busy streets. She swallowed her fears and followed the two girls he had only known for a few minutes, Wilma and Simone, to an unknown destination.

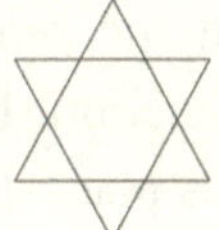

thirty-one

THE TWO STRANGE girls could have been leading Alina anywhere. But they brought her to a looming dark building that stood behind an iron gate. Alina looked at the fortress, and for a moment, she considered running away. But what was the point? She had nowhere else to go. Next door to the large building and behind the gate, Alina saw a beautiful cathedral with stained glass. *This is a church, but I have no idea what religion it belongs to.* When they entered the stone building, it was very quiet, even though many young women were scattered about the house. Some were washing windows or floors. Others were hurrying along the corridor. Some of the women wore long black dresses with headpieces that covered their hair. Alina recognized their uniform because she'd seen them before in Germany. They were nuns.

"Come on, I'm going to introduce you to the Mother Superior," Wilma said. "Don't be afraid. You look like you've seen a ghost. This is a nunnery. The nuns help us find work. Sometimes we babysit for children, or we go and help crippled, old, or sick people. Sometimes, we just clean houses. Jobs like that. You won't need any real skills. But I'll tell you right now that the nuns expect us to be well-behaved, and we do have a lot of chores. Still, they feed us. Some of the girls have even decided that the church is their calling.

"This is all part of the Catholic Church. You look like you've never seen anything like this before. So, I assume that you must be Lutheran?"

Alina nodded. "Lutheran, yes."

"I am, too. But when I came from Germany, I met up with a group of lovely girls from Ireland. They were living here, and the nuns helped them find work. My grandmother had sponsored me, but by the time I arrived, she'd passed on. So, I was glad to find this place. I'll introduce you to the girls who live here after you get approval to stay from the Mother Superior. Tell her you're Catholic."

Wilma knocked on a heavy, looming wooden door. The dark mahogany shone like it had recently been polished. "Come in." The voice that answered the knock was calm but authoritative.

"Reverend Mother, this is my new friend, Adelheid Strombeck. She just got here from Germany and has nowhere to go. She has no family and no one to turn to. She's a Catholic."

The Reverend Mother looked at Alina. "The first thing you must realize is that there is no room for lazy girls here. You will have to pull your own weight."

Alina nodded. "I understand."

"Sometimes we are able to find you girls jobs like nannies or housekeepers. That sort of thing. But until we find you work, there is cleaning and cooking to be done right here, and there is to be no complaining. We don't take well to ungrateful girls. Do you understand?"

"Yes, ma'am."

"Very well. Go with Wilma; she'll find you a place to sleep."

They walked through the long corridors. Wilma put her finger over her lips. "It's important that we don't make a lot of noise here," Wilma whispered. Alina didn't say anything. She just continued to follow Wilma. She had no idea what life in a convent would be like. But she was grateful to have a place to stay. At least she wouldn't be alone in the park after the sunset at the mercy of those hungry, desperate men. Alina shivered when she thought of how their eyes had bored through her. No matter what the nuns expected of her, it had to be better than that.

"Thank you for bringing me here." Alina's voice was choking up with gratitude.

"They do work us hard, and they expect us to be decent women, but all in all, it's not so bad. Don't get me wrong, it's not easy, but it could be much worse. Anyway, I want you to meet some of the others. Especially Eileen. She's the girl from Ireland who brought me here. She's funny and very witty. You'll like her. Her sister Coleen is here too. She's going to be a nun."

Alina smiled. She tried not to think of her family or Johan or of being Jewish. This was a new page in her life. She had to be flexible if she was going to survive.

thirty-two

Alina

THE MOTHER SUPERIOR had not lied when she said there would be hard work. Alina learned quickly that living in the convent meant adhering to strict rules.

She watched young novices begin their journey to become nuns or sisters, as the girls called them. The girls were required to dress in clothes that underplayed all feminine aspects of their bodies. Even their undergarments were subject to approval. If they didn't own proper clothing, the nuns provided it, and the girls were required to attend church services. The services were not so different from the ones she'd attended sometimes on high holidays at the synagogue when she was a child. But because her family wasn't religious, she didn't attend very often. At the convent, the mandatory attendance in the church was much more frequent, and sometimes she wished she didn't have to go when she was tired or just wanted time to herself. But there was no refusing. Great dedication was required of the nuns and priests. They were expected to remain chaste for their entire lives, and Alina wondered how they could manage that.

But every day, Alina suffered from anxiety because she knew that soon her pregnancy would be visible. If anyone at the convent discovered that she was pregnant out of wedlock, there would be hell to pay.

So, she knew she had to make up a story to explain her pregnancy to the Mother Superior. She lied and said that her husband had died on the ship. She told herself it wasn't really a lie. They would have been married had it not been for the Nuremberg laws. And if he had lived, God bless his soul, Johan would have married her as soon as they could. But that wasn't the only lie she was living with. She had told them at the convent that she was Catholic.

It only took three weeks for Alina to be sent out on a job as a live-in nanny and maid for an elderly couple who were caring for their ten-year-old grandson. Both of the child's parents had perished in an automobile accident. So he'd gone to live with his only relatives, his father's aging parents. The old couple were originally from Germany and had migrated to the US before the First World War. However, they had not even attempted to learn English. Since they were Catholics and had come to America before the war began, they were recognized by the church as Americans. When the couple had put in a request for help, several German-speaking girls were called to interview for the position. Alina was one of them. She was asked if she could tolerate caring for an elderly woman who was ill, an elderly man who was in a wheelchair, and a young boy. Of all the girls interviewed, she was the only one who said she could handle the job.

When the door was opened to the apartment where the couple lived, Alina was hit in the face by the unpleasant odor of filth. She should have expected as much. The elderly occupants could not clean, and the child was too young to care. It took her the first three days to clean the apartment and put the place in order. Gunther and Hilda Meister were kind but very sickly and feeble. There was little interaction between the couple and Alina. Most of the time, the Meisters were in their bed asleep. Alina brought them food, but neither of them accepted her offer to help them bathe, which they rarely did. She did what she could, but there was nothing more she could do for them.

Until Alina arrived, the boy, Hans, had been running wild without supervision. Although only ten, he was already smoking in the house and had been caught stealing. He hovered in the alleyways with a group of rebellious boys older than him. These boys used him to break into homes and burglarize because he was still small enough to fit easily through windows. Something had to be done before Hans ended up in prison. The grandparents discussed sending Hans off to a brownshirt camp for the remainder of the summer. They knew he was a handful and far too much of a delinquent for Adelheid to control. The brownshirt camps, although they were filled with Nazi propaganda, offered a healthy outdoor setting and plenty of discipline.

The grandparents hoped that being away from his friends would benefit Hans. One afternoon, when Alina brought Mrs. Meister's lunch to her bed, Mrs. Meister asked Alina to sit down and talk with her. Alina was glad for the company. So she sat on the edge of the bed. The room had a putrid, musty odor.

"Adelheid, my husband, Gunther, and I are having plenty of problems with Hans, as you know."

"Yes, I know." Alina nodded.

"When we hired you, we hoped that somehow you would be able to control him with a strong hand. But that was foolish on our part. He is much too far gone. I see that he doesn't listen to you either. He needs discipline, and neither Gunther nor I are able to control him. We are thinking that maybe we will send him to one of the Bund camps. Personally, I don't like the Nazi ideology that they teach. After all, I don't want to get into trouble here in America. Gunther and I have a comfortable life here. If, for some reason, the United States decided to deport us, it would be terrible. But as you know, Mr. Meister and I don't have much money to spare, and we live on very little. The summer camp through the Bund is inexpensive, and from what I hear, they are very strict and will help him get on the right path."

Nazi camps for children in the United States? Right here in New York? Alina felt woozy, like she might faint. She'd run all the way across the ocean, she'd suffered losses and made sacrifices all to escape from Hitler, but his shadow was still here, hovering over her. Who could ever have thought that there would be Nazi summer camps in the United States?

"Nazi camps for children?" Alina asked, hoping she'd heard wrong.

"Yes, they are summer camps where the children get a lot of exercise outdoors. They keep them busy and out of trouble, but more importantly, they get a lot of discipline. It would take him away from the neighborhood and from that crowd of hoodlums who have become his friends, at least for the summer. Unless, Adelheid, you truly believe that you can turn him around. It won't be easy. Mr. Meister and I know he is a difficult boy, and we won't fault you if you feel it would be too difficult. What do you think?"

"I am not sure what to think. I mean, I don't know if I can handle Hans. He doesn't listen to me at all. But, well, Nazi summer camps for children in America?"

"I usually don't like to tell anyone this, but Gunther is a member of the Bund and was very involved before he became ill. I didn't approve. But that didn't matter to him. He is a man. You know how men are. They do what they want to do, and once they are married, their wives have to put up with it. But now, he's too sick to participate. He has no energy for it anymore. It doesn't matter anyway because after Kuhn was arrested in 1939, everything with the Bund started slowing down. Kuhn was the leader, you know, and he was a terrible man. He stole a lot of money from the members. That's why he was put in jail."

"I don't know anything about the Bund or anyone named Kuhn."

"Well, you just got here from Germany, didn't you, Adelheid?"

"Yes," Alina replied, deciding it was best to keep her mouth shut and listen rather than say anything that would bring suspicion to her.

"Well, anyway, like I was saying, Kuhn was arrested. But Gunther refuses to believe that Kuhn is guilty even though he was convicted. Gunther's quite sure that it's an American conspiracy to destroy the Nazi Party in the United States. And as I said, between you and me, I am glad my husband has stopped being so involved. We don't need any trouble. I thought that after Kuhn was arrested, the camps for children would be gone. But one of my lady friends told me a few summer camps are still in operation. If Hans weren't such a difficult boy, I would never consider sending him. But what can we do? He is getting into more trouble every day. I am afraid he is going to end up in prison, maybe for a long time. Who knows? Maybe his whole life. He is going in the wrong direction. And, Mr. Meister and I are too old to take hold of him. When we hired you, we hoped that you would be able to straighten him out. But now we see that a young girl is not strong enough to control a boy like this. It's not your fault. But of course, you understand that we cannot afford to keep you and send Hans off to camp, too. It has to be one or the other. I am sorry."

Alina looked down at the ground. Hilda Meister was right; she wasn't strong enough to handle Hans. And now he was going to become another Nazi in the making, and she was going to go back to the convent as a failure. She nodded, feeling defeated.

She'd only been with the Meisters a month, and she had already been fired. Alina packed her bag and left. She was not ready to face the Reverend Mother, who would be so disappointed in her. She would have to explain why she'd not been able to keep her job. The Reverend Mother would not accept her backing down from the challenge. Alina was sure she would say that Alina should have been able to handle Hans.

Heartsick about her future, Alina walked through the streets, not ready to return to the convent. The nuns would probably not send her out on another job for a long time. She might even be punished with extra chores. What was she going to do with the rest of her life? She couldn't live in the convent forever.

Some other girls had decided to join the order and become nuns, but this was not even a consideration for Alina. She needed time to gather her thoughts, so she stopped to sit on the ground under a large maple tree in a small park. Over the past month, she had learned a little English when she'd gone to the markets to buy food for the Meisters, but she still did not know enough to get along on her own in America. Well, at least she knew her way back to the convent, so she wouldn't have to go through the misery of finding someone who could speak enough German to give her directions.

Her empty stomach growled with hunger, wishing she had something to eat. It was not good for the baby that she had not eaten in hours. Alina sat in the park for a long time, wishing she could talk to her mother about how she felt. She needed Michal now. Her body was changing with the pregnancy, and she wasn't sure what was normal and what was not.

When Alina was young, this was not how she imagined it would be when she grew up and had a family of her own. She always thought that her mama and papa would be by her side. Her husband would be excited about the arrival of his child. And all would be right with the world. But that was before Hitler had blown the top off the mountain of dreams she'd kept in her heart and turned her life into a volcano spewing hot lava.

"Don't cry," Alina told herself. "If there is one thing you must have learned from all of this, it is that crying doesn't ever help anything." Alina sighed. What was she going to do? She couldn't talk to the nuns or the other girls about having a baby. She had been forced to tell the nuns that she was pregnant and that her husband had died on the journey to America. However, instead of the lie working in her favor, it turned everything in her world upside down. The Mother Superior kept insisting that she give the baby up to a wealthy family for adoption as soon as it was born. The very idea of losing touch with her child horrified her. This baby was all she had in the world.

But what other choice did she have? She had no income. Fortunately, she still had a little money Johan had given her but no husband. There was only one person who might be able to help: Johan's father. But Johan had warned her about him. Still, she had to try. Her mind began weighing her options. The well-worn yellowed paper with Johan's father's name and address was still in her bra. She'd kept it there so no one would ever find it. She took the paper out with trembling hands and read the name aloud. "Trevor Powell." This was Johan's biological father. She looked down at the paper and read his address. She would show the paper to strangers and ask them how to get to this location. Once she finds Trevor Powell, she will tell him everything. In exchange for his help getting settled, Alina would swear never to tell his wife about Johan. His wife need never know about his affair in Germany and the child he left behind. She wouldn't blackmail him. She would only ask for a little help. Being devious wasn't her way of doing things.

Instead, Alina would beg with all of her heart for him to allow her to work for him and his family as a maid so that she could have her baby and keep the child. It was farfetched. Trevor Powell would probably deny he ever had a son. He would probably throw her out, and she would have wasted money on carfare. But she had to try.

So Alina, or Adelheid, as she was known in America, got up and began looking for a woman to ask for directions. It was dangerous to approach a man and let him know that she was alone and lost. She passed couples and men alone but did not see a woman until she looked into the window of a coffee shop. A heavyset middle-aged woman with graying blond hair was at the counter serving food. Alina walked in. Her mouth watered from the smell of the food. At that moment, she thought about going back to the convent. At least she would be assured of something to eat. But she was so ashamed of being let go from her job that she couldn't face the sisters. Sitting on a stool at the end of the counter, she waited for the waitress to come over and try to take her order. In the best English she could muster, she stumbled over the words.

"*Bitte*, you can help me?" Alina put the paper with the address down in front of her. "*Wei kann* I go to this address?"

"Let me have a look, honey," the waitress said, taking the paper in her hand. "Let's see. This here address is located in a pretty damned nice part of town. You can take the A train for three stops, then get off and walk three blocks to the north..."

Alina's eyes were glued to the woman as she spoke, but Alina only understood bits and pieces of what the woman was telling her.

"You don't understand me, do you?" The woman smiled. Then she yelled across the counter, "Anybody here speak German?"

"Who the hell would want to speak Kraut?" One of the businessmen at the counter dressed in a suit and tie said, "I hate those bastards."

An older man at the counter said, "Yeah, Doris, I speak a little German. I learned it when I fought in the Great War. What do you need?" His hair was combed back neatly, and he wore a clean button-down shirt.

"This gal here needs some directions. She's tryin' to get to this here address, but she don't speak English. So, I can't help her. Can you give her a little help, Joe?"

"Yeah, sure."

Joe's German wasn't perfect, but it was enough for Alina to figure out how to navigate her way to Johan's father's house.

"*Danke, danke so Viel,*" Alina said to Doris and Joe, and then she left the restaurant and walked down the stairs to the subway station.

Twice, Alina went the wrong way and got lost because she had trouble reading the signs, but by seven that evening, she arrived at the home of Johan's birth father. The house was large and well-maintained, as were all the homes on the block. This was an expensive area. They were all brick or stone with beautifully landscaped lawns. Her head ached from the full day of travel, and she wished she felt more confident in what she was about to do. If Trevor Powell sends her away, she will have to return to the convent. Soon, it would be getting dark outside.

And to make matters worse, she was lost. She had no idea how to get back to the convent because she'd taken such a roundabout way to get to Powell's house. Sweat trickled down her armpits and pooled under her bra. Her fingers felt for the small roll of dollar bills she'd stashed inside her bra, and once she was sure they were still there, Alina straightened her back, knocked on the door, and waited.

A tall man with a semi-bald head and slender build answered the door. "I'm sorry. I don't want to buy anything."

"Are you Trevor Powell?"

"Who are you?" the man asked suspiciously, and Alina felt her stomach sink.

She stammered, "I can come please inside and talk to you."

"I am not interested." He began to close the door.

Alina was exhausted. Her shoulders and neck were so sore that she reached up and rubbed them. She felt tears stinging behind her eyes. "Bitte, please…"

"Who are you?" the man asked in perfect German.

"I am Alina Margolis. But, my papers say I am Adelheid Strombeck. My betrothed was Johan Strombeck. Please, I need to talk to you," she answered in German.

The man studied her. Then he shook his head. "I should have expected this," he said. Then, to her surprise, he added, "Come in."

"Sit down," he said, speaking to her in German. "My wife, she should rest in peace, passed on last month. If she were still alive, I could not have welcomed you in. She knew nothing about my indiscretion in Germany."

"Johan said not to come. He said you would not help me. But I had no place else to turn."

"And I would not have. But I guess fortune is in your favor," he said, sounding bitter. "So, what? You need money?"

"I need help. I need work. I am pregnant with your grandson."

The man got up and walked to the window. "Pregnant? Where is Johan?"

"He died on the ship on the way over from Germany."

"Oh."

"*Bitte*, don't send me away…"

Trevor Powell paced the room with his hands clasped behind his back. He didn't speak until he stopped and looked out the big picture window in the living room. Then, without looking at Alina, he said, "Well, I suppose I could use a housekeeper. My wife managed everything in the house. She supervised our housekeeper and our cook. After she passed away, I fired them. That was an act of insanity. Of course, I realize that now, but I was rather out of my mind at the time. I just wanted to be alone. There were too many people in the house. It's very strange, but I am still grieving my wife. I didn't realize how much she had done for me when she was alive. I suppose you can say I took her for granted. Now, I am lost without her."

Alina looked around and noticed that although the house was not as filthy as the Meisters' home had been, it was in disarray. She could see that he had neglected it for a while. "I could take care of your home, do the cooking, and manage things for you. I would stay out of your way. You wouldn't even know that I was here." Alina cast her eyes to the marble floor. "Mr. Powell, please, I need help. I desperately need a place to stay."

"Hmmm, I suppose you could work for me. My Norma, my wife, could not be hurt by learning about my past anymore, so it really doesn't make any difference. You don't know the guilt I've felt for so long over the affair I had with Johan's mother in Germany. Thank God Norma never found out," he said, shrugging his shoulders. A deep line between his eyebrows grew deeper when he talked of his past.

"I would be so grateful to you," Alina whispered.

"There is a room on the second floor for the housekeeper. You see, Norma and I never had any children of our own. She loved children, but she couldn't have them. I want you to understand that it would be just you and I together in this house. How do you feel about that? Would that be all right with you? People might get the wrong impression. A young girl living alone with a man who is not her husband."

"I don't have the luxury to care what people say. I need a place to stay. I need work."

"All right then. Go up the stairs, turn left, and the housekeeper's room is the second door on your right, just after the bathroom. I will pay you a small salary. Mostly, your payment will be in the form of room and board. If that is alright with you, you can start work tomorrow."

"Yes, it is wonderful. Thank you, thank you."

He nodded. "Yes, go now, please. I need to be alone."

thirty-three

Alina

1941

ALINA FOUND life in Trevor Powell's home to be pleasant. He was an undemanding employer. In fact, he hardly spoke to her, and she was very quiet, making it a point to stay out of his way. Still, she prepared his food and kept the house immaculate. Her heart sang with gratitude for the roof over her head and her unborn child.

Trevor didn't go out much, so he didn't dress up very often, but when he did, she immediately pressed the shirt and trousers that he'd worn so he always looked well-dressed. Slowly, Trevor began to open up and talk to Alina. It seemed that he was beginning to enjoy having human companionship. Since he spoke perfect German, they were able to converse easily. Never again did he mention his affair with Johan's mother, and Alina didn't ask any questions. Of course, she wondered how they'd met, what had happened between them. She wondered if he'd ever seen pictures of Johan or if he'd ever even thought about him. But if she had asked those questions, it could easily have changed the congenial atmosphere that Alina and Trevor shared, and she wasn't about to lose her home over mere curiosity.

For the first two weeks, Alina was nothing but a servant to Trevor.

She ate alone in the kitchen while he ate alone at the dining table. However, one evening, Trevor asked her to join him for dinner in the dining room, and from that day on, they had their meals together. Soon, they began going for long walks in the afternoon, sometimes taking the subway to Central Park and bringing lunch for a picnic.

Trevor was a great deal older than Alina. Although she dared not ask his age, she assumed from Johan's age and Trevor's appearance that he was around fifty. As the weeks went by, she could see in the way Trevor looked at her that he was beginning to find her attractive. Perhaps it was her youth and his loneliness, but Alina could see that he wanted something more from her. And because he had never really known Johan, he didn't see her as a daughter-in-law. Instead, it began to feel as if he was courting her. Alina wasn't sure if he expected her to be his mistress or if he wanted a wife. So far, he had not shown her disrespect by attempting to take her to his bed or kiss her. Alina was glad for this, but she knew instinctively by how he looked at her that it was only a matter of time. This caused her distress because she was getting further along in her pregnancy, and she knew that if she rejected him, she would risk being back out on the street.

Trevor enjoyed having the company. Since he'd lost his wife, he had been drifting, in many ways even waiting for his own death so that he could join her. He'd been a terrible husband in his youth, mean sometimes, difficult, and unfaithful. In fact, there had been more indiscretions than just Johan's mother. But Johan's mother had been the longest and most serious affair he'd had. And, as far as he knew, Johan had been his only child. But as the years rambled on, the sexual hunger that had once driven him to have affairs faded, and he and Norma became more than husband and wife—they became best friends.

He sometimes wondered if she ever knew about the other women. If she did, she never mentioned them, and he never told her. But it wasn't until she was gone that he realized how her constant presence had comforted him through their years together. She'd listened to his problems and never questioned him when he traveled for months. The truth was, Norma had loved him. No one else in his life had ever really loved him.

Trevor was abandoned at birth and raised in a Catholic orphanage. He never knew his parents. But from what he had been told, it was believed that his mother was an unmarried teenager who'd abandoned him on the steps of the orphanage late one night when he was just an infant. A week before little Trevor was found on the steps, a young girl from a farm had arrived in town. She'd taken a room in a flophouse a few blocks from the orphanage. The neighborhood people noticed her because she was not accompanied by a man and was obviously pregnant. In fact, she was the topic of gossip among the ladies because no one knew where she'd come from. Then, from the day that the infant was found on the steps, the girl was never seen again. This was all Trevor knew about his background.

However, although he was born into poverty, Trevor was not about to spend his life after the orphanage in a flophouse. He was willing to work hard, as hard as was necessary, to rise above the stigma of his shameful birth. Over the years, he'd made every effort to befriend important people at any cost. He became involved in the building of skyscrapers. Money was his first love. Women and illicit sex were his second. When he met Norma, she was young and very beautiful. But more importantly, she was from a wealthy and respected family. Trevor saw the opportunity to leave his pathetic background behind. So, he seduced her, and she became pregnant. Of course, this was exactly what he wanted, and he married her. If Trevor could have had it his way, he would have fallen in love with her. Instead, he found himself resenting the loss of freedom that came with marriage. And because all of his success depended on Norma, he resented her too.

Once his father-in-law took him into business, he began to earn substantial amounts of money. But his rebellious side refused to be satisfied. He went out at night and found prostitutes to prove to himself that he was still in control of his own life and that although Norma's family controlled the money, he was still his own man.

Norma loved being pregnant and couldn't wait for the baby to be born. The truth was that he really didn't want a child. To him, that would be just another rope around his neck. In Norma's seventh month of pregnancy, she miscarried. After that, due to the complications of the miscarriage, the doctor recommended that she not become pregnant again.

Trevor believed at the time that he had willed that miscarriage and blamed himself for what happened. He was sick with guilt. Instead of being kinder to Norma, he hated her even more. He felt trapped and felt as if he'd been cheated out of his life. Then, to make matters worse, because of Norma's condition, he was told that he must curtail their sexual life to prevent her from becoming pregnant again. He thought he might go mad with the need for release. Careful not to get caught, he went out several nights a week to visit the prostitutes.

Then everything changed. Trevor's father-in-law had a stroke and died within days. Now Trevor had no one to answer to. It no longer mattered if he got caught. There was no one to turn him out. So, he became even more promiscuous. Then Trevor got tired of having to be home every night. He wanted even more freedom, so Trevor lied to Norma and told her he had to go out of the country on business. She was a mouse of a girl, quiet, sweet, and adoring. She never questioned him. Trevor was gone for weeks at a time. He would return home and have affairs that lasted for several months. Trevor would stay with a lover until he grew tired of her and found a new one.

Then he went to Germany and met Johan's mother. He loved the country as well as the great sex he had with the woman, so he stayed for almost six months. Finally, he returned home. Norma welcomed him back without question. Strangely enough, throughout their marriage, Trevor never told Norma that he loved her because he didn't know that he did, at least not until she was gone.

After Norma died, Trevor fell into a dark depression. He rehashed his mistakes and had so many regrets. That was until this lovely young girl, Alina, came out of nowhere and illuminated the darkness in his soul.

Alina was like a beautiful butterfly that alit in his home. She was young and delicate. Her smile made him feel warm inside, and he enjoyed her company. Age and the loss of his wife gave Trevor the need for stability, a family, and a legacy to leave behind when his time came. Even more importantly, he wanted to be sure that if he became ill or feeble, there would be someone there to care for him. Those were the thoughts that went through his mind when he decided that he wanted to marry Alina. If he could keep her with him, maybe he would never feel that terrible emptiness in the pit of his stomach that he felt when he was alone. He doubted he would be much good to her as a lover; his body had begun to fail him, but he was willing to try. A wife would do him good. And Alina and her unborn baby needed a home. It seemed like a perfect match.

Of course, Trevor would never reveal the truth about his humble beginnings to Alina. If he did, he was afraid he would be less in her eyes, so he wanted her to believe he had been born into the wealthy class. And now, with his wife, Norma, and all his in-laws gone, she had no way of ever learning the truth. Trevor Powell could be anyone he chose to be, and he liked it that way.

thirty-four

THE END of November cast a chill upon New York City. Trevor proposed to Alina. She told him that she wanted a little time to think it over. He wasn't happy about that, but he agreed. Later, when she was alone that evening in her room, she considered the proposal. She should have been happy and excited. Trevor was wealthy. But, instead of being elated, Alina wanted to say no to him. He was much older than she was, and the thought of a physical relationship with him repelled her. But she was afraid that Trevor would be hurt and angry if she refused. Then, he might decide to throw her out in the street. If he did, she would be homeless and destitute again. So, she thought it through a little more. Even though she wasn't attracted to him romantically, she reasoned that he seemed kind. He seemed to care for her. This marriage would give her the security she needed for her unborn child. So Alina closed her eyes, took a deep breath, said a prayer, then went to Trevor's room and knocked on the door.

"Come in, Alina," he said.

"Yes, Trevor, I'll marry you."

He smiled. "It will be good for all three of us," he said. "You, me, and the baby…"

Yes, and especially my baby. My baby will grow up safe, in a secure home, and not wanting for anything.

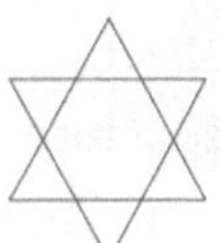

thirty-five

Alina

THE FOLLOWING MONTH, Japan bombed Pearl Harbor, sending the United States diving headlong into the war. Everywhere on the streets of New York, Alina saw Americans ready to fight for the country they loved. Boys were enlisting in the armed forces left and right. She saw posters of Uncle Sam and boys looking smart in their pressed new armed forces uniforms.

Trevor was too old and unhealthy to enlist, so he and Alina were married instead. The bombing on American soil shook the country to its very core. This was a time for the immigrants to stand up and show that they, too, were true Americans. This war was personal for Alina. She prayed that with the help of the mighty United States, Hitler would finally be defeated.

For several years, the world had been watching as Hitler was on his way to conquering all of Europe. Alina was worried sick over the fighting between Britain and Germany because Gilde was there. She'd heard that Germany had been bombing London relentlessly. Every night, she said a prayer that Gilde was safe. She'd tried to write to Gilde and Lotti but had received no answer from either of them. All that she'd left behind, her parents, her sister, her friends. What had become of them? She had no way of finding out.

Alina and Trevor Powell were married on the fifth of January. Alina gave birth to Johan's son three months and five days later. Sometime during her childhood, Alina learned that in the Jewish religion, people named their children after their loved ones who had passed away. She knew she wanted to name the baby after Johan. And so she followed the Jewish tradition to the best of her recollection by taking the first letter of Johan's name and calling their son Joseph. When Joseph was first born, Trevor loved the baby. However, Trevor wasn't used to having an infant in the house, and soon he grew ill-tempered. The child cried, kept him awake at night, and needed all of Alina's attention. And, because Alina was so taken with the baby, Trevor also grew tired of Alina.

Before Joseph was born, Trevor fancied himself the center of Alina's world. Now, since she became a mother, she was different, and his needs came after the needs of her noisy, annoying child. Trevor began to make sarcastic remarks that hurt his wife. However, she never said a word. Alina would just look at him when he said terrible things, with her eyes glassy and her heart heavy. The marriage that had seemed so right now felt like a prison.

"You realize you will never get your pre-baby figure back, right?" Trevor said one day, Alina sat on a chair, nursing Joseph.

Alina shrugged. But secretly, she felt fat and unattractive. As time passed, Trevor found little ways to dig at her insecurities and make her feel inferior. He had tried to make love to her several times since Joseph was born, but he was unable to keep an erection, and for this, he blamed her. When they were first married, he claimed that he didn't want to hurt the baby, so he didn't touch her at all. But after Joseph was born, he tried to make love to her and failed. That was when he began making comments about her body. And Alina believed him. Finally, he gave up trying to make love to her, and she was glad that she didn't have to remove her clothes in front of him anymore.

Trevor decided that it was best that Alina move back into the bedroom where she'd lived before they were married. "The baby wakes me up crying during the night. It's probably best for you to stay in the same room as your child. You can keep him quiet. That way, I can finally get a decent night's sleep," Trevor growled.

Alina watched the lines grow deeper in Trevor's face as he snarled at her. He looked so old and selfish that it sent a shiver up her spine. Every night, Alina said a silent prayer that Trevor would grow accustomed to having a baby in the house. That he would become more tolerant and maybe even loving towards Joseph.

But if she were completely honest with herself, Alina had to admit she was glad to sleep in the smaller room with a cradle for her son. When she'd first married Trevor, she believed that, in many ways, he was her savior. He was going to make the world right for her and the baby. But now, every time he said something hurtful or critical of her or Joey, as she called him, she was more repulsed by him. Sometimes, she felt guilty for being ungrateful. But it had gone beyond a lack of gratitude or a mild dislike. Alina was beginning to hate her husband. She tried to put those horrible feelings out of her mind and somehow make her shattered marriage work, if not for her sake, then for Joey's. But whenever she did something kind for Trevor, he pushed her kindness aside, leaving her feeling unloved and useless. She would have been miserable if it had not been for little Joey.

Alina missed her family even more since Joey was born. They would have loved him if they had all seen him. She was sure of it. Every week, she tried to send letters to Lotti and Gilde but never received an answer. Nor did the letters return to her as being undeliverable. So, she had no information about her family or Lotti and Lev. If only the Nazis and her migration to America had all been nothing but a nightmare. If somehow, by the grace of God, she could wake up at home in her own bed with her sister in the room down the hall, with her parents in the kitchen, and her friends living down the road. If only… But it was not a dream. None of it was a dream. It was all real. Even Johan's death. Poor Johan.

Alina still cared deeply for him, but perhaps because of the circumstances of their lives, she had never allowed herself to fall madly in love with him the way he was with her. During their short courtship, she'd been in a constant state of worry. The changes in her life then—and still—were coming too rapidly, and her emotions were stunted. Perhaps it was the fear of loving and losing again. Still, sometimes, when she was alone and Joey was asleep, Alina would whisper to Johan in the darkness. She would tell him about Joey, and sometimes, in her mind, she could hear him answer. Then she would feel the tears slip down her cheeks and wet the pillow. Oh, how she missed having a man take care of her and treat her kindly.

Little Joey was a lot of work, requiring constant attention. Regardless of how much effort she had to put into caring for him, Joey was his mother's one true joy. Joey was the only reason Alina ever smiled anymore. And finally, one day, he smiled back. It was late spring, and Alina had made a friend at the park. She was a mother close to Alina's age. They were sitting under a tree with their children in carriages when Joey smiled.

"Look, look, Maria, he's smiling."

"It's gas. My mother said when a baby smiles, it's gas," Maria answered, laughing. She was a short, pretty girl, a little chunky, with long dark hair. Her parents had come to America from Italy, but she was born in New York. Alina had learned enough English to communicate a little with Maria. Whenever she and Maria met, Maria would help her learn more. One Sunday, Maria invited Alina to bring Joey to her family's house for dinner.

"Bring your husband along. My mama makes a wonderful Sunday sauce."

"I would love to come. But my husband will probably be out of town on business. He's always having to go somewhere," Alina lied. The truth was she didn't trust Trevor to behave. When he met Maria and her family, he might make obnoxious comments. Although she'd never been to their home before, Alina was fairly sure that Maria's family was not wealthy. Certainly not in Trevor's financial class. She knew him and she knew he would tell her that her Italian immigrant friends weren't suitable companions for the wife of a Powell. Since Trevor controls all of the money, if he forbade the friendship, she would be forced to listen to him or risk his anger and any consequences his rage might bring. He had ways of punishing behavior he didn't approve of. The less he knew about Maria, the better. So, she decided not to invite Trevor. She liked Maria and enjoyed having a young female friend to talk to. Their children were close in age, so they shared a great deal in common.

He paid no attention to her comings and goings. In fact, he was so glad when she took Joey out of the house that he never asked where she went.

On Saturday, Alina baked a cake to bring to Maria's house. Then, on Sunday morning, she dressed Joey in his nicest clothes and stepped into a white summer dress that was tastefully covered with red roses. Trevor saw her getting ready to go out, but he never said a word. He just scoffed and walked into his room. Without looking back, Alina gently laid Joey in his carriage and walked almost a mile to Maria's house for dinner.

The food was wonderful. Maria was right. The sauce on the noodles her mother had prepared made her taste buds explode with delight. Alina had never tasted anything like it. Maria's parents were much older and mainly spoke Italian, but her husband, her two brothers, and her younger sister spoke perfect English. Whenever the parents said something in Italian, one of the younger family members carefully explained what the parents were saying so Alina would not feel left out. Alina's English was still not good enough for her to understand everything that was said. Still, she instinctively knew that no one was talking badly about her. As she watched the family laughing and kidding with each other, she felt the warmth of the love they shared.

Everyone was very kind to her; she was grateful for their generosity and happy for them and all they had. But just sitting with all of them gathered together around a table only reminded Alina of her life such a long time ago, a life she might never have again.

Alina and Maria continued to meet in the park twice a week. They arranged the times for their visits to begin a few hours before their children took their afternoon naps. However, when Maria asked Alina to come to dinner again, Alina made an excuse and declined.

One afternoon, after meeting with Maria, Alina had left the park.

It was a hot summer day, and she was walking back home when she saw a familiar face. Her eyes lit up. The man she recognized was crossing the street and walking towards a big white truck. When he looked up and saw her, his handsome face broke into a smile. He waved and called out, "Alina."

She recognized his face. He was the Russian she'd met on the boat. She couldn't remember his name. She waved. He ran over to her. "How have you been?"

"Fine," she said, trying to smile. "This is my son, Joey."

"Hi, Joey," He said. He spoke perfect German, but his Russian accent reminded Alina so much of her father that she couldn't decide whether to embrace him or cry. "You forgot my name?"

She shrugged. "Yes, I'm sorry."

"Ugo, Ugo Blok. I remember your name. Your real name and your not-so-real name. You're really Alina Margolis, but you go by Adelheid Strombeck."

"Good memory," she said.

He laughed. "How could I forget such a pretty smile?"

"I have another name now. I'm Adelheid Powell. Or Alina Powell, if you prefer. I got married."

"Congratulations," he said, thinking she quickly met someone after Johan's death. But that happened often to immigrants. It was easier for a woman to be married than to be alone in this country. "So, what do you prefer to be called, Adelheid or Alina?"

She thought she saw a quick flash of disappointment flare across his face when she said she was married. But then it was gone.

"Alina. I prefer Alina. I suppose I always will. I can't get used to being Adelheid."

"Alina it is." He smiled. "Well, I guess I should be going. It's good to see you again."

"Yes. It's very good to see you," she said. He began walking away. Something in her gut made her panic. If he left, she'd never see him again. She'd never hear that voice that sounded so much like her papa again. "Ugo," she said. He turned around. "I just wondered if you ever saw anyone else from the boat?" She felt stupid. Now that she'd called out to him, she really had nothing to say.

"No, I don't remember anyone else that was onboard. You and your husband were the only people I talked to," he said. Then he must have seen something in her eyes because he cocked his head and stared at her. "Alina, is something wrong?"

She hardly knew this man, but she wanted to tell him everything. She'd grown up believing every woman needed a strong man to lean on. Ugo was that sort of man. And he reminded her so much of her papa that she would have liked to tell him everything. If only she could open up to him and talk about Trevor and the loss of her family and the joy it brought her to hear someone speak with her father's Russian accent. But how could she? So Alina just shrugged and shook her head. "No, nothing is wrong. I'm fine." Then she couldn't control the tears, and she began to weep.

Ugo's coworker, who stood beside the white truck, called to Ugo, "Come on, let's go. We gotta deliver another piano before dark."

"Wait a minute. This is an old friend of mine. I have to take a few minutes to talk to her. I'll be right there." He spoke to his coworker in broken English. But his English was much better than Alina's.

"What's wrong? Talk to me. You can talk to me," Ugo said to Alina in German. Her head was hung low, and he crouched down so their eyes were level.

She shook her head. "I can't."

"You can."

"Not here, not now, not like this in the middle of the street." She took out a handkerchief and wiped her eyes and nose. "I'm sorry. I don't know what came over me. I guess I just felt so nostalgic seeing someone from the boat. It made me think of Johan." She lied. She hadn't been thinking of Johan at that moment. In fact, she didn't know what she wanted from Ugo. All she knew was that she didn't want to say goodbye.

"I have an idea. I am taking an English class one morning a week. It is made up mostly of Russian students. But I think it will help you learn the language. Would you, maybe, like to come to class with me?"

She knew he was married. She had seen his beautiful wife. And momentarily, she felt a bit envious of the striking redhead. Because Trevor had made her feel overweight and matronly, she was suddenly insecure. But she didn't want to walk away from Ugo forever. Alina thought she must be going out of her mind. What was she thinking? After all, she was married too. But she heard herself say, "Yes, I would like to come to class. I want to learn English. I need to learn English."

"The class is on Saturday morning. I'll meet you right here, and we can go together. Can you make it by nine o'clock?"

Saturday morning? On the Sabbath? Why was she thinking about that now? She hadn't celebrated Shabbat in years. So, what had brought that to mind? Even Trevor didn't know she was a Jew. "I'll be here," she said, wondering if some wild and free spirit had suddenly taken possession of her.

"Good. I'll see you then," Ugo said. "I'm sorry, Alina. I have to go now. I deliver pianos, mostly. But sometimes heavy furniture too."

Her father made furniture. The similarities between Ugo's Russian accent, his job working with furniture, and the memories Alina held dear of her father touched her heart. *Don't start crying again.*

"Goodbye," she said, glad she would see him again.

"Goodbye for now…" he said, smiling as he turned and ran to the truck. He opened the door and hopped inside.

God, his accent sounded like her father's. *I miss you so much, Papa. I wish you could see your grandson.* Alina turned the carriage around the corner towards the home she shared with a man she could never love.

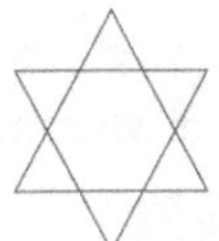

thirty-six

Alina

ALINA MET Maria in the park, as they did every Friday. Both babies had fallen asleep from the rocking of their carriages as their mothers walked to their meeting place. Alina knew Trevor wouldn't care if she went out on a Saturday morning. It seemed as if he had lost interest in her entirely. As long as Joey was quiet, she didn't see or hear from Trevor at all. He expected the house to be clean and meals to be prepared. In fact, their relationship was just as it was when she'd first arrived. Only now, she was bound to him by law and by promise. So, he no longer paid her any money for her services.

"Joey is asleep?" Maria asked. Alina nodded. "Alberto is asleep too. Ahh, it's good to have a break from the babies and just relax."

Alina nodded. "I have a big favor to ask you," she said to Maria in broken English. "Tomorrow morning I am going to go to a class to learn English at nine o'clock. I was wondering if maybe you could watch Joey for me for a few hours."

"Of course. Can you bring him to my house?"

"Yes, to your mother's house where we had dinner?"

"Yes, that's right. We all live there together. It's easier to afford to pay all the bills if we all live in one place and pitch in. I know. Too

many people in one house with only one bathroom. But we manage."
Maria smiled.

"Will you need my help every Saturday morning so you can go to this class?" Maria asked.

"Yes, if you can help me?"

"Yes, of course, I would be happy to help you."

Alina wished she had money to pay Maria, but Trevor watched every penny he gave her for food. Still, perhaps she might be able to skim a little off the top. She wouldn't offer Maria any money until she was sure she could take a little every week from her food money.

"I wish I could give you some money to pay for your babysitting."

"Don't be ridiculous. I am at home with Alberto anyway. So, what's another baby? I don't mind at all."

"Ridiculous? What does that word mean?" Alina asked.

"Silly, foolish."

Alina cocked her head. She didn't really understand. "Thank you for watching Joey. It means so much to me."

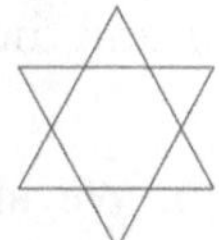

thirty-seven

THE FOLLOWING MORNING, Alina hurried to drop Joey off and then be on time to meet Ugo. But Joey had woken up cranky, and it had been difficult for her to get him ready. By the time she arrived at the corner of the street where she and Ugo had agreed to meet, she was fifteen minutes late. Alina was sure that Ugo would be gone. If he waited, he would be late for class. After all, he wasn't even sure she would show up. But to her surprise, he was waiting there. He had even dressed up in a dark suit and tie. When he saw her approaching him, Ugo smiled.

Alina's eyes locked with his, and she felt her heart leap like a tiny bird fluttering in her chest. Then she remembered he was married, and thankfully, so was she.

"You look very pretty," Ugo said. He was so outspoken that Alina blushed. She looked away so he wouldn't see that she was embarrassed but also flattered. Trevor hadn't told her she was pretty since Joey was born, and it felt good to know that a man still found her attractive. "Where is the baby?"

"Oh, I dropped Joey off at a friend's house so I could go to the class. I couldn't bring him with me. He's too young, and he would disturb everyone when he starts crying."

"That was a wise decision. You'll see that some of the students are having a tough time with English. A crying baby would make it even harder for them."

She nodded. For a few silent seconds, they stood on the sidewalk looking at each other, longing to say more, to let the other know somehow that a kind of magic was happening between them, and they both felt its power. But neither spoke.

Finally, Ugo said, "Well, come on then, we should go. We are running late."

They walked quickly. Ugo's legs were long, and it was hard for Alina to keep up, but he remembered to slow down every time he got too far ahead so she could catch up.

"Sorry to walk so fast, but we must get to class, or they will lock us out. If you are late, they close the doors, and then they don't like to let you in."

"Oh no!"

"Don't worry." He smiled. "I've been late before, and I talked them into letting me in. But if we can make it on time, it saves us a lot of trouble."

Alina nodded. She longed to ask Ugo if his wife would be in the class because Alina wasn't sure how she would feel if she met his wife face to face. Although she knew she had no real reason to feel anything at all about the woman. Ugo was just a friend who was going to help her learn English. That was all there should ever be between them. She couldn't help but find him handsome, but that didn't mean that either of them would ever let anything come of it. And besides, what would he want with a frump like her when he had such a beautiful wife? She glanced up at him and suddenly felt bad, like she'd lost something. Trevor had won. She felt ugly and undesirable.

However, she knew this class would be good for her, even life-changing. If she could speak better English, she could get a job. Then, with a bit of luck, she might somehow be able to afford to leave Trevor. *God help me. I wish I didn't have these terrible feelings about getting away from Trevor, but I can't see spending the rest of my life with him. Still,*

I am such a coward. I am so afraid to be alone again like I was when I first got here, on my own, without the safety net of a man to fall back on. Ugo opened the door for her, and they entered the classroom.

thirty-eight
Alina

EVERY SATURDAY MORNING, Alina and Ugo met and went to class together. Alina found it hard to deny that her feelings for Ugo grew daily. Not only did he remind her of her father, but he made her feel at ease when she was with him. Ugo gave her that comfortable feeling of safety that could only come from the strength of having a man to take care of her.

And strangely enough, when she and Ugo were together, she didn't think of his wife. He had a wonderful way of saying the right things that made her feel young, desirable, and even pretty again. Feeling close to Ugo came easily. This was something that never happened with Trevor. Even during their early days when Trevor had been so taken with her, he'd always had a hard, cold outer shell, which kept her at a distance. She'd never quite trusted Trevor. At first, she'd attributed it to what Johan had told her about his father, but later, Trevor had proven to be as nasty as Johan had promised he would be.

Ugo's wife never attended the class, and he never mentioned her to Alina. And although Alina knew Ugo was already married, she some-times wondered what it would be like to be his wife. He might have tried to take her to bed if he were a different kind of man. Even though she tried to hide it, she thought Ugo could tell she was terribly lonely. And out of the need to be touched and to feel loved, she might very well have slept with him. But he was always a gentleman. Ugo never acted inappropriately and never took advantage of her neediness. And the more he treated her with respect, the more impressed she was with his integrity and honor.

Sometimes, during class or as they walked together, she would glimpse him looking at her with a loving gaze or hear a softness in his voice when he said her name. She would feel such tenderness that it made the reality of the emptiness in her life even more painful. There were nights when she tossed and turned, unable to sleep because she felt so trapped in her loveless marriage. She was exhausted every day from trying to keep Joey out of Trevor's way and thought she could pass out as soon as Joey fell asleep, but it would be just the opposite. As soon as she heard Joey's gentle breathing, her mind began to race. Marriage was forever, wasn't it? She had been so hard on her mother when her parents had separated. She wished now that she could talk to Michal and tell her that through living, she had come to understand so many things she did not understand as a child.

Had she really doomed herself to a life with this terrible man? The very idea was so painful that it made her stomach ache. Then she couldn't help but think about Ugo. *Does Ugo have any feelings at all for me? Does he sometimes lie awake with thoughts of me running through his mind like I think of him? What if?* She asked herself every day, what if? What if Johan had not died? What if she had not married Trevor? What if Ugo was not married to such a beautiful woman? And they were both single? What if I didn't have a child? That would always be the 'What if?' question that sent her back to reality. She had a child, and she loved her son. The fact was that she was Trevor's wife, and Ugo was a married man, and that was just how the cards had fallen.

Alina would have remained faithful and tried her best to be Trevor's good wife if he had only been civil to her son.

It was a rainy night, nearing the end of a sweltering summer. Joey awakened from the crash of thunder in the wee hours. He cried, then went back to sleep, only to awaken in another fit of screaming the next time the thunder roared. Nothing Alina could do seemed to soothe him. He wouldn't take her breast. She carried him in her arms as she paced the room, rocking him back and forth and singing softly, but he continued to wail. When she kissed Joey's cheek, it was warm and clammy. *Oh dear God, please don't let him be sick.* Every night, Alina stayed with Joey in their room, and the door was closed. This was usually enough to keep Trevor from hearing Joey cry. But this time, Joey was screeching louder than he'd ever done before. Alina knew the noise was bothering Trevor because she heard him walk down the stairs and enter the kitchen, then return to his room and slam the door.

Still, the baby continued to wail. Finally, Alina was so frightened that something might be wrong with Joey that she went to Trevor's room to ask for money to call the doctor. He refused, telling her Joey was spoiled and crying because he wanted attention. Alina had no money of her own. If she had, she would have taken Joey to the doctor right away. She even thought about asking Maria for the money, but the rain was coming down so hard in thick, heavy sheets of water that she didn't dare try to take Joey with her to Maria's house. All she could do was wait and see how Joey did through the night. The storms continued relentlessly throughout the following day and into the evening. But Joey did not get better, and his crying did not subside. Finally, he fell asleep at a little after ten the following evening. Alina was relieved. She kissed him gently on his forehead, which felt hot under her lips. A bolt of terror surged through Alina; her son was burning up with fever. If only she could convince Trevor to give her the money, she would have gladly gone in the rain to bring the doctor back. But when she asked him again, Trevor refused. She cried and begged him, but he just turned away and left her standing there with her heart pounding with fear. *Please, God, please don't let my son die.* The hours passed, and although she was worn out, Alina lay awake in bed listening to Joey's hoarse wheezing. If she knew where Ugo lived, she would go to him in the morning and ask for help. But they had always met on the street before class. She had no idea where to find him.

Sometime during the night, Joey let out a high-pitched scream that broke the silence of the house. Alina was not asleep, but the sound still startled her. She jumped to her feet in the darkness and lifted Joey in her arms. Her throat felt dry, but she began rocking him softly. He was quieted by the motion and just whimpering now. However, Joey's screech had awakened Trevor, and he came into the room without knocking. He grabbed the baby from Alina's arms and shook Joey hard. Joey cried even louder.

Alina screamed. Trevor tossed the baby back to Alina, who caught him in her arms and pressed him to her chest. Joey's eyes were wide, and he was shrieking again. Trevor's entire body was shaking. He had no patience for a child and realized that marrying Alina had been a mistake. Still, the way he had behaved that night frightened him. He knew he should not have done that to the baby. His hands were cold and trembling.

"Shut him up. I can't bear this anymore, Alina," Trevor said, afraid that he might do something he would regret.

Alina was unnerved, and she began crying, too.

"I'm sorry. I didn't mean to hurt him," Trevor said. "But you'd better find a way to keep him quiet." Then Trevor left the room.

At that moment, Alina realized that she hated Trevor. Joey was screaming even louder. Any gratitude she'd once felt towards her husband was gone, and she didn't care. She no longer felt guilty. She was angry with him. But even more, she was scared, terrified that he might have done some irreversible damage to Joey by shaking him so hard.

Several hours passed before Joey fell asleep again. Alina took him into her bed and slept with him beside her, cradling him in her arms as her tears wet the pillow.

She barely slept that night. Her mind was moving like a freight train. She rehashed all the mistakes she'd made in her life. After this terrible marriage, she thought a lot about how she'd judged her mother. If only she could see Michal again and tell her she was sorry. Alina was born when her parents were separated. So, it was not until Alina was around five that her parents reconciled, and she came to know and love her father. Alina had been too young to remember much, but she knew that during the breakup, her mother had taken a lover, Otto. She somehow remembered his name. He was a writer of children's fables. But it wasn't Otto that stuck in her mind; it was his sister, Bridget, who was twelve. Bridget became the older sister that Alina never had. They had formed a real bond. Then Otto died, and Bridget went to live with relatives from far away. She couldn't remember where. But she remembered resenting Michal for sending Bridget away. She had been so confused, not understanding much of what was happening. But then her mother reunited with her father. The details were jumbled in her mind. But she smiled when she thought of how she'd first been afraid of her papa. He was a big, strong man, not a slender, gentle man like Otto. And for a short while, Alina was angry at her mother for bringing this strange man into their lives. But slowly, her papa won her heart with his love and kindness. He was like a giant bear with arms that could embrace and protect her. He was generous with his heart, not only to her mother but also to her. And she felt his love so deeply that as time passed, she began to feel angry at her mother for having had her affair with Otto. Then, her sister, Gilde, had come along. Instead of feeling threatened by the addition of another child, Alina adored Gilde from the first moment she saw her.

Gilde took the place that had been vacant in her life when Bridget had gone away. But, now, the roles had changed. When Alina was close to Bridget, she was the little sister. Now, Gilde was her baby sister, and Alina nurtured her like a mother. Alina shook her head in the darkness. It was hard to say why her parents had separated before she was born, but now that she was an adult and had lived through so many things, she no longer held any grudge against her mother. In fact, she wished more than anything that she could tell Michal how much she loved and appreciated everything that Michal had done for her. At the time, she'd been so angry. But now she knew that adults did things for reasons children couldn't comprehend.

Joey slept as the morning sun crept through the window shade. Gently, Alina pressed the back of her hand against his forehead. It had cooled down. Had her prayers been answered? Had God spared her son? She kissed his cheek and listened. His breathing was regular; the wheezing was not entirely gone, but it had subsided a great deal, and he seemed comfortable. Alina was deep in thought as she looked at her child asleep on his side with his thumb in his mouth.

I have to find a way to earn my own money. After last night, I know that I cannot ever put my life or the life of my son in the hands of a man again. No matter what I have to do, I will find a way to become self-supporting. Joey could have died last night, and because I was dependent on Trevor for everything, I was powerless to help him. That must never happen again, never. But how will I ever find work? How? I have no skills. Alina bit her lower lip. *Well, the English class is where I have to begin because if I can't speak the language in this country, I will never survive on my own. Being married to Trevor or any other man is not the answer. The only person I can really trust and depend upon is myself. But how?*

The next day, Joey was much better. His fever was gone, and he was smiling. Alina was amazed at how quickly he'd recovered. Whatever had been wrong with him had passed as the angel of death had passed over the homes smeared with lamb's blood on Passover, leaving him alive. She thanked God repeatedly. Her son had been spared. He'd been given back to her. However, she'd learned a valuable lesson, and her marriage to Trevor had suffered beyond repair.

It was as if Trevor crossed an invisible line that night, and from that day forward, he no longer tried to control his foul temper. During an argument several days later, he slapped Alina across her cheek when she pushed him away from Joey. His language when he spoke to Alina was coarse and disrespectful. When the baby woke him at night, he didn't think twice about banging on the locked door of Alina's room and shouting at her that he would like to kill that good-for-nothing bastard. Alina was terrified of him, not only for herself but mostly for Joey.

She had to find a way out.

Meanwhile, Ugo had become a constant in her life, a good friend.

The classes they shared became the highlight of Alina's week. He was always offering to help her. When she needed to buy clothes for Joey and didn't want to ask Trevor for money, she casually mentioned it to Ugo. The following week, he appeared at their meeting place with a bag of clothing for a baby. "I have these things from when my daughter was little. Many of them are yellow, so you can't tell if they are for a boy or a girl. Try them. Maybe they will fit," he said.

The clothing was clean, and Alina appreciated that he remembered it. Ugo had that same quiet kindness, that same thoughtfulness her father had. When she was depressed, Ugo made her laugh with jokes about the way people misunderstood his English because of his Russian accent. His easy sense of humor always gave her a feeling of well-being. But Alina knew that she dared not think about falling in love. It would only make her more dependent on another person. And a married man at that. Nothing good could come of an affair between her and Ugo. Right now, she has to concentrate on finding a way to support Joey and herself so that she can escape from Trevor. If she'd learned anything from her past, it was that going from one man to another man for security was not the answer. Alina had to have her own money to make her own decisions and care for her child without asking for help from anyone.

━━

Because she had become such an involved student, the English class proved priceless to Alina's development. She worked and studied hard, learning quickly. Her hatred for her husband motivated her. She would work hard until she could speak well enough to keep a job. Then, she could get away from Trevor. And as much as she tried to resist it, the friendship between Alina and Ugo deepened. It was hard not to like him. He was so kind and understanding and so easy to talk to. Ugo was walking her back home from class one afternoon, and they were having a conversation. Whenever they were together, they made it a point to practice their skills by speaking only in English. He was far too attentive for a man who had a wife. It angered her because his sweetness nurtured the fire in the feelings that were growing for him in her heart. Feelings she wanted to extinguish. They were pointless and counterproductive to the future she'd been planning.

"Aren't you married?" Alina asked Ugo rather curtly.

"I was. My wife left me. She took my daughter. She won't even let me see my child because of how badly I behaved when she left me. I am ashamed to tell you what happened."

Alina cocked her head. What had he done? It was hard to imagine that Ugo could have behaved the same way Trevor did. Did he hit his wife? Did he hurt his child? But now that he mentioned it, Alina had to know. "We're friends, Ugo. You can tell me what happened."

Ugo looked away from her and said, "My wife became a whore." He coughed a little but still did not turn to look at Alina. "She works in a whorehouse. It was my fault. I was a disappointment to her. You see, I couldn't earn enough money to keep her happy. She was never satisfied with what I could give her. Nothing I did or tried to do was enough for Klara. I sent her and my daughter to America before I came here. We didn't have enough money to pay for passage for all of us. I wanted to ensure she got out of Russia as quickly as possible. I mean, with the war and Stalin. I wanted to take care of them before myself. My little girl is Lada. Her formal name is Christina, but I affectionately call her Lada. It means goddess of beauty. Lada wasn't even a full year old when she and Klara came here. I was afraid to send her on the journey, but I was more afraid not to." Finally, he turned to look at her.

Alina thought she saw his eyes turning glassy with tears. But he didn't cry.

Ugo continued. "After I knew Klara and Lada had arrived in America safely, I worked at any available job just to earn enough money for passage for myself. Sometimes, I worked sixteen to eighteen hours a day. It took me a year to save enough because I also sent money to them during that time. That delayed my journey, but I wanted to make sure that I took care of them as much as I could. When I got to the United States, I didn't know it, but Klara was already working as a prostitute. It was hard to find my way here initially because of the language, but I found this job delivering heavy furniture. Believe me, I did my best to support my wife and child and to be a good husband. But I couldn't earn enough to give her the finer things in life. We were just surviving, and barely. But I began to notice that she was somehow getting jewelry and nice clothes. I couldn't understand how. So, I asked her. That's when she told me that she was working as a prostitute. In fact, she said she was glad I asked because she was planning to leave me and move into the whorehouse where she could work full-time. I failed her. I never even came close to making the kind of money that she could earn there at the brothel. It makes me sick. I feel worthless."

"I'm sorry to hear it," Alina said. She didn't say what she was thinking, but she wondered if the child was really Ugo's. Perhaps his wife had been selling her body in Russia before she'd ever left to come to the US.

"Your parents are here?" Alina asked.

"No, the people I am staying with are my aunt and uncle, but I've been calling them Mama and Papa since I was young. They are like parents to me. She's my father's sister. She married an American during the Great War, and they sponsored my wife, my daughter, and me to come into the country."

"Your parents are still in Russia?"

"They are dead. My aunt and her husband are the only real family I have. Except, of course, my daughter, who lives with her mother."

Alina saw the shame on Ugo's face. His shoulders slumped. His hands were stuffed in his pockets. And his features seemed to crumple as he talked. Alina stroked his forearm. She felt bad for him and had no doubt that he'd done all he could to make his wife happy. "I am so sorry that you went through all of this," she said gently, not knowing what else to say.

"Yes, well, I'm new to this country, and I hope that once I speak perfect English, I can get a better job and earn more money. Then I will get married again. A man should be married and have a family. I believe everyone needs someone to come home to after a hard day of work. Someone to share their lives with. You know what I mean? And for this, I will need to earn more money and get a better job."

"A better job, yes. I am sure you will get a better job." Alina liked Ugo a lot. He was a kind and honest man. A good man with a good heart. And now she knew he was single. But she'd had her fill of love and men, and she was never going to fall back into thinking of marriage as her safety net. Not anymore.

thirty-nine

Alina

ALINA KNEW that Trevor kept wads of cash in the top drawer of his dresser. After all, she washed and ironed all his clothes, then carefully put them away as he'd demanded they be arranged. Since the day she came to work for him, she has always seen the roll of American dollars when she puts the piles of neatly folded clothes into the drawer. She'd never touched the money. In fact, she'd never even dared to count it. But now that she thought about it, she realized that she had never seen Trevor count it either. He trusted her. Alina decided that he shouldn't have. Not the way he treated her and Joey. And as time went on, he only became meaner. He'd slapped her again on several occasions when he'd asked her a question, and he hadn't liked her answer. And now Alina was convinced he had married her so she would be his cook and housekeeper without expecting to be paid.

She began to think about taking money from the drawer. Then, several times when Trevor was out, and Joey was napping, Alina held the money in her trembling hands. The bills felt strange and cold in her hands. Her own thoughts terrified her. If she took all the money and ran away, Trevor would call the police, and she would end up in jail or deported. However, what if she took small amounts every so often and hid them away? In time, she would have enough to start her own business. The idea made her stomach sick with fear, but she was also excited about being free of this man and this marriage. She had never stolen anything from anyone before. But she could see no other way out.

The first time Alina stole from her husband, she took a single dollar and hid it under her pillow. All night, she worried that Trevor would notice and say something. Every time she saw him, she was terrified that she would be found out and he would beat her. But days passed, and he never mentioned the missing money. The following week, she took another two dollars. Again, he didn't notice. So, from then on, she began to take a few dollars weekly. She had no firm plan, but she knew that when the time came to go, at least she would have the money to survive and, most importantly, to take care of Joey. She longed to tell Ugo what she was doing. It would be good to talk to someone about all the guilt and fear she held like a secret in her heart. Ugo had become her closest friend; somehow, she knew he wouldn't judge her. But she decided it was best not to tell anyone about the crime she was committing. Every time Trevor said or did something that hurt her or Joey, she thought about that money, and the very thought that she'd taken it from him comforted her. As time went on, Alina grew bolder and began taking more. Trevor still didn't notice. Her little pile of cash began to grow. In fact, now it was too big to hide under a pillow, so she cut out a space between the mattress and the box spring and tucked the bills inside.

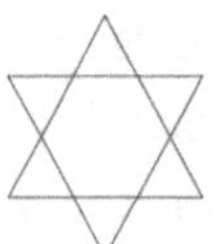

forty
Michal

April 28, 1942

RAVENSBRÜCK HAD PLENTY OF SPIES, women who had found out information before the rest of the prisoners. Because of these spies, a rumor began circulating that Himmler was planning a second visit to Ravensbrück. The last time he came, he'd walked through the camp surveying the broken women. He was making sure that all of his orders were being carried out.

Michal remembered the day of Himmler's first visit. The entire camp's population had been standing in a line at roll call. He'd marched by with his chin high and hands clasped behind his back, smiling at the woman guard to let her know he was pleased with how well things were going at the camp. Heida had warned Michal to keep her eyes down as he walked by her.

"Don't look him in the eye. You hear me? Don't draw any attention to yourself," Heida warned.

"I know. I know," Michal answered her. And when he arrived that day, she tried to do as Heida had told her. She'd kept her eyes on the ground. But as he was passing by, engaged deeply in conversation with the female guard, who Michal noticed had curled her blond hair for the occasion, Michal quickly looked up. Neither Himmler nor the guard saw her, but Michal couldn't help herself. She had to see him. She had to look directly at the man who had orchestrated such a hell for helpless women.

And there he was: Heinrich Himmler. He was just inches away from Michal. If she reached out, she could touch him. If she had a knife and the courage, she could kill him. His polished black boots caught a ray of sunshine as he laughed at something the female guard said. Michal shivered. Looking at him, she felt as if she'd seen the devil walking the earth. It wasn't so much the way he looked. Himmler was an average man, rather unattractive, wearing thick glasses, his tailored uniform, and a hat. It was something else, something far more sinister. He had a dark and terrible smell of death, an odor his expensive cologne could never mask. And long after he'd gone, whenever someone talked about him, Michal would still feel the evil heaviness of his presence and smell the invisible odor that followed him.

A frightening rumor was circulating like a virus among the prisoners that Himmler was planning to return. No one knew why. Perhaps it was just to see how the camp was faring. Maybe to be sure that no one was being given too much food or water. It was hard to say, but everyone, even the guards, was uneasy. The prisoners feared for their lives, and the guards feared for their comfortable jobs. But all waited in anticipation of Himmler's visit.

A deep bond of friendship had formed between Heida and Michal. To the others in the camp, Heida appeared hard. She barely spoke, and when she did, she gave one-word answers. But she'd finally opened up and talked to Michal. Michal was quiet and kept to herself; she didn't gossip or complain, so Heida felt she could tell Michal things without worrying about her secrets being shared indiscriminately. And so, Heida told Michal her story. Heida said she hadn't known that she was a lesbian until she met Iris. In fact, when she and Iris met, Heida was married with a young son, Ludwig. It wasn't an unhappy marriage, but from the beginning, something was missing. Even when she was with her husband, Gerwig, Heida said she felt alone. Sometimes, she would lie in bed beside him and feel pain in her throat from holding back the tears. Gerwig tried unsuccessfully to be a good husband, but Heida admitted he was a wonderful father. When Heida met Iris, Iris was studying to be an architect.

"An ambitious career for a woman," Heida told Michal, smiling, "but that was Iris. The male students were not quick to accept her. However, she was not easily discouraged. My husband had gone back to further his education. He was studying to be an engineer at the same university Iris attended. I met Iris when my husband came down with a terrible flu. He was very ill and asked me to pick up and deliver his classwork every day so that he would not be behind in his class. Every morning, I would dress Ludwig and take him with me to the university to pick up Gerwig's work. One of the mornings, when I arrived, Iris was waiting in the office. She had a private meeting with her professor, and he was late. It was the main office where I went to pick up Gerwig's work from his professors. Iris and I began to talk. I'd never met such a strong, ambitious woman. And this might sound strange, but somehow, within the first few minutes of speaking, I knew that she embodied the real me. Does that make any sense to you? What I mean is that being with her helped me to know who I was." Heida smiled. "Then she seemed to be at the office at least twice a week when I arrived. She later told me that she felt the same way about me, that I did about her and had begun to find reasons to be at the office when I came in to pick up and deliver my husband's work. Then, when my husband got well and returned to his classes, I didn't want to say goodbye to Iris. So, I went to the university. But this time, it was only to meet with Iris. After that, we began planning to meet outside the university, at the park. Then at cafés or restaurants. One thing led to another, and well, it just happened. And once we made love, I knew beyond a doubt that I'd finally come home. Now everything made sense to me. I understood why things were never right with Gerwig. I guess you could say I finally knew myself, and I also knew that this woman was my true love. Iris was very political. She and I became very involved with the Communist Party. As time passed, I became even more involved than she had been. I guess I was and still am enraptured with ideals of equality. That's probably why the Gestapo was keeping an eye on me."

"Did you stay with your husband even after you realized you were in love with Iris?"

"Yes, at first. But then… my son was murdered. Kidnapped and murdered." Heida coughed.

"You don't have to tell me anymore if you don't want to," Michal said.

"I want to, I have to. I've lived with the guilt for all these years. I need to tell someone what happened. Iris and I were together. We were alone in my flat, making love on the day that my little boy was killed. I had sent Ludwig to play with one of his friends who lived only a street away so that Iris and I could be alone. I have never forgiven myself.

"He was only five years old. He should never have been outside walking alone. I should have taken him to his friend's house and brought him back. But I didn't. Instead, I was selfish. I told him to walk to Earl's house. He was so excited to be allowed to go out all alone. 'I am such a big boy now,' he said to me before he left. You see, I wasn't thinking. Iris and I had very little time alone, and I craved every minute I could get to be alone with Iris. Between Iris' schedule and Gerwig's, it was hard to arrange a time when she and I could be together. That day, we had two hours before Gerwig was to return.

"I watched Ludwig walk down the street. He turned back and smiled at me. Oh God, Michal. Then Ludwig was gone, gone forever. Somewhere between our house and Earl's house, he met with someone who took him away from us forever. Gerwig didn't even know about Iris and me, but he blamed me for not watching Ludwig better. He was right. I should have taken better care of my little boy. But Gerwig didn't have to punish me. I punished myself. Every day, the guilt and misery of losing my child grew stronger. I had to tell

Gerwig the truth. The truth was eating me alive. He had to know everything. You see, I wanted the blame. I wanted him to yell and scream and condemn me to hell for the rest of my life. And he did. He threw me out. I went home to my family, but Gerwig had told my parents about Iris and me, and they kicked me out, too.

"I avoided Iris for several months. I felt that God was punishing me for loving her, and the best thing to do was to stay away from her. So, I had to survive. I had no place to go. I found a job as a maid, scrubbing the floors in a brothel. I was on my hands and knees, my knuckles bled, and I was glad for the punishment. Well deserved for what I had done, I thought. But my soul cried out for Iris. If I could see her, talk to her, tell her everything, I might be able to close this gaping wound in my heart. So, finally, I went to see her. She let me in and never asked me why I had been gone from her life for so long. We sat in silence in her living room for a quarter of an hour. Then I told her everything, all about what happened, where I was working, everything. She listened, and then she took me in her arms, and I wept. Iris asked me to move in with her, and I did. And even though the neighborhood shunned us and even though I'd lost my little boy, I found a ray of sunshine in this world. My Iris, my love.

"For a while, we were happy. Then the Nazis came. I was arrested. Every day, I pray that with God's help, somehow Iris got away. I don't know for sure that she did. I was arrested on the street while she was at home. It happened when I was going to the butcher shop. Someone, one of our neighbors, I am sure, told the Gestapo that Iris and I were lesbians. They picked me up in a black car, and well, here I am. I have not seen Iris since. Every day, I pray for her, and I pray that God is a forgiving God and not a punishing God."

"I believe he is a forgiving God," Michal said as she patted Heida's arm.

"Do you believe that my sin with Iris was what caused Ludwig's death?"

"No, I don't believe love in any shape or form is ever a sin. What happened to your son is a terrible tragedy, but it is not your fault. You must believe that."

"I am trying. Every day, I try. I should have taken half an hour to walk him to his friend's house and ensure he arrived safely."

"I did some terrible things in my life, too. And there were times that I wondered the same thing as you: Is God a forgiving or a punishing God? But as I said, I believe he is a forgiving God."

"You couldn't have done anything as bad as I did."

"I grew up in a religious family, and so when I was separated from my husband, and I took a lover, a man I was not married to, a voice in the back of my mind always reminded me of the Ten Commandments. You know, the one about adultery. So, yes, there have been times that I wondered if I have been condemned to this prison as a punishment for my sins. However, I refuse to believe that God would do this to me. No, Heida, it is not God who has put us in here but horrible human beings. Men of flesh and blood created this place, not God."

"If there really is a God, I wonder why He doesn't do something to stop them," Heida asked.

"Free will? I don't know. My first husband was a Talmud scholar; he used to talk about God giving us free will. Maybe that's it. I don't know. I wish I had an answer. I ask myself all the time why God has abandoned us here."

"It is hard for me to keep believing. But, I must. If I don't believe there is a God, then there is no one I can even hope might help Iris. I can't imagine you taking a lover, Michal. You seem like such a straight-laced girl. What happened?"

"Well, at the beginning of our marriage, my husband Taavi and I had a lot of problems. Something terrible happened to me, and because of it, there was a wall between my husband and me. Let me explain. I was married to another man before my marriage to Taavi. His name was Avram. It was an arranged marriage. But he was a kind and good man. We had a nice marriage. He was killed when the Cossacks invaded our village. They murdered Avram, and one of them raped me. Taavi saw it happen. In fact, if it weren't for him, I would probably be dead. He saved me by killing the Cossack. Then he got me out of the village during the attack. I fell in love with him and married him. But I was damaged by the rape, and it stood between us. I felt dirty, and I couldn't even stand to think of a man touching my body. And so I was unable to be a true wife to Taavi."

"You mean you couldn't make love with him."

"That's right. I couldn't. I tried, but it was too difficult. It brought back memories of the rape. At the time, Taavi was young and eager. He was hurt and offended, but still, I couldn't change what I was feeling. One night, he'd gone out with a friend and had too much to drink. He came home, and in desperation, he forced himself on me. He didn't know it until much later, but I got pregnant that night. Anyway, after he forced himself on me, we fought, and then we separated. It's a very long story. But during our separation, I fell in love with a man who wrote children's stories. We had a beautiful affair. He was kind and gentle, and because he was so patient, I was finally able to fall in love with him. His name was Otto, and he helped me in so many ways. But then I found out that he was bisexual, and I was appalled. I treated him badly. I guess it was the shock and the pain of what I considered a betrayal. Now I see that everything worked out how it was supposed to. My relationship with Otto actually brought me back to Taavi. But at the time, I was cold and terrible to Otto. He begged me to try to understand, but I couldn't. So I took my daughter, Alina, and left him. Then Otto's sister came to me and told me that he was sick and he was dying. I went to him to tell him I was sorry, but he was already unconscious, and then he was gone. I wish I'd had the chance to talk to him."

"Sometimes it happens like that. We regret the things we couldn't or didn't say."

"Otto could not give me all of himself; he wasn't made that way, and I didn't understand at the time. But, after Otto died, I was able to forgive Taavi. We got back together, and I was finally able to be his wife. It was then that I introduced Taavi to his daughter, Alina. He was a wonderful father from the beginning. Then, from that day on, Taavi and I began to build our lives together. So, I owe Otto a great deal."

She smiled. "I'm sure wherever he is, wherever people go when they die, he knows you're sorry."

"I hope so."

It wasn't long before Michal and Heida found out the reason for Himmler's visit. He'd come to recruit guards and kapos for his new project, a prison camp the Nazis were putting together called Auschwitz.

forty-one
Michal

ONE THOUSAND PRISONERS were chosen the following day to become kapos at Auschwitz. It was a time of upheaval, which always meant danger in Ravensbrück.

The women were called out to roll call that morning. As usual, the prisoners lined up. Then, the selection began. The guards were told by Himmler to sort through the prisoners and find the cruelest and toughest among them to be sent to Auschwitz. Some of the women were already known to be hard and heartless; they were chosen first. Among them were a woman who had run a brothel, a well-known prostitute, several unbreakable political prisoners, and, to Michal's surprise, a group of Jehovah's Witnesses who she was sure did not possess the cruel streak that the guards were seeking. From where Michal stood, she could see Heida. One of the young female guards known to be brutal to prisoners had pulled Heida out of line. Michal wasn't able to hear what was being said. But she saw the guard putting a gun in Heida's hand and pointing at another prisoner. The other prisoner got down on her knees. The prisoner's whole body was trembling. It was like watching a silent horror film. From where she stood, Michal knew the prisoner was crying. Then Michal heard the guard yell, "Shoot her, and you'll come with us as a kapo." Everyone knew that the kapos got better food and better treatment.

The guard was ordering Heida to kill. Heida held the gun pointed at the prisoner who was kneeling on the ground.

"Shoot," the guard said again. "Shoot, or I will kill you."

Michal was shuddering so hard she was afraid she might fall over. She'd learned to stay quiet, to be as invisible as possible. This was the way to survive. But now she couldn't. Her friend was in trouble, and she had to do something, even if it meant her life. Michal ran out of line.

"Where are you going? Get back in line," another guard screeched, but Michal had already reached Heida.

"You have one second to kill her. If you do, you will go to Auschwitz, where you'll get better rations and a better bed. A bed without lice. You'd like that, wouldn't you? If you don't kill her, I'll shoot you."

Heida's hand was shaking so badly that she could barely keep the gun from falling to the ground. She couldn't do it.

Michal looked at Heida, and she knew Heida couldn't do it. There was less than a second to make a choice. In less than a second, Heida would be dead, and there would be no way back.

Michal could hardly breathe, but she grabbed the gun. "I'll do it. I'll kill her."

"A brave little Jew. Go ahead, let me see if you can kill her, and if you do, I'll send you and your friend, Heida. Yes, why not? Do it, and you both get out of here and go to Auschwitz. Don't do it, and I'll kill you both," the guard said, clearly amused.

Now that she was close enough to see the woman on the ground, Michal felt the fire inside of her going dim. How could she kill this woman? The woman was so thin that her tall body looked like a broom handle. There were angry red patches on her bald head. She was crying, whimpering. *Don't look at her eyes*. Michal told herself. She felt the bile rising in her throat.

"Kill her, or I'll kill your friend," the guard said. "This is beginning to bore me. Do it now. This is your last chance," she was shouting.

The guard turned a gun on Heida, and for a brief second, Michal wanted to shoot the guard, but she knew that if she dared, more guards would come, and both she and Heida would be killed on the spot. So, she aimed at the woman on the ground and pulled the trigger. Blood spattered on Michal's face. Michal felt vomit rise into her mouth, but she dared not puke or cry.

"Oh, you surprise me, little Jew. Is this woman your lover?"

Neither Heida nor Michal answered. There was no right answer. They were at the mercy of this guard. She would do whatever she chose with them.

The pretty young Nazi guard laughed. Then she shot Heida. Michal gasped. She turned the gun on Michal, but when she fired, the gun didn't go off. She tried again and failed again. Then the Nazi shrugged and looked at Michal. "It's your lucky day, Jew. You won't die today. But you won't go with us to Auschwitz either. Get back in line and make it fast."

After roll call was over, Michal watched as the prisoners took Heida's body away. Heida had been her only friend in this pit of hell, and now she was gone. "Go to God, my friend, and be at peace," Michal whispered as the prisoners pulling Heida by her arms and legs disappeared behind a building.

That night, Michal woke up sweating. She'd had a dream of the woman she shot that day, and it was so real that she relived the horror of the murder. "I'm so sorry," Michal said in her dream. "I didn't want to do it." As she lay awake remembering the dream, she knew this nightmare would haunt her forever.

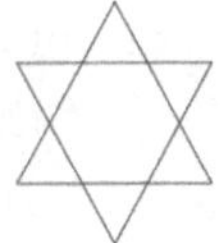

forty-two

Taavi

Autumn 1942

TAAVI DID AS LOTTI RECOMMENDED. He stayed out of sight. He went off into the country and slept in barns and cellars. He ate what he could find or steal. But he could not begin to imagine how he might find Michal and his family; without his wife and children, life was meaningless.

At night, when the weather was good, he slept under the stars and thought about all the wasted time he and Michal had spent apart because of his arrogant stubbornness. He thought about his daughters and remembered how Alina would run to him with her arms outstretched, crying, "Daddy, look at the picture I drew for you." Or Gilde would say, "Daddy, Daddy, watch. I am going to sing and dance for you."

When those memories came rushing at him, drowning him in their wake, he almost wished he would have died in prison. After all, he was their father, the man of the house. It was his responsibility to care for and protect his family. And he had failed. Failed miserably.

From living in the forest, Taavi learned never to sleep deeply. It seemed he had become accustomed to hearing unfamiliar sounds in his sleep. And he'd learned to awaken in seconds, be on his feet, and go from sleep to running without even a moment's pause. Somehow, he had managed to learn to live off the land, even in the dead of a terrible winter. It was not easy; he'd nearly frozen to death a couple of times when he could not find a vacant barn or cellar. He was always lean and hungry. But he'd survived and believed that if he continued to hide and keep moving, he would make it through until all of this ended one way or another. Either Germany would be victorious, and that would mean disaster for the Jews, or with God's help, somehow the Nazis would lose their power.

But what did all of this mean to Taavi? He couldn't wait for the outcome of the war. He needed to find his family now. He couldn't rest until he found them; if it meant taking a risk, it was worth it. Because Taavi hadn't been in contact with a living soul since he'd left Lotti's home, Taavi did not know that America had entered the war against Germany. All he knew was that he hid when he saw German troops come through the countryside. Taavi had no idea how far Hitler had gone in his pursuit of power. But, he refused to believe that Michal or his daughters might be dead. The very thought was so painful that it left him breathless, his stomach aching. He bit his lower lip. He could no longer hide like a frightened animal. He had to go back and speak to the only person he knew who had enough influence and plenty of friends in the Nazi Party to help him.

Frieda. He had hurt her far too many times. And, he knew she felt betrayed again. If circumstances had been different, he would never have gone to her the first time, and he certainly would not be considering returning to her again. Even though Frieda was still caught up in the sexual depravity of the bygone Weimar era, and she was a stubborn, strong, and successful businesswoman, she had a weakness. Her weakness was Taavi. And Taavi knew it. He knew that Frieda was infatuated with him. And because of her feelings for him, she would put herself at risk to save him. After all, she'd done it once. She was a smart woman. Frieda knew when she got him released that if she were caught, she would have been punished for even attempting to help a Jew. But she had not given in to fear. Instead, she had not hesitated to pay that Nazi bastard Braus for his release. Taavi was grateful to her. He was more grateful than he could ever express to her. Because Taavi knew that the only gratitude that Frieda would understand was his willingness to surrender his love and his life to her. But he was not able to give this.

Now, he was about to see her, and instead of getting down on his knees and begging her to take him back, he would be selfishly asking her to put her own feelings aside. Again. Taavi would have to hope that Frieda's love for him was strong enough that she would be willing to help Michal, the woman who made her heart ache with jealousy. He would have to pray that somewhere inside the coarse and brazen Frieda was a golden beam of light that would make her soften to his pleading. Taavi hoped that she would make her take pity upon his desperation. And Taavi was desperate. He had to beg Frieda to help the woman he loved as he had never loved Frieda, not even in the heat of their affair. And if she, by some miracle, agreed, he knew that she would once again be putting herself in danger for him. However, once again, she was his only hope. And she was Michal's only hope. So, even though he felt terribly guilty about what he was about to do, he would go back to Frieda, get on his knees, and beg her to help him just one more time.

forty-three

Taavi

HE WAITED IN THE DARK, hiding outside the nightclub until after it closed. Taavi knew from years of working with Frieda that once everyone was gone, she would sit at the empty bar and have a shot of whiskey before going home alone. He hovered in the shadows in the wee hours before dawn, hugging the side of the building where he could not be seen, and watched as the staff left. Then, just to be sure it was safe, he peeked into the window.

Frieda was sitting on the same stool, wearing her man-tailored suit. But instead of looking strong, exotic, and enticing, Taavi could see that her hard life had begun to take its toll on her. She was painfully thin. He knew that she'd gone through periods of addiction to opium and then, sometimes, cocaine. Over the time they'd spent together, they'd shared a sordid relationship filled with sexually perverse games that often included other players and left Taavi drugged and spent. He'd grown tired and disgusted with the lifestyle, but he doubted she had. He looked at her and felt a pang of pity. How lonely she must be. After all, she was no longer young. Once Taavi had left that life, he never missed it. He'd loved being a married man with children. If only Hitler had never come into power, he would have lived his life out in peace. But that was not to be his fate.

Taavi took a deep breath. The crisp, clean fall air filled his lungs. He watched as Frieda poured a second shot. She looked like a broken doll. Her slender shoulders slumped forward.

First, Taavi looked in all directions. Once he was sure there was no one around, he came out from behind the building and slipped through the door to the club.

When she heard the door open and then close, Frieda looked up from her drink.

"Taavi?" Her face lit up. "What are you doing here?"

"I've come to see you."

Frieda rose quickly. "Come. You must hurry. I have to hide you in the back room. Did anyone see you?" She grabbed his arm and, moving quickly, escorted him to the apartment behind the nightclub.

"No. I don't think so," he answered.

She followed him in and closed the door behind her. "Taavi." Her voice was a whisper, but even though he could hardly hear her, he felt her emotions. Frieda stood with her back against the door as if holding it closed from intruders. Even though she'd locked it and no one had seen them enter.

"How are you, Frieda?"

"How should I be? You want a drink?" she said.

"Yes, please. I could use a drink."

She walked over to the small bar in the apartment's living room and poured him a whiskey. He downed it in one swallow.

"You look good," he lied, the guilt already growing inside him for what he was about to do.

"Do I? I am aging, Taavi. Ahh, well, I suppose it beats the alternative, eh?"

"You are a constant, Frieda. You'll always be a glamorous woman. You're ageless."

"Yes, that sounds very nice, even though I know it's a lie." She smiled and then lit a cigarette. "So, as much as I'd like to believe you couldn't live without me, I know better. So, Taavi, tell me, why did you come here?"

"I came to see you."

"Ahh, how I wish that were true, Taavi, but you've always been a lousy liar. And, I must tell you that you look and smell atrocious. But I am sure you must realize that. So, come on, Taavi, enough already. Out with it, what do you want? Why did you really come?"

He was afraid to ask for her help. If she turned him down, there was nowhere else for him to go. He had to sweeten the deal. He had to reawaken her feelings for him, or she would never help him.

Taavi walked over to Frieda and gently kissed her on the lips. She sighed as if she'd yearned for this moment for a very long time. He pulled her to him until her chest was pressed hard against his and kissed her again. This time, he placed one hand in her hair and tugged gently. She trembled with passion. Taavi forgot his guilt. It had been a long time since he'd made love, and his body ached for release. Frieda bent to her knees and began to unzip his pants. For a brief moment, Taavi thought of Michal, and guilt welled inside him. He was enjoying this too much. But then nature took over, and his feelings of guilt were washed away by the flood of his need.

Once it was finished, Taavi was sick with shame. For him, the moment satisfied a physical need, like the need for food or the need to sleep. Once satisfied, the real reason he'd come to Frieda resurfaced and pounded like a drum in his mind. Frieda lay in his arms. He'd planned to do this devious thing to her for several days in the forest before he arrived. It was his only hope, but it still felt so wrong. Frieda was happy now. He could hear it as she sighed, breathing softly. He felt it in the way her hand caressed his chest. He had won her over. She would help him now. After all the years they'd spent together, he knew how her mind worked. Even if he had to promise that he would never go back to Michal and stay with Frieda forever, Taavi decided that he would make that vow to Frieda if it meant saving the lives of Michal and his daughters.

"I've really missed you..." Frieda moaned, her head buried in his chest. "I am not going to ask you any questions about anything. To be quite honest, I don't want to know. I am just glad you're here now."

He patted her back. *Slowly. Take this slowly. Don't ask her for help quite yet. Stoke the fire, Taavi. Take your time.* He must not rush this;

though every minute could mean danger or even death for those he loved, the urgency he felt made his body shiver. Frieda misinterpreted his trembling and held him tighter.

"You've missed me too," she whispered. "Taavi, Taavi, you were always the one for me. I think you know that I have always been in love with you."

He grunted. She giggled. "What does that mean?"

"It's hard for me to express emotion," he said. *Taavi, try.* He was disgusted with himself for needing to manipulate this poor woman's feelings.

"There is no need to speak. Just lay here and hold me, Taavi."

Frieda fell asleep. Gently, Taavi moved her up to the pillow so that she would not lie on him. Then he turned his face away from her to look at the wall. *What other choice did I have? What else could I have done?* He knew he'd acted badly, taking advantage of Frieda's feelings. Poor Frieda, she'd been nothing but kind to him. What kind of man had he become? Still, there was no other option if he even hoped to find a way to save Michal and his girls.

forty-four

Taavi

AGAIN, the following morning, as Taavi lay awake with Frieda beside him, breathing softly, he had to remind himself, "Don't rush this." He looked at Frieda, and his stomach ached for her. She didn't look well. The night before, he hadn't noticed how much her hair had thinned. But now, he could see that not only had she lost a great deal of hair, but the skin on her neck and arms hung off of her and creased like the skin of a lizard. He felt deeply saddened. He knew he had given her the impression that he cared for her. *Taavi, Taavi, what kind of man are you? Not the kind of man you always believed that you would be.*

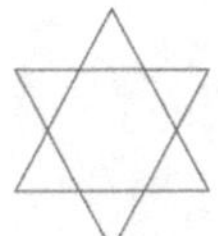

forty-five

Taavi

ALMOST A WEEK WENT by before Taavi decided that he couldn't bear to wait any longer. He'd allowed Frieda to share his bed every night. Her face glowed with joy, and she smiled and laughed again. She constantly told him she loved him and even asked him if he loved her. He'd changed the subject to avoid answering. How could he answer? He wanted to scream, to tell her that somewhere, his precious wife and daughters were suffering, and he could not do anything to save them without Frieda's influence. "Calm, Taavi. Be calm," he told himself one morning as Frieda returned from the bakery with two buttered sweet rolls and two cups of real coffee.

He was still in bed in his underwear when she turned the key in the lock. Taavi cringed as Frieda walked in and set the coffee and the greasy brown bag from the bakery on the table. Then she sat on the bed and smiled at Taavi. She bent to touch his face. Her eyes shined with caring.

"It's real coffee and real sugar, too. Hard to get, no?" she said.

"Yes." He nodded. "I'm impressed. But then again, Frieda, you've always been able to do the impossible."

"Yeah?" She laughed. "I hoped you would enjoy it. Here." She got up and handed him a cup of the steaming hot liquid.

It smelled wonderful.

"Thank you," he said and took a sip. She had friends everywhere. The coffee and sugar reinforced that fact. There was no doubt about it. If Frieda would only help him, he could probably find Michal and the girls.

"Frieda?" his voice was soft.

"Yes, my darling."

"I have to talk to you about something very serious."

"Of course. What is it?" Frieda put her arm on his bare shoulder.

"I care for you, Frieda. I always have. You have been such a good friend to me." He hesitated for a moment.

"A friend?"

"Yes," he tried again. "A friend, a great help, and a lover." Taavi cleared his throat. "I will stay with you for the rest of my life—"

She interrupted him. "I love you, Taavi."

He nodded. "I know. I know. But, Frieda, I need a favor. I need something from you."

"Opium? Morphine? Anything."

It was almost impossible to get the words out because he feared the consequences so greatly. Frieda had the power to destroy Michal and his daughters, to destroy him. But she also had the power to save. *Oh God, help me say this correctly so she doesn't turn against me. Please, I beg you. I don't care what the cost is to me. Just make her help my family.* Taavi was still holding the coffee cup, but he took Frieda's hand with his other hand. "Frieda. I need you to help Michal and my girls. I don't know where they are. I don't even know if they are alive. All I know is that Michal was arrested in 1938 when she went to the police station looking for me. I need you to see if your friends can find her and my girls. I promise you I will not leave you and go back to my wife. I will even divorce her. Please, Frieda, do what you can to save their lives."

Frieda freed her hand from his and stood up. She turned away from him. There was a thick silence in the air for several minutes. Then she said, "You still love her. You love her so much that you would stay with me to save her." Frieda cleared her throat and nodded. "Yes, Taavi, you love her in a way that you will never love me."

"Frieda. I will be yours. Just save her life. And my children. Frieda, please. That is all I ask. I will divorce her and marry you."

"You care that much for her, don't you, Taavi?" She smiled bitterly. He could see that her heart was broken. "No one in my whole life has ever felt that way about me."

"I do love you," Taavi lied.

"I wish you did." She walked out of the room, closing the door behind her.

Taavi was overcome with worry. If Frieda wanted to, she could cause Michal even more problems. Would Frieda go to one of her friends and see to it that Michal was murdered? He wanted to follow Frieda, to fall on his knees and beg her. But he knew enough about women to know that Frieda needed time to think alone. He'd just opened his heart, and now Frieda knew the truth. If she helped him, he would marry her, but she would never be his true love. Would that be enough? Would she at least help his daughters? Everything, his entire life, lay in her hands. What would she do next? Only time will tell.

Frieda returned in less than an hour. She didn't knock before entering.

"I'll contact a friend of mine today. A high official in the Nazi Party. I will see if I can find your wife and daughters. There are no guarantees. From what I have heard, they are killing Jews left and right. So, I do not know what I will uncover. But I will do my best for you, Taavi. Then, if I can find your family, I will send them to safe work camps where they will not be hurt. If possible, they will survive all of this, but you must promise me that you will never see Michal again. So, do you agree to this?"

He nodded. Frieda had turned from the woman weak with love for him back into the shrewd businesswoman who had built her nightclub into a popular, money-making hot spot where top Nazi officials came to fraternize. She looked at him, firm and strong. At this point, Taavi would do anything she wanted and agree to any terms as long as she could promise him that his family would be safe. Frieda could lie to him. He knew it was possible, but he had to take that chance. There was no other option.

"You have my word," Taavi said, and he meant it.

"Very well. I'll let you know when I get some information," she said, then she lit a cigarette and looked him square in the eyes. "I have work to do. I'll be back later."

After Frieda left, Taavi said a prayer of thanks and begged God to watch over his wife and daughters because he was powerless and could not.

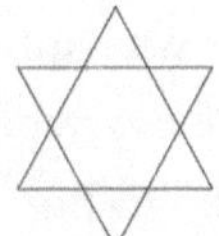

forty-six
Frieda

FRIEDA WALKED into her office and took a bottle of whiskey out of the drawer of her desk. She didn't bother with a glass. Instead, she drank it straight from the bottle. It burned as it rolled down her throat, and she liked how it felt.

Taavi, Taavi, Taavi, what was it about that crazy Jew that drove her so insane with passion? She'd never felt this way about any other man. Eh? Maybe it was the circumcised penis? Frieda laughed bitterly. She'd been with other men who'd been circumcised, and the love-making was nothing like it was with Taavi. Maybe it was the fact that she could not ever possess him. He was hers, but not completely.

He'd never really been hers, not even when he and his wife were separated, and she and Taavi were a couple. Not even then. Frieda lit another cigarette. She'd taken quite a risk getting Taavi out the first time. Yes, she had friends at the Party, but people turned on each other in the blink of an eye, and Frieda wasn't about to find herself in prison over Taavi's wife and his children by her. She'd been willing to go out on a limb for him, but not for this woman who was nothing to her but her nemesis. Frieda took another swig from the bottle. She wasn't sure what to do. Then it came to her. If Taavi thought Michal was dead, he would get over her. If Frieda demanded it, he would not leave the little room behind her nightclub. After all, he was not free to search the streets himself. Taavi was only safe because she provided him a place to hide. Frieda had no plans of bringing unwanted attention to herself. She would not ask any officials any questions about Jews.

Only one man knew that she had Taavi hidden; he was quiet because she had continued paying him plenty of money even when Taavi wasn't with her. But now he was back, and he belonged to her. If Taavi thought Michal and his girls were dead, he would have no choice but to get over his feelings for his wife. After all, chances were good that they were dead. The way they were killing Jews, in fact, if they were alive, it would have been a surprise. But Frieda had no intentions of finding out. She was going to wait a day or two and then tell Taavi that she'd been informed by a reliable source that Michal and his daughters were all dead. He would mourn; she expected that from him. But then he would have no more distractions from his relationship with Frieda and no chances of reuniting with Michal and their children. He would have to start his life over, and she would be the logical choice. If she didn't think it was so dangerous to call attention to herself, she would go to someone and see to it that Michal was murdered and out of the way. However, with the climate in the country right now, talking to officials about Jews was not a good idea. It would alert them and make them want to know why she was so interested. It was worth it to her to pay any amount of money to keep Taavi safe from harm, but it was not worth it to her to risk her life for Michal or Michal's children. She would just cross her fingers, and with luck, they were all gone already.

The next day, Frieda told Taavi that she had someone looking into the whereabouts of his family. She promised Taavi that she'd spared no expense to find them. Knowing him the way a woman knows a man she loves, she could see in his eyes that he believed her.

"All I can do now is wait until my connection contacts me. It could take a while. I couldn't push him to hurry, you understand. Just asking him to do this thing for me put me at great risk."

"I know, Frieda, and I will always be indebted to you."

Good. Taavi will realize how much I love him and fall in love with me for my kindness.

"You realize that I would do anything for you, Taavi," she said, touching his shoulder.

"Yes, I know. And I am very grateful to you."

She smiled. "I'd rather have your love than your gratitude."

"I love you…" he said, justifying the word's deceptive use in his mind by thinking that he did love her. He loved her like a man loves a good friend, but he couldn't and never would love another woman like he loved Michal.

"Do you, Taavi?" she said. Her voice cracked, and she sighed the way people sighed when they finally got something that they'd wanted for a very long time.

He nodded. He couldn't bear to say it again. The look on her face and the lump in his throat stopped him.

Frieda smiled and gently stroked his cheek with her long red nails. "My sweet Taavi."

He swallowed hard and felt his Adam's apple move up and down. It had been so much easier to make love to Frieda when he and Michal were separated. Then, times were so different. It was all about pride, and life and death had not hung in the balance. Michal had bruised his ego, and he was going to have sex with any willing woman to prove to himself that he was sexually desirable. Then, when Frieda came along, she gave him a good job and plenty of money and led him on a path of depravity. He'd followed willingly, then. But Taavi was not the same man anymore. Wild parties filled with hedonistic abandonment, sex, drugs, those things that had once brought him pleasure no longer enticed him. In fact, when he remembered some of the things he did in the past, he was ashamed. She didn't realize it, but the man Frieda had fallen in love with was gone. Still, Taavi kept his mouth shut. He needed her help, so he would go along with whatever she wanted.

"Kiss me," she said.

He took her in his arms, trying not to appear mechanical, and pressed her against him. She had never been beautiful, but she was attractive in her youth. Now, he could hardly look at her, but it didn't matter. It wouldn't have mattered if she were beautiful. Taavi knew that real love was the only thing that mattered, not beauty, not money, just love. Family, wife, home. These were the things that were precious. It took losing them—but also coming close to death—to understand just how much he valued the gifts God had given him in Michal, Alina, and Gilde.

Taavi felt Frieda's body melt into his and wondered if he would be able to get an erection. The other night, he was able to perform because it had been so long since he'd been with a woman. But now? Dear God, he didn't want to do this. Not now. Maybe after he learned Michal was all right, he could at least fake his way through it. Maybe then. Frieda's perfume saturated his nostrils, but instead of being seductive, it made him feel sick to his stomach. Somehow, he had to trick his body into cooperating. In the past, when he was in the camp and felt that he was drowning in misery, he'd masturbated, thinking about Michal. At that time, the only joy he could find was in the memories that lived only within his own mind. Then, he'd been able to become aroused. But now, it was difficult to bear the pain of thinking about Michal while trying to make love to another woman. If he tried to think about Michal, he knew it wouldn't help. And there was no hiding the fact from Frieda that he was not aroused. She reached down and felt his lack of desire for her. What lie could he tell her?

"I'm sorry. I'm tired, and I am weak. Besides, I am just so worried about my family. Forgive me, Frieda."

But she didn't stop. Frieda continued as if she never heard him. She seemed instinctively to know what he needed. She bent down and took him into her mouth. The power of his need overcame him, and Taavi closed his eyes and saw Michal. Michal, he whispered in his mind. Then, his natural instincts took over again.

After Frieda slipped out of bed the following morning, Taavi got up and showered. He scrubbed his body for a long time but could not wash away his guilt. He brushed his teeth and combed his hair. Then he vomited.

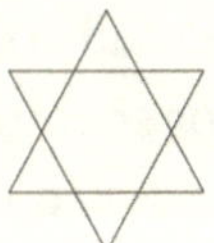

forty-seven

Michal

Winter 1943

RAVENSBRÜCK WAS UNBEARABLE BEFORE, but it was even worse without Heida. At least when Heida was alive, Michal had a friend with whom she could talk and share her feelings. Now, she was utterly alone. She'd lost her family, her daughters, her husband, and now she'd watched her best friend die. In fact, Michal had even done the unthinkable. She'd murdered another woman. The crime she'd committed against God and another human being followed her every moment of every day.

Her body had become a mass of lean muscle and skin covering bones. She worked until the sweat-soaked her uniform, and she was beyond exhausted. But at night, instead of finding rest, she was haunted by her own mind. Deep purple puffy circles had formed around her eyes, and her hair fell out in clumps on the straw where she slept. Michal was doubtful that she would survive this prison, but then her mind began to disconnect from reality. She started to see the faces of those she loved in her mind's eye, and she could speak to them and hear them answer in their voices. Many times, she was sure they were right there beside her. It gave her such comfort to speak to Taavi and hear his advice and promises for their future. She spoke to Alina and slowly began to create an imaginary life. A world that existed only in her mind. Michal imagined Alina was engaged, and she and her daughter planned a wedding. She talked to Gilde, who grew into a beautiful and precocious young woman. And she had long conversations with Heida, who told her to forgive herself for shooting that poor woman. "It wasn't your fault," Heida said. "You did it to try to save me."

"But you're dead now," Michal answered Heida in her mind.

"It's all right, I am with Iris. I am fine here. Don't worry about me," Heida said, smiling.

Michal's mind played tricks on her. Maybe it was the hard work or the frostbite that had caused her to lose three toes or the near starvation. Michal began to have difficulty separating reality from fantasy. Her body continued to follow the rules that were set before her by the cruel Nazi guards, but her mind had escaped the prison and entered into another realm.

But even though Michal tried, she could not see or talk to the woman she murdered. All she saw was a shadow of the woman's eyes, which terrified her.

One day, as Michal was waiting in line for soup, she heard someone call her name. "Michal!" Was it in her mind, or was it real? It was a woman's voice, a familiar voice. But she couldn't place it. She took her bowl and sat on a rock, shivering from the cold. The little finger on her left hand had turned black. She noted that it would probably fall off soon. "Who was that voice?" she heard Alina ask in her mind.

"I don't know," Michal answered, still shivering.

Then, a woman came over to her. Was she real? The woman wore the uniform of a Nazi guard. The gray jacket, the culotte skirt, the black leather boots, and a little hat. "Michal Margolis, is that you?"

Was this real, or was another person talking to her in her mind? She couldn't distinguish between the two anymore. "Do I know you?" Michal squinted, looking up at the guard.

"It is you. It's me, Bridget. Otto's sister."

Otto. That was a name from her past. Otto, he'd been her lover so long ago, in another lifetime. She remembered Bridget, his sister. What a sweet girl. "Don't you recall how close Bridget and I were?" she heard Alina say in her mind. "Yes, I do, Alina," she answered, but not aloud.

"Michal, Michal…" The girl who called herself Bridget was talking to her, trying to get her attention. Obviously, she didn't hear Alina.

"Yes, I remember you," Michal said.

Bridget looked like she was going to cry. "I had to take this job. There was no other work…"

Bridget was rambling on and on, but Michal couldn't hear her. Michal's mind was traveling back to the days when she and Otto were living together, and Bridget and Alina were like sisters.

"I'm going to help you." Bridget had tears in her eyes. "I am going to get you another job. A job where you are not outside in the elements all day. There is a laundry in town that uses slave labor from Ravensbrück. At least you would be out of the cold. I will have you transferred there. Stay here. I'll be right back."

True to her word, Bridget returned with a heel of bread and gave it to Michal. "Eat this. I'll try to get you more. You are so skinny. My God, how did it come to this? I am so sorry, Michal. But I must keep up a front, too, or I will be a prisoner instead of a guard. I'll do what I can to help you. But I can't speak out. I must not tell them that you are my friend. I am ashamed, but it is the only way to survive here. Do you understand?"

Michal nodded. Yes, she understood. She understood everything. Michal smiled. Was this real, or just another vision? It didn't matter. Nothing really mattered. She was eating the bread but also thinking about how grown-up Bridget was. Why, the last time she'd seen her, Bridget was just a child going to live with her aunt and uncle, and here she was, a woman.

"Alina would love to see you," Michal said. "She loved you so."

"Alina, how is Alina?"

"She is fine. We talk often. You probably haven't heard the news, but she is engaged. She and I have been so busy planning her wedding." Michal smiled and took another bite. She noticed her little finger hanging by a thin piece of skin. *It will be gone by tomorrow.*

It was then that Bridget realized that Michal had escaped Ravensbrück, which was the only way she could. Michal had lost her mind.

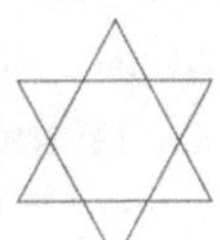

forty-eight
Bridget

BRIDGET KNEW that truckloads of women were being taken away every day to be gassed and murdered. Most of the women chosen for extermination were sick with tuberculosis or other diseases. Still, healthy women were being murdered as well. Bridget wished that she didn't know the truth. She'd taken this job because she was desperate for money and rations, too. She felt terrible about what she saw. But what could she do? She was only one person. Still, even if she could turn a blind eye to the misery of strangers, she could not stand by and allow Michal to be tortured and killed. And she was certain that once the guards realized that Michal had gone insane, she would be exterminated immediately.

Bridget asked that Michal be transferred to work in the laundry in town. But the laundry was only taking twenty prisoners, and at the present time, they had a full staff. It wasn't easy work, but it was better than Michal's present job. Bridget was pretty sure that she could probably have bumped someone and put Michal in her place, but she had another idea.

Siemens Electric had opened a plant adjacent to the camp. They used slave labor to build parts for rockets for the war effort. The hours were long, twelve-hour shifts. But it didn't matter where

Michal worked; all the jobs required at least twelve-hour shifts. It wasn't always that way, but once Himmler learned that some of the women were working eight-hour shifts, he adjusted his rules and said that all women at all jobs were now required to work twelve or more hours a day. If she could have Michal put on an assembly line, Michal might be able to do her job. It would be repetitive, perhaps even dangerous. She would try to find the job with the least risk factors. And then, maybe by some miracle, Michal might slip by unnoticed. At least Bridget was hoping this would be the case. Since Bridget was well-liked by her superiors at the camp, she thought she might not have had too much of a difficult time arranging this for Michal. She had to be careful how she approached it because no matter how much the officers liked her, Bridget knew that it was not safe to become known as a Jew lover.

The superior officers liked and respected Bridget's willingness to work hard. They took notice of her strong, athletic body. She fit the ideal of a *Deutsches Mädchen*. And it didn't hurt that Bridget always tried to please them. So when she explained that Michal had been a teacher of hers and she wanted to have her transferred to the Siemens electrical factory, permission was granted. A few days later, Michal was sent to work at Siemens. Bridget told herself that at least Michal was inside. At least she was warm. However, even though she knew this, it still didn't alleviate the guilt that Bridget carried like a weight on her shoulders, but it helped.

forty-nine

Michal

SINCE MICHAL'S mind had left the earthly plane, she was spared the trauma of seeing her fellow prisoners tortured. When a woman was being whipped to death, Michal's mind simply turned off like a hose in the garden where the spigot had been twisted until the water stopped running. Michal answered when questioned, but things said to her often did not register in her mind.

Bridget came to Michal's block at night whenever she could bring bits of extra food for Michal.

Michal was always happy to see Bridget, and she reminisced with Bridget in a faraway voice about Otto as if he were still alive.

It was strange to Michal that Bridget always had glassy eyes, as if she'd been crying. Once, Michal asked Bridget why she seemed so sad, and Bridget just smiled and shook her head. But tears flowed down her cheeks. Michal wiped them away just like she did when Bridget was a child and Michal took care of her.

Michal was surprised that it took two days for her finger to fall off. The other appendages had been much quicker. It happened one afternoon when she was working at Siemens. It had been a long time. In fact, she could no longer remember how long since she'd had any feeling in that finger. She picked up the black finger and held it for a moment, looking at it as if she wasn't sure what it was or whom it belonged to. Then she tossed it into the trash in the factory and continued working. Her job was easy, but repetitious. Her hands did the work just as she had been instructed, but her mind was not at Siemens; her mind was at home with Taavi and the girls. Softly so no one could hear her, she sang the song she and Taavi had always sung to their children when they were small.

"You've got to have a little mazel because mazel means good luck. If you have a little *mazel*, you'll always have good luck."

A smile came over her face as she closed her eyes and saw her daughters and their father sitting on the living room floor, singing this song along with her. She kissed Gilde's cheek. *It's so good to be home.*

fifty
Bridget

BRIDGET DID what she could to keep watch over Michal, but it was difficult. She was training to be a guard, and to survive, Bridget had to work hard and make sure her superiors were pleased with her. If she didn't, she would lose her job, and she desperately needed the money. Besides all of that, she was afraid she might be pregnant. She had a boyfriend, and they had become lovers just a few months ago. Now, her period was late. Other guards had given birth at the camp, and they were not chastised. The babies were sent to live with their families, but at least they were permitted to keep their jobs and their income. If she was pregnant, she would have to send the child to live with her boyfriend's sister. That was, of course, provided his sister was willing to take the baby. With all this on her mind, Bridget still tried to steal food and bring it to Michal at night. It was easy to see that Michal's mind was slipping away more every day. There was nothing Bridget could do. Perhaps it was better. At least Michal was not suffering. One night, Michal was so delusional that she told Bridget that she'd spent the day with Gilde and Alina. Bridget thought of her brother and how much he loved Michal. Alina had been like a sister to her, and Michal like a mother. All Bridget could do was pray that Alina was still alive and safe somewhere.

As Michal got worse, Bridget became afraid for her. It was only a matter of time before one of the guards realized how mentally ill Michal had become, and when they did, it would all be over for Michal. Bridget had been forced to witness a gassing of a group of women once. She couldn't forget the horror of it, and the very idea of Michal suffering the way those poor women had suffered was unbearable to her.

One frigid night, when Bridget came into the block to see Michal, she noticed that Michal lay on her side, hacking. A small trickle of blood made a jagged line from her lips to the pillow. The wrenching cough would surely attract the attention of the block guards. Bridget shivered. Michal could be sent to the hospital, where she would probably be instantly killed. But if they didn't kill her, they were sure to discover that she was insane. Not only was she mad, but she was a Jew. The Nazis had been euthanizing the insane for a long time.

Bridget feared that Dr. Treite, the camp doctor, would not euthanize Michal, but he would torture her until her inevitable annihilation. Dr. Treite was known to be a sadist. He had created a special room for the insane. Bridget heard the other guards talking about the terrible experiments he was performing, using the prisoners as subjects. He enjoyed the suffering. Bridget cringed at the idea of Michal enduring such terrible pain. Between coughing fits, Michal was shaking. Could it be tuberculosis? Bridget pressed her hands hard against her temples. If she left Michal on this block, she'd probably be transferred to Dr. Treite by morning.

Bridget smoothed Michal's hair. "You'll be all right."

"Is that you, Bridget?" Michal asked. "Where is Alina? I haven't seen her all day. And I don't feel well. It's very hard to breathe."

"She'll be here soon." A tear formed in Bridget's eye, but she knew what she must do. "You just be still and try to relax. I'll be right back with some medicine that will help you," Bridget said, and a memory of a picnic she shared long ago with Otto, Alina, and Michal flashed across the screen of her mind. "Don't think," Bridget told herself. "Leave the past in the past."

Bridget sneaked into the hospital. It was easy for her to get in because the nurse on duty was one of the guards she'd become friendly with.

"What do you need?" her friend asked.

"We have morphine, don't we? I can't sleep."

"Yes, but, you can't just take it. If you get caught—"

"I won't get caught if you don't tell on me."

"Have you taken it before? Do you know what you're doing?"

"Of course. I've done it before. I just need a little to help me sleep."

"All right," the nurse said. "But don't tell anyone that I gave you the key."

"Heidi, do you think I would ever get you in trouble?"

"No, I know you wouldn't." Heidi hesitated. "Bridget? Listen, can you do me a favor, too?"

"Sure. What?"

"Can you keep an eye on this place for me for a half hour? I'm not supposed to leave. But I'm starving. I want to go and get something to eat."

"Of course I will. Go on, and when you get back, I'll go and get the morphine."

"Are you sure?" Heidi asked.

"Certainly." Bridget smiled.

As soon as Heidi left, Bridget went into the medicine closet and took two small tubes of morphine. She carefully wrapped them in the handkerchief she always carried and stuck the package deep into her pocket. Then she sat down at the desk and waited for Heidi to return.

When Heidi got back, she accompanied Bridget to the medicine closet, and not knowing that Bridget had already taken two tubes, she allowed Bridget to take a single dose of morphine and a needle to inject it.

"Now, you promise you won't tell?" Heidi asked again.

"I won't tell. I am upset and can't fall asleep. Boyfriend problems, you know? I appreciate your helping me out with this."

"You know that morphine is addictive, don't you?"

"Yes, I've heard. But don't worry. I only use it when I absolutely can't get any rest. It's not often enough to worry."

"All right. Just keep quiet about this, Bridget."

"I will. I would never want to get you into trouble. Good night, Heidi, and thank you."

—

Bridget's hand closed around the vials of morphine, and she felt the tears swell behind her eyes as she looked at Michal lying on the filthy cot sandwiched between two other pathetic women.

"You came back? I am so glad to see you again. I am just a little under the weather today. Did you say you were bringing medicine? I have been so rude. I must ask, how is your brother? I hope he understands that I had to leave and reunite with my husband." Michal was smiling, her eyes glassed over, her face skeletal, a pool of blood drying in her tangled hair.

"He's doing just fine. I'm sure he understands," Bridget said. Michal was lost in her madness. She'd forgotten that Otto was dead. "I brought you something to help your cough." Bridget took the three doses of morphine out of her pocket. She had no medical background. But she was fairly certain that it was enough to end Michal's life.

Michal nodded. "Thank you, Bridget. You have always been such a good girl. You and my Alina are like sisters. Did you talk with her recently?"

"Yes. I saw her earlier today." Again, Bridget lied to comfort this poor woman who had comforted her as a child.

"Good. How is she? I haven't seen her today. But yesterday, she came by to show me the fabric she wanted me to use for her wedding gown. She is getting married, you know? Such a nice boy. His name is Benny."

"Yes, she told me," Bridget said, smiling. Now, tears had begun running down her face.

"We'll have a beautiful wedding. You'll be there, of course, Otto too? I hope he will come. I hope he isn't angry with me."

"Yes, of course, he will. He told me he is not angry with you at all," Bridget said. She could hardly catch her breath. Better this way than for Michal to endure the pain Dr. Treite would surely inflict upon her. *God help me. I wish I could just run away from here, from all of this.*

Then Michal began to cough again. When she stopped hacking, blood ran from her lips, and she was gasping for breath.

"I think you should give me the medicine. This cough is getting worse," Michal said. For just a flash of a second, something in Michal's eyes seemed to tell Bridget that she knew what Bridget was about to do and that she was grateful. Then, the clarity was gone as fast as it had appeared, and the madness returned. It was easy for Bridget to see the change in Michal's face.

"And as you must realize, I have so much to do for the upcoming wedding. I have to get rid of this cough so that I have the strength." Michal smiled. Her voice cracked, but she continued talking. "It's too bad that Gilde is too old to be a flower girl. She was such a cute toddler; she would have made a lovely flower girl. But of course, that might have stolen some of the attention from Alina. I don't think you ever saw Gilde as a toddler. Ahhh, she was a beautiful child." Michal smiled, then gently Bridget took Michal's arm and stretched it out.

Again, the flash of clarity. "I'm ready. Please give me the medicine now." Bridget was shaking. Sweat was trickling down her back under her uniform. She tore a piece of fabric from Michal's shirt and tied it around Michal's upper arm. Then Bridget found a strong vein in Michal's arm and inserted the needle as gently as she could. *Please, God, make this swift and painless.* Bridget bit her lower lip so hard that she tasted blood. Once the morphine tube was empty, keeping the needle inserted, she switched to the second tube. Michal's eyes were blinking slowly as if they were weighted down. But before she closed them completely, Michal reached up with her other hand and gently squeezed Bridget's arm. Then Michal softly smiled at Bridget and winked. Then, in a whisper, she said, "Thank you."

Bridget's hands were trembling as she finished the last tube. "Goodbye, Michal. I couldn't bear to think of anyone hurting you. You were like a mother to me when I was a child. God help me. I hope this was the right decision." Bridget whispered as she caressed Michal's cheek.

The following morning, Michal was found dead in her cot. Three women shared the bed with Michal, but if any of them saw or heard anything the night before, no one said a word.

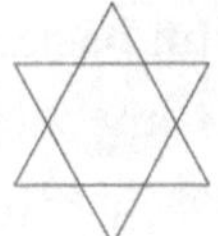

fifty-one

Taavi

Early Spring 1944

TAAVI ASKED Frieda every day if she had heard anything about Michal or the girls. And every day, Frieda said no, nothing. Of course, she had not asked anyone. She was waiting for what she thought was a reasonable amount of time to tell Taavi that her connection had told her that Michal and his daughters were dead. Taavi was always on edge, nervous, and unable to sit still. He was not at all the man she remembered. And quite frankly, Frieda was growing tired of the new Taavi. The exciting and often cruel man he'd been when they had been lovers years ago was gone. In his place was a man as jumpy as a prey animal, who was lousy in bed. And if truth be told, it was his sexual expertise that had been Frieda's main attraction to Taavi. He was an awe-inspiring, experimental, wild, and untamed lover in his youth. Now, he was none of those things, and Frieda had begun to dread making love with him. Often, he was unable to perform, which was frustrating and embarrassing for him. Even worse, every time she saw him, she could count on him to mention his wife or family. She found him irritating.

Frieda was fed up. One evening, she went to see Taavi. That was to be her final effort to separate him from his attachment to his family. Tonight she would tell him that she'd spoken with her Nazi officer friend, and the Nazi had told her that Michal and the girls were dead. She would be sympathetic, a shoulder to cry on if he needed one. Then, perhaps, with some luck, the news would change him back to the old Taavi. Maybe this was what he needed to let go of his wife's hold on him. If it didn't work, Frieda thought that she might just stop paying the blackmail to keep him safe and have him sent back to the camp. What good was he to her this way? Frieda had begun to realize that what she had once believed was love for Taavi was nothing more than the fire of primal lust. Without the oxygen of great sex, that fire was rapidly extinguished.

She walked into his room to find him seated on a chair, reading the newspaper she'd given him the previous day. He'd begged her for a radio, but she refused. She knew Taavi wanted to listen to the BBC, which was against the law. It was bad enough that she was harboring a Jew, and the penalty for that was death. She was tired of trying to please him. If one of her other employees happened to come in early or stay late and hear the radio, especially the BBC, Taavi would be discovered, and she would be arrested. Frieda wasn't going to take any more risks for him. He just wasn't proving worth the effort.

"Did you hear anything?" he asked as soon as he saw her.

The same boring question. Frieda thought she might lose her mind from his obsession with his family. "Yes. And the news is not good. I'm sorry, Taavi. They are all dead."

Taavi stood up, and the paper dropped to the floor. All the blood drained from his face. He put his palms on his eyebrows and began to pace the room. "My God. My God…" he repeated over and over. *This can't be true. Lotti said Gilde went to England. That would mean she may be safe. But what if she was returned home? That would mean Frieda is correct, and everyone I love is gone. Dear God, let this not be true. If it is true, I have nothing left to live for. My family is all gone.* However, he believed it was true, and his heart ached with the knowledge.

"I'm sorry." Frieda went to him and put her hand on his shoulder.

He shook her off and kept walking, repeating, "My God, my Michal. My God, my children, my girls…"

Frieda thought it best to leave him alone, to let him digest his grief and then mourn so that he could get on with his life.

Again, she said, "I'm sorry, Taavi." And she left.

fifty-two

Frieda

FRIEDA GAVE Taavi a couple of days to be alone before she returned to his room. In the past, she was always eager and filled with anticipation before an encounter with him, but now it seemed more like an obligation than a joy. Frieda decided this was her last attempt to fix her relationship with him. Every month, she paid one hundred reichsmarks to that bastard Braus as protection money to keep Taavi safe. Now, she was beginning to feel annoyed. It was becoming obvious that she was not getting anything in return for the money she was spending and the risk she had been taking. Since the club first opened, years before Hitler came to power, plenty of men walked through the doors every night. In the past, since Frieda first met Taavi, she hadn't wanted anyone but him. None of the others excited her or kept her fascination for very long. However, Taavi had changed. He no longer excited her, so she began looking for another lover. With the cabaret as busy as it was, it didn't take long, and recently, Frieda had met Bernd, a student half her age, handsome and physically fit. Most importantly, he flattered her and made her feel young and excited about life again like Taavi had once made her feel.

She had taken Bernd home to bed with her the previous two nights and found him to be quite the lover. In fact, Frieda was so satisfied with Bernd that she would have liked to have him move into the apartment behind the club where Taavi was living. It would be a good deal for him as he would not have to pay any rent, and for her, well, he would be available whenever she wanted him. He was not a Jew, so she wouldn't have to be watching her back constantly and paying exorbitant amounts of money as ransom for his safety.

She knocked on the apartment door, suddenly wishing she could rid herself of Taavi and all the trouble that came with him.

"Come in," he answered. She heard the pain in his voice. It seemed he was so needy, and she was very tired of comforting him.

"Taavi, so, how are you feeling?" Frieda said. She looked at him. He was sitting on the edge of the bed, his hair disheveled. She could smell that he hadn't bathed even from across the room. *Disgusting.* When he'd first come to her from that camp, she'd been so filled with a desire for him that she hadn't cared how dirty he was. But now she was repulsed.

He shrugged. "How should I be feeling? Michal and my daughters are gone forever. I failed them all. I failed as a husband and as a father. It was my job to protect them, Frieda. But I couldn't. I couldn't."

This was the first time she didn't want to touch him. In fact, as she looked at him, he turned her stomach. She'd tried to delude herself into believing he loved her, but he never loved her. She had to accept it now. As she studied him, she could no longer see any trace of the handsome, sexy young man he'd once been. His hair was thin and receded. His body was hunched, and even though he'd started eating regularly again, the skin hung on him where starvation had eaten his muscles. His eyes were shadowed and sunken in with despair. But most of all, his spirit was broken.

"I'm truly sorry, Taavi. I'll leave you alone. It's probably best," Frieda said.

He just nodded. He didn't protest, didn't beg her to stay.

Frieda gave him one more pathetic glance, then turned and left. The next morning, she called Braus and told him to come and arrest Taavi.

"If I do, I'll have to arrest you too. You have been hiding him in your club. I don't suggest you stop paying the ransom if you know what is good for you," Braus said.

"I have a lot of friends. You know that. If I go down for this, you will go down with me. I will tell everyone about your part in all of this. They will believe me, and you'll end up a prisoner instead of a guard."

There was silence on the other end of the phone.

Then Braus began to speak. "Very well. Here is what you do. Tonight, throw him out. I'll arrest him on the street. That way, you won't be involved at all."

"What time?" Frieda asked.

"Eleven tonight."

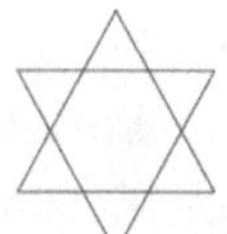

fifty-three
Taavi

WHEN FRIEDA DEMANDED that he go, Taavi was more than willing to leave. He was glad not to have to cope with her wanting more from him than he could give anymore. He would hide in alleyways until he could get back to the forest if he could. Taavi didn't care if he was arrested. He really had no reason to go on living.

He left through the back door of the cabaret like a thief in the night, sliding between buildings, staying out of the streetlights. Taavi's muscles contracted and jerked as his senses went on high alert. The loud laughter of two uniformed men walking through the street sent him careening into the side of the building, where he tore his shirt and bloodied his shoulder. His heart and soul would have easily welcomed a quick end to the pain, but the God-given life force inside of him still fought against death. The blood ran down his arm, but he paid no heed. All he could think of was getting away from the city, where he could be alone to grieve in peace. Somewhere in the distance, a woman giggled, breaking the early morning silence again. Her voice sounded like tiny bells, and it made Taavi want to weep. Then he heard the bustle of working people as the city came alive. He moved faster. Dawn was breaking; the sun had begun to light the sky. *Hurry, get out before daylight.*

Finally, after over two hours of ducking into the shadows, Taavi slipped out of the city. It was easy to see that he'd left the madness of Berlin behind because the greenery became more lush. *Michal*, he thought, whispering her name softly.

He remembered the first time he saw her so long ago, in that little settlement in Siberia. It was mid-afternoon, and she was on her way to the market. He'd been on his knees in the carpentry shop working on something. He couldn't remember what. But then, an invisible nudge had made him look up from his work. There she was, the most beautiful girl he'd ever seen. If he recalled correctly, Michal was fifteen at the time, on the brink of womanhood. Her appearance just slightly revealed the magnificent woman she was to become. But somehow, just glancing across the road when his eyes met hers, Taavi knew he would spend the rest of his life loving her. And he had, and he would until his very last breath.

Then he remembered Alina. She was so afraid of him when he and Michal had first reunited. But slowly and gently, he'd won her over. What a smart girl his Alina was. She'd wanted to be a teacher. In his mind's eye, he saw Alina's face. She had just begun to blossom when her life was stolen away from her. "Alina," he whispered.

In his mind's eye, he saw golden curls. Gilde's curls, little Gilde, always happy, always singing. She was only ten years old. Neither of his daughters would ever be married, nor would they know the joys of motherhood. Tears spilled down his cheeks. He would gladly have traded his own life for any one of them. Taavi was so lost in thought that he was shocked when he felt a sharp pain in his upper back, sharp enough to knock the wind out of him and throw him to the ground. At first, it all felt so unreal that he was confused. He had no idea what had happened. But then, as he lay with his face in the dirt, he tasted blood in his mouth and realized that a bullet had entered his body, like a searing knife cutting him in half between his shoulder blades. His body convulsed and writhed in agony on the ground. His eyes closed against the pain and the world of men, and he saw visions so real that he believed them to be true.

There was Alina, his daughter, his beautiful, sweet Alina, always so serious. She was in the living room of their old apartment, reading a book. She looked up and smiled at him. Then his little Gilde came running towards him, reaching her arms to the sky for him to pick her up and put her on his shoulders. "Carry me around and show me the world, Papa," Gilde said, as she had always done every day when he got home from work. *The world, my Gilde, you want to see the world? The world?* A tear fell from his eye and wet the ground. What a terrible world he had brought his children into. "I'm sorry, Gilde, I'm sorry, Alina." And then, when he felt his life slipping away as the blood of his ancestors poured from his body, he saw her, Michal, his one true love. She was so close to him that he could feel her breath on his cheek. Taavi looked into her eyes; they were so clear in his mind. He heard her voice. "Taavi, come to me," she whispered.

"I'm here, Michal. Take me with you." Taavi whispered. He felt her take his hand as another bullet entered his body. The hot lead burned through his aching soul and pierced his already broken heart, shattering it and ending his life on earth.

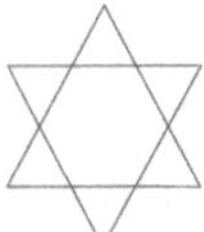

fifty-four

Alina

Summer 1944

ALINA LOOKED in the mirror at the purple and yellow bruise on her cheek and wondered if she should skip class today. Ugo would ask all kinds of questions about what happened to cause the bruise. And she would be forced to tell him the truth. Trevor was hitting her more and more often. His violent outbursts against Alina and Joey had become more brutal, and he no longer slapped her. Instead, he hit her with his fist, hairbrush, or belt buckle. Alina knew that if Ugo found out, he would want to confront Trevor, and that confrontation would no doubt land Ugo in prison. But Alina had other ideas. Alone in her room every night, she'd had plenty of time to think things through. She'd acquired a fair sum of money, and she knew that she wanted to open a business of her own.

After what she'd been through with losing everyone she loved and then marrying a man who treated her and her child like they were less than human, Alina knew that the only way to survive in the world was to be independent. Only then could she escape the fear that made her grit her teeth when she heard the dreaded sound of Trevor's footsteps on the wood floor. She had come to live in constant fear. If Joey was crying too loudly, it was only a matter of time before Trevor would fling the door to their room open wide until the door handle made a dent in the wall. He would glare at Alina, his eyes red with rage. And although she trembled in terror, every time it happened, she would stand between her child and this horrible man she called husband. She would keep him from Joey until he was so angry that he ripped her away from her son and began beating her instead of taking his anger out on Joey.

Her hatred for Trevor grew stronger every time he had an outburst. She dreaded the painful days of recovery following a severe beating, but she would rather he hit her than ever touch Joey. Sometimes at night, after a day of particularly sadistic behavior on Trevor's part, she would lie in bed and think about killing him. In her mind, she would see herself taking his gun out of his desk drawer where he kept it and shooting him until she was sure he was dead. But then she would remember the consequences. *Don't be a fool*, she told herself. *If you are in prison, no one will take care of Joey. He will grow up alone on the streets of New York.* The only way for Joey and her to survive, she decided, was to find a way out of that house and that marriage. She tried to find a job. But she had no employable skills. And with no skills, what kind of business could she possibly open? She realized that she could marry Ugo. He would agree to it, but that was not a solution. It was only more of the same. She would go from being dependent on one man to being dependent on another. Alina Margolis was not going to do that again.

She got up and began getting dressed. Her mind was racing, but she couldn't come up with a solution.

Well, maybe I don't have an answer right now, Alina comforted herself, *but if I want to be independent, I have to keep going to the English classes. I can't worry about what Ugo will think of my bruises. I won't miss my English class because something in my appearance might upset a man. My son's future is at stake.*

Alina combed her hair and put on her hat. Then she dressed Joey, and the two quietly slipped out of the house. Joey was on his way to Maria's, and Alina was on her way to meet Ugo and attend class.

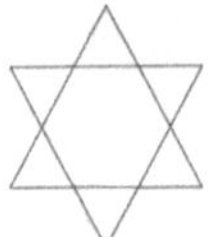

fifty-five

Alina

MARIA WAS WONDERFUL WITH JOEY. She refused to accept money to watch him. So Alina brought her gifts. Today, she'd made a batch of cookies for Maria, which she wrapped in a pretty kitchen towel.

"Hello, Joey! Hello, Alina," Maria said when they walked in.

Maria was pregnant again, and her belly was getting big. She and her family were poor, but they were rich in love, and that was something Alina missed. Once upon a time, her life was filled with love. When she'd lived with her parents, who she missed desperately, and her sweet little sister, who by now would be eighteen years old, a woman. Alina couldn't imagine Gilde all grown up, and the idea brought tears to her eyes. Gilde was no longer a child, and she'd missed all of those years with her, years she could never get back. Then she thought about Lotti, her dear friend and mentor. *Lotti, I pray for you and Lev every day, and I wish more than anything that I could sit at your kitchen table and talk to you, hear your voice, at least for a moment.* But, of course, there was no way to talk to Lotti. In fact, she couldn't even get a letter to Lotti in Germany. America was deep into the war.

American troops had landed in a bloody battle for Normandy in early June, only two months ago.

But most of all, she missed Johan. Not because she was in love with him, but because he was in love with her, and she knew that he would have protected her as long as he was alive. However, as much as she missed Johan, she would never allow herself to lean on anyone the way she had leaned on him. The day he died, Alina knew for the first time what it was like to be alone in the world. And marrying Trevor had turned out to be worse than being alone.

Joey loved going to Maria's house. The first few times Alina left Joey, he'd cried when Alina left for class, and she'd been sick with guilt. But now, as soon as he saw Maria, he reached out to Maria with his chubby little toddler arms, beckoning her to pick him up. Maria constantly told Alina to stay after class and have coffee with the other students. "Joey is fine here," Maria would say, smiling. And Alina knew it was true, but she felt guilty because she wasn't really with all the other students. She was with Ugo. However, Alina didn't know how to explain the friendship between herself and Ugo to Maria. Also, she couldn't tell Maria about her terrible marriage or the bruises on her face. But Maria never asked, and Alina was glad that she hadn't. She thought that perhaps Maria knew or at least had some idea, but she was too kind to ask.

That day, Ugo waited patiently on the sidewalk a block away from Maria's apartment. Alina loved turning the corner and seeing him standing there, dressed in his nicest clothes, smiling, happy to see her. Sometimes, she thought, he reminded her of Johan, the way Johan had been so understanding, but more often, he still reminded her of her father.

"What happened to your face?" Ugo frowned as he looked at the bruise.

"Nothing. I fell."

"You fell and hit your cheek? Hmmm. You expect me to believe that?" Ugo asked, shaking his head.

"I am asking you to respect my privacy." Alina could not meet his eyes.

"There is no privacy between us. We are friends. Alina. You know that you can tell me anything."

"Yes, Ugo. I know."

"Then talk to me, please. Is your husband hurting you? Is he hurting Joey?"

She shook her head. "Just stay out of this, please, Ugo. I know what I am doing."

"You expect me to stand by and let some man hit you and not do anything to stop it? You should know me better, Alina." He stopped walking and firmly put his hands on her shoulders, turning her to face him.

"I don't want your help. If I wanted your help, I'd ask for it," Alina said more harshly than she wanted.

"I'm sorry," he said. Then he released her shoulders and looked away.

They walked in awkward silence all the way to the English class. She took her seat, and he took his, but neither of them said a word to each other. Class began, but Alina couldn't concentrate. She was trying to protect Ugo from serving time in prison. If he had the chance, she knew he would physically assault Trevor. And if Trevor survived, she had no doubt he would file charges. Alina could see Ugo in her peripheral vision as they sat at their desks. He was writing something in his book. Her heart melted a little for the man who meant so well. If she studied him, he wasn't handsome, not in a classic sense. His nose was too big, his jaw too strong, and his cheekbones jutted out. But he was kind, and she knew he cared about her. He meant well, and she was sorry for being so abrupt with him earlier.

The young female teacher was holding up a vase and saying "vase" as the class repeated the word after her. Just then, a woman opened the classroom door and entered without knocking. She had hair the color of ripe strawberries and a tight black dress with high heels. The teacher frowned at her for interrupting the class.

"Can I help you?" the teacher said curtly.

"I must speak to Ugo Blok. I was told I could find him here," the beautiful redhead with the almond-shaped, gold-flecked topaz eyes said in broken English. Her voice was a little too loud, and the way her body trembled gave Alina the indication that she was distraught about something. Alina studied her and decided that she was quite beautiful. She wore black silk stockings. No one Alina knew owned silk stockings because they were difficult to come by. Her magnificent red hair was caught on one side with a shiny gold clip. Looking at her made Alina feel inferior, especially since she asked for Ugo.

Ugo rose to his feet. His voice cracked as he asked, "Klara, what are you doing here?" Then, before Klara could answer, Ugo said, "Excuse us, please," as he took Klara's arm and led her outside the classroom door.

Alina leaned back in her seat. This woman must be his ex-wife.

Klara. Ugo had called her Klara. Alina knew her name. Alina was ashamed of herself but couldn't help but be jealous of the striking woman. She had no right to be. After all, she'd been pushing Ugo's affections away for months. She leaned her head on her hand and looked down at the desk in case anyone watched her. She didn't want them to see the range of emotions that were flitting across her face. She hated to think that Ugo and Klara might be reconciling their marriage, even though she had no right to feel that way. But even if they were, there was still no reason for her to come to his classroom to find him. Why had she come? Money? A million questions were running through Alina's mind. But the most disturbing of them all was that she had to face the possibility that she might be losing Ugo. All the feelings she'd been denying for him were now flooding her heart and mind, and a deep pang of fear stabbed the pit of her stomach. Until today, Alina believed that Ugo would always be there waiting for her no matter what. Now, she was not so sure, and as much as she was afraid to love him, she was also afraid to lose him.

The teacher was still speaking to the class, but Alina wasn't listening. Her palms were sweating; her face was flushed. All she could do was wait until Ugo returned. And even then, what could she ask him? She had made it quite clear to him on several occasions that she never wanted another serious relationship with a man. It was true, wasn't it? Alina wanted nothing more than independence, her own money, her own home, and a place to raise Joey where he would be safe from Trevor. That was why she'd been rejecting Ugo's affection. If she left

Trevor and married Ugo, she would be taking Joey from one man who was not his father to live with another man who was not his father. Over the past several months, she believed she'd come to know Ugo well enough to know that he would not be cruel to her son. But still, she had no guarantee. And if she married Ugo and put her savings together with his, she might end up penniless again. Alina bit her lip and tried to make sense of her life. After Joey was born, everything changed. Where in the past she could afford to make mistakes, now she had to be sure Joey was cared for properly. Letting a man into her life threatened that security. *Damn it, Ugo, you are not what I want.* Alina tried to concentrate on what the teacher was saying. But it was hard to focus. Her eyes kept traveling back to the door, and she wondered what was happening outside between Ugo and that woman.

Finally, Ugo came back in. He gathered his books together and picked them up. Then he leaned over and whispered in Alina's ear.

"I need to talk to you. Can you come outside the room for a minute? I don't want to disturb the class."

Alina nodded and got up. The teacher gave them both a look of disdain for disrupting the lesson. They walked out the door and into the hallway.

"My daughter is very sick. I have to go and see her. Klara needs money for a doctor. Apparently, she has spent everything she earned. I don't care what she does with her money.

"In fact, I don't care what she does at all. But I have to go and help my child."

His hands were shaking. It broke Alina's heart to see Ugo this distressed. Ugo had never shown such weakness. He'd always seemed so strong and in control.

"Let me come with you," Alina said, surprising herself. She was always pulling away from him, but now, something in the trembling of his hands made her want to reach out to him. To comfort him, to help.

"Alina." He turned to look directly into her eyes. "I can't ask you to do this. You do realize where I am going? My daughter lives with her mother in a house of prostitution."

Alina felt her face flush with heat and embarrassment. But Ugo was so vulnerable. "I'll go. I want to go with you."

She saw the raw emotion come over his face, and at that moment, she knew for sure that he was indeed in love with her. Alina took his hand and squeezed it. A million emotions raced through her mind and body. She'd sworn to herself that she didn't love him. In fact, she'd convinced herself that she wasn't capable of romantic love. Her devotion, she told herself, was only to her child, and there was no room in her heart for anyone else.

"Are you sure you want to do this?" Ugo's voice cracked.

"Yes."

"Then come with me."

"Let me go back into the classroom and get my books," Alina said.

When they left the room and walked into the hall, Klara had left. She had already gone back to her house.

"Do you know where this place is?" Alina asked.

"Yes, I know," Ugo said. Even in pain, he took her books and carried them for her. It was a natural instinct for him, and Alina was touched that he kept his manners as a gentleman even now when he was distressed.

fifty-six
Alina

ALINA WAS EXPECTING the bordello to be an obvious house of ill repute. She had anticipated something outlandish and vulgar. But it was nothing of the sort. In fact, it was an ordinary two-story brownstone in a less prestigious part of town. Ugo knocked on the door, and Alina and Ugo were ushered in by a woman in a flimsy robe with her hair in pin curls. Other girls were sitting around a kitchen table looking disheveled. Alina thought that the prostitutes would all be as glamorous as Klara. But then she realized that Klara had dressed up to go out. It was ten thirty in the morning. The girls were probably not expecting company until the late afternoon at the earliest.

"I am here to see my daughter. My wife is Klara Blok," Ugo said to the woman with the pin curls.

"Oh yeah, the gal with the sick kid."

"Yes, the child is my daughter. Her name is Christina Blok." He knew Klara used Christina's given name, but she never called her daughter Lada. That was only his special name for their child.

"Stay right here. I'll see if it's okay to let you go up."

The woman disappeared for a few minutes, giving Alina time to look around. There was a large living room with many chairs, two huge overstuffed sofas, and a shiny black piano. The red velvet drapes were thick enough to keep out prying eyes.

"It's all right. The two of you can go upstairs. It's the fifth room on the left-hand side. The kid has a room attached to her mother's. So, just go on into Klara's room, and she'll direct you from there."

They walked up the flight of stairs to the second floor. Ugo leaned over to Alina as he opened the door. "I can't stand to think my daughter is growing up here with these women. I want her to come to live with me and my family. But Klara's been fighting me about it, and she has a better lawyer. I think he must be one of the customers she met in this place. But maybe once Christina gets well, Klara might see how it would be better for her to be away from this house and these women. I am hoping she will finally agree to let me take my daughter out of here."

Klara was standing in the doorway between the two rooms.

Ugo didn't care that Klara heard him. He just glared at his ex-wife.

"She's right in here." Klara directed Ugo. Alina followed.

Ugo ran to the bed and knelt beside his daughter while Alina stood helplessly beside him.

The child was crying. "Shhh," Ugo said, and he picked her up into his arms, held her close to him, and rocked her. He put his lips to her forehead. Then he turned to Klara. "She's burning up with fever. Go and get the doctor. I'll pay him."

Klara didn't speak. She nodded and left.

"Can I hold her?" Alina asked.

Carefully, Ugo put Christina in Alina's arms. The child didn't recognize Alina, so she pushed away. Alina could see that the little girl wanted her father, so she put her back into Ugo's arms. "I think you're right, she's very hot, she has a fever."

Before the doctor arrived, Christina vomited on Ugo, but he didn't seem fazed. In fact, even with vomit all over his only suit jacket, Ugo still didn't put Christina down. He kept pacing and rocking her.

The doctor arrived and began examining the two-year-old. Ugo whispered in Alina's ear, "She looks so tiny lying there."

"I know. She'll be all right. You'll see." Alina tried to be encouraging.

"Her throat is very red," the doctor said, "and she's running a high fever. Keep her warm, make sure she drinks a lot of liquids, and wash her down with rubbing alcohol to bring down her fever. I'll come back in a few days to see how she's doing."

Ugo stayed with Christina, not leaving her side.

Alina went home later that afternoon but returned with home-made chicken soup the following day.

Three days passed, and Ugo still did not leave his daughter.

Alina dropped Joey off for an hour at Maria's apartment and came by to check on Christina every day. On the fourth day, Christina seemed to be getting better. She was smiling and more playful. She no longer had a fever, and Ugo and Alina were relieved.

Once Ugo felt that Christina was well enough for him to leave her bedside for a few minutes, he went to talk to Klara and insisted that the brothel was no place for a child. He tried to convince Klara to let him take Christina home, telling her that it would be easier for her to work if she were free of the responsibility of caring for a child. "She will live with me. You can come to see her any time you want to."

Klara was not convinced. She was still not willing to let Ugo take Christina.

That afternoon, the doctor returned and said Christina was fine. She was well. Ugo felt it was time for him to leave the brothel. But he decided from then on that he would return at least once every week to visit with his Lada. He deserved to see his daughter grow up.

Alina was with Ugo when the doctor said Christina was well, and the relief she saw on Ugo's face touched her heart.

That night, Alina was at home in the little room she shared with her son. Joey was asleep, and she was reading a German novel when the phone rang. It was rare for anyone to call, so she ran down the stairs to answer the phone.

It was Ugo.

"Can you come quickly? Christina is very sick again. I don't know what's wrong with her, but she can't move her arm or leg, and she can't lift her head."

"I can't leave Joey with Trevor, and it's very late. I know you need me, but I can't come until tomorrow. I can take Joey to Maria's house in the morning and then come to you."

"Will you? Will you please?"

"Of course," she said.

And Alina would have gone, but during the night, Joey began running a fever and vomiting. He was coughing and throwing up so much that Trevor was concerned that the illness might be contagious, so he agreed to pay for a doctor.

Alina called Ugo. She had to call the brothel. He had given her the number when Christina had first gotten sick. It was late that night, but one of the women answered and called Ugo to take the phone.

"Alina?" he asked.

"Joey is sick now, too," she said. "A doctor is on the way."

"Oh God, that's terrible. Christina is getting worse. She can't breathe. I sent for the doctor again."

"I am sorry, Ugo. I can't come in the morning. I can't take Joey to Maria's in this condition."

"I understand."

"I'll stay in touch," Alina said.

Neither Alina nor Ugo wanted to voice their fears, so they both stayed at home with their children and each, in their own way, prayed that this was not the dreaded disease that they feared: polio.

fifty-seven

Lotti

A DAY DIDN'T GO by that Lotti didn't think of Lev. She missed her true love and all of her friends. The other women in the building where she lived were kind but distant towards her. During the day, she worked and that kept her busy. But when night came, she was alone and terribly lonely in the small apartment she'd once shared with Lev.

When she'd first started her job, she had tried to make friends, but rumors had circulated about her marriage to a Jewish man, and it caused the others to keep their distance. Every day, Lotti brought her lunch to work and sat alone at the end of the long table in the lunchroom. She was only thirty-six, but she felt much older. Perhaps it was the loneliness that made her feel so old and tired. Perhaps she had resigned herself to the fact that she would never love again. But when she felt exceptionally lost, she talked to Lev in her mind, and sometimes, she could even hear his voice in her head.

During the long winter nights, she would recall some of her fondest memories of when she and Alina had worked at the orphanage together. How wonderful it had been to spend the day working with her best friend and then coming home to Lev's warm arms at night. Now, she was alone, a woman of pure German blood but hated by her own kind. And yet, if Germany lost the war, things would be even worse for her. Because if the Russians came into Berlin, she would be treated as a Nazi. No one would believe her that she had been against the Nazis from the beginning. All they would see was a German woman. And from what she'd heard, the Russians were just itching to get into Germany. They wanted to punish the women for the loved ones they'd lost during the war. People were speaking in whispers everywhere. They were saying that Germany was not doing well.

Lotti would be glad to see the Nazis destroyed, but she also knew that she would go down with them. No matter what she said or did, she was doomed either way. Damned Hitler and the Nazi Party. They had destroyed her life and taken everything she loved.

Then, at the end of February 1945, a young girl came to work at the hotel where Lotti worked. She was a little pixie of a girl, and her name was Bernadette. Bernadette couldn't have been more than seventeen, and in some ways, she reminded Lotti of Alina. Bernadette kept to herself. Lotti noticed that she sat alone when she took her meals and didn't seem interested in joining the group of young girls who met every day at lunchtime and giggled together at the other end of the table. Instead, Bernadette just ate quietly and spoke to no one. This intrigued Lotti, and at this point in her life, very little intrigued her. One afternoon, Lotti saw Bernadette sitting alone and decided to walk over to introduce herself.

The worst that could happen would be Bernadette would ask her to leave. And Lotti had heard that before from plenty of other women.

"Hello, I'm Lotti Strombeck. I work on the phones. Can I join you?"

"Sure, I'm Bernadette Schmidt."

Lotti sat down. "I work on the switchboard."

"I am in housekeeping. I clean the rooms and the toilets too. It's a job, you know?" Bernadette said; her voice was bitter.

"Yes. I understand."

"It's sometimes a filthy job. But at least I have a little bit of money coming in." Bernadette smiled wryly.

"We have a position open on the switchboard. It opened last week. One of the older ladies passed away. Would you like me to ask if they would consider hiring you?"

"Would you? I would love that. I would love to work on the phones instead of cleaning up other people's messes."

"Of course. I'll ask Mr. Mueller today right after lunch."

"It would be a lot easier than my present job, that's for sure."

Lotti did as she promised, and Mr. Mueller agreed to set up an interview for Bernadette the following morning.

Bernadette came in looking like a delicate flower. She wore a white blouse and a navy skirt. She and Mueller were in his office for a quarter of an hour before Bernadette came out smiling. She walked over to Lotti and whispered, "Thank you so much. He hired me! I start on Monday."

While Bernadette and Lotti became fast friends, she was not friendly to other people. In fact, she hardly spoke. She answered when someone asked her a question, but for the most part, she kept her head down and did her work.

Two weeks later, Lotti invited Bernadette over for dinner. Bernadette was glad to accept the invitation. It was a Friday evening, and Lotti stopped on her way home to pick up a sweet roll from the bakery. A rare treat, something she would never have purchased for herself. But she was looking forward to having company, and it seemed fitting to celebrate Bernadette's new job. Then, she raced back to her apartment to prepare dinner. Bernadette arrived on time with a thick rye bread she'd purchased on her way over from the bakery on the corner.

"I'm so glad you came," Lotti said as she ushered her new friend into the apartment.

They had a simple dinner of soup and a thick piece of bread that Bernadette had brought. Then Lotti took out the sweet roll and cut it in half, giving her guest the larger piece.

"So, the women at the hotel talk, as you know," Bernadette said. "I have heard that you were married to a Jew."

"Yes, it's true," Lotti said. "I loved him very much."

"Where is he now? In a camp?" Bernadette asked.

"No, he's dead. I miss him every day," Lotti said, looking at the floor. She had not spoken openly about Lev since she'd seen Taavi, and talking with this girl brought back so many memories. "Does it bother you?" Lotti cleared her throat.

"Does what bother me?" Bernadette asked.

"That my husband was Jewish?"

"I don't care. I have nothing against Jews. That's Hitler's war, not mine. I have enough trouble just trying to survive, you know?"

"Yes, I do know. I feel the same way. But of course, you realize that befriending me might cost you the friendship of the other workers at the hotel. I'm an outcast."

"So what. I don't need their fake friendship. They sit and talk like best friends, and as soon as one of them leaves the room, they gossip about her as if she were their worst enemy. Who needs a friend like that? Not me, surely."

Lotti nodded. This was a strange young woman. She had a beautiful young face, but her eyes were deep and dark, as if she'd seen more than her fair share of tragedy. But Lotti would not ask questions. She would listen.

"You can call me Berni."

"Alright, Berni it is. Do you live near here?"

"I share an apartment with several women about four blocks north. It's very crowded, and I hate it. But my parents threw me out, and I needed a place to live."

Lotti didn't want to pry, but the conversation was lagging behind. She had to think of something to ask. "So, do you have a boyfriend?"

"Me, no. I have no interest in getting involved with anyone, not now, not ever."

Not now, not ever? Lotti thought. Berni was so young to be so jaded. What had happened to this poor child?

They sat quietly and nibbled on the coveted sweet roll.

"So, you were married. You want to talk about it?"

"Well," Lotti said. "My husband, Lev, was my best friend. I loved him very much. But my parents rejected him. They threw me out, too. I understand how hard it can be to get along with family."

"You can't know what I have been through. No one could understand," Berni said, her eyes hard as glass.

"Do you want to talk about it?"

"No."

"That's all right then. You don't have to discuss anything. We can just sit here and enjoy our time together," Lotti said.

Berni nodded. Lotti saw that Berni's eyes were no longer hard. They'd softened into a deep well of sadness. Lotti wished she could help in some way.

The evening was awkward, and Lotti was convinced that the friendship with Berni would fade away. It didn't. There was little talk between them. Berni was quiet and withdrawn, but she did kind things for Lotti, things Lotti hardly expected. When Berni brought food to work, she offered to share it with Lotti. They sat together when they ate lunch. And even though the conversation was minimal, a bond was forming between them, and for the first time in a long time, Lotti felt she had found a friend.

They had more dinners together at Lotti's apartment and occasional walks through the park and the Berlin Zoo when they had the same days off. One afternoon, as they walked through the zoo, Berni stopped and held on to the fence. Her knuckles were white, and her face was cramped in pain.

"What is it?" Lotti asked.

"Nothing, I'm fine." Berni shook her head and began to walk again. Then she collapsed on the ground, and Lotti saw a thin line of blood running down Berni's thigh.

"Oh my God, help me, someone help me. This girl needs medical attention!"

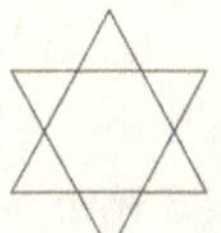

fifty-eight
Alina

THE DOCTOR DIAGNOSED Joey with polio. Trevor would have never paid for a doctor if he had not been afraid of catching Joey's illness. When Joey first showed signs of being ill, Alina and Trevor fought because he didn't want to pay for the doctor to make a house call. Trevor had raised his voice, and Joey whimpered. He stood in front of the door to Joey's room, insisting that if Alina just let the boy sleep, he would be fine. A chill ran up her spine, and Alina came to believe that Trevor wanted Joey to die. She glared at Trevor and looked deeply into his eyes. She knew she had to leave him. As soon as Joey was well enough, they would go. She had no idea where or how, but she would take the money she'd been hiding and run. "I'm telling you, Alina, you baby this child far too much. Leave him alone. Sicknesses make a child stronger. Your constant catering to him is making him weak," Trevor said.

"He might be contagious, Trevor. You could catch this. You are not a young man. It might kill you," Alina said, knowing that would scare Trevor.

She saw his expression change once she lit that fire in Trevor's brain. He was afraid for himself.

"Call for the doctor," he said, stomping out of the room.

"Give me the money," she said. She could have used the money she stole from Trevor as she planned, but if she could get it from Trevor, why not?

Trevor went into his room and came back with a wad of bills. Alina grabbed it from his hand.

Then she scooped her son into her arms and ran two blocks to the doctor's office. Joey was burning up with a fever. It was raining. The rain was pouring down in sheets. Alina's hair fell drenched into her eyes, but she kept going. She didn't think she was strong enough to carry Joey like that. In fact, she'd never been able to do it in the past. But somehow, this time, she didn't feel his weight. Instead, this time, all she felt was the urgency of getting her only child the help he needed to survive. The doctor examined him and sent them home. "Polio," he said. It was a hard go at first. The doctor could do nothing for Joey.

Alina sat at his bedside, wiping the sweat from his brow while bargaining and pleading with God for his life. She locked the door and did not eat or sleep. When Trevor knocked and had the nerve to ask if the doctor told Alina whether Joey was contagious, she told Trevor to go away. Finally, after three days of walking on a tightrope between life and death, Joey slowly began to recover. His fever broke, and he was breathing more easily. Joey got well, but not completely. The disease had left him with some damage to the right side of his body. His arm hung limp, and his little legs were slightly twisted. But he would live.

It was several weeks before Alina returned to her English class. She had not called Ugo, and he had not called her. Two weeks after Alina returned to class, Ugo showed up at the classroom. It was then that Alina learned that Ugo's daughter had polio, too, but she had not been as fortunate as Joey. Ugo's daughter died. When Alina heard the news, she felt sick to her stomach.

"I'm so sorry, Ugo." Alina touched his arm, but Ugo looked away. He couldn't meet her eyes. She knew it was because he hated to show pain and weakness.

"Thank you," he said, clearing his throat and squaring his shoulders.

For several minutes, there was an awkward silence.

"Joey had polio. He made it through. I mean, he is alive, but it crippled him," Alina said. She couldn't help but wonder if she'd brought the polio germs home to Joey after she'd gone to see Christina with Ugo.

Dear God, her son, her only child. He could easily have died. She felt guilty for thinking of herself and Joey while poor, dear Ugo was in so much pain. He was her best friend, and she couldn't find the right words to say to help him get through this tragedy. If it had been Joey who died, she would be beyond despair right now. In fact, she wasn't sure she would have ever been able to recover. It's hard to say what one would do when confronted with such tremendous loss.

She thought again as she glanced at Ugo. He still was not looking at her. She longed to take him in her arms and comfort him but couldn't bring herself to do so. Alina was at a loss. She just stood across from him and shook her head as tears threatened to spill from her eyes. Ugo had not been able to spend much time with his young daughter before he'd lost her forever. It was frightening for Alina to think of how fleeting life could be, especially when it came to children, to Joey. There was no known treatment for polio. It was all a matter of luck, Alina thought. Some lived, some died. And when she was at home, and she looked at Joey's deformed little body, her heart would moan in desperation because although she was filled with the deepest gratitude that he was alive, she couldn't help but worry about how hard his life would be as a cripple.

Ugo pretended to be strong, but Alina saw the pain in his eyes. She could do nothing for him. And then they began meeting on the corner again and walking to class together. They never talked about Christina. Instead, he attended class and quietly pushed through his sadness.

Maria and Alina had not met at the park for a couple of weeks, but once Joey recovered, she went to Maria's house to explain why she hadn't been around.

"Joey was too sick to come over here, and I didn't want to expose your children to the disease, either," Alina said.

Maria understood. She crossed herself and said a prayer.

"I am worried about Joey. How will he get through life? What kind of work can he do?" Alina said. "His body is so mangled."

Maria was silent for a moment. Somewhere, a crow cawed. Then Maria cleared her throat and took Alina's hand. "President Roosevelt had polio, and it didn't stop him in life," Maria said. "He is a great man, and he is the president of the greatest country in the world, yes?"

"Yes," Alina answered. But Roosevelt was one in a million. How would little Joey Powell get by? Joey had Trevor's name, but that was all he had and all she wanted from his stepfather. Alina was the only one who loved that little boy. And now, with Joey being crippled, she would have to try even harder to make sure that he had plenty of money because he would need to get a good education. He would never be capable of manual labor. His body couldn't withstand it. She looked into the buggy where Joey had fallen asleep, and she knew that she would do anything for her son.

fifty-nine

Alina

ALINA WAS ready to leave Trevor. She packed all the personal possessions she could take and moved in with Maria. She left Trevor a note but was afraid to confront him. He had proven he could be violent, and she didn't know how he would react to her leaving.

It was Maria's suggestion that Alina bring Joey and stay with her. Maria told her that she and Joey were welcome to stay as long as they liked. However, the apartment was crowded, and Alina needed to find a job and a place. Maria had offered to watch Joey while Alina worked. Maria even insisted that she didn't want to be paid for babysitting. Alina was uncomfortable taking so much from her friend. After all, she was living with Maria's family rent-free. This couldn't go on. Alina was desperate to earn money. Every day, she went out looking for any kind of work. She found nothing. She would be in trouble if she took an apartment and went through her savings. She had to find a way to earn a living.

Ugo was there for Alina. He was supportive in any way she would allow him to be. He offered to help her move the rest of her things, but she didn't want to return to the house and see Trevor. Thus far, Trevor had not found her. But she knew Trevor would be angry, and if she brought Ugo with her, there was bound to be a fight. Because

Trevor had so many friends in the police department, he could probably shoot Ugo and Alina and get away without being arrested. Then what would become of Joey?

The material things she had to leave behind were not worth the price she might pay for going back and trying to take them. As time passed, it was obvious to Alina how much Ugo cared about her because he did wonderful, kind things, like bringing a whole bag of groceries to Maria's house when he got paid. He spent money on small toys for Joey.

He was so sweet, and a part of her hungered for the touch of a lover, but she knew it would complicate her already complicated life far too much. However, his hand would occasionally brush hers, or she'd smell the clean fragrance of his freshly washed hair, and desire would send a little shiver through her. Desire? She'd never felt this way about any man before, not poor Benny, not Johan, dear sweet Johan, and certainly not Trevor.

Ugo never talked about how much he missed his daughter, and Alina didn't pry. He was not the kind of man to cry on her shoulder. No, Ugo was the type of man who suffered silently and alone. Alina knew a lot about him, and sometimes, she wished he could talk to her. She couldn't give him the love she knew he needed, but she could be there for him as a best friend and confidant if he would only let her. He'd bottled up so much pain that she worried about his sanity.

One afternoon, Alina heard that the butcher needed an employee. Immediately, she got dressed and went to apply for the job. She assumed the butcher would probably want to hire a man, but she had to try. The idea of working with meat, killing animals, and cleaning up blood made her sick to her stomach. But if by some miracle he hired her, she would find a way to do what had to be done. She needed a job, any job.

"I've come here looking for work," Alina said when the butcher asked her what she wanted.

"Wait until all the customers are gone, and then we can talk about employment," the butcher told Alina. She saw the lecherous look in his eyes, and a feeling of depression came over her. What was the difference between having a demanding old boss who was groping at her or a terrible husband? Not much. It would take a constant effort to keep his hands off of her. She dreaded the idea of working every day with a man like this. Well, at least Joey wouldn't have to have any contact with him.

She stood outside the butcher shop and waited as the owner had told her to do. It began to drizzle, and then the drizzle turned to heavier rain. It was early March, and the rain was like a cold shower; the wind blew a chill through her wet hair.

"Are you Alina?" The voice and face were familiar, but Alina didn't recognize the woman at first.

"I'm Klara, Ugo's ex-wife." Klara was not dressed up the way she'd been when Alina saw her in the classroom and at the brothel. In fact, today, Klara looked like an average woman going shopping for food. That glorious red hair was covered with a scarf, and she wore a shapeless wool coat.

Oh dear. What did Klara think of her? Was this going to be a problem? Did Klara think she'd stolen her husband? *Please don't start yelling. Not now. Not when I am trying so hard to find work.*

"Yes, I do remember you," Alina said. Then, hesitating just a little with honest sympathy, she said, "I'm sorry about your daughter."

Klara shrugged. But Alina saw the sadness cross Klara's face. Then maybe it was the sorrow, but Klara seemed to soften. "I am going into the butcher shop. Do you want to come in and get out of the rain? It's cold as hell out here."

"Yes, it is. I'm freezing. But I can't come in." There was something soft and warm in Klara's eyes that made Alina feel she could talk to her. This was strange because there should have been a discord between them because of Ugo. And yet, Alina felt connected to Klara in a way she couldn't explain. Maybe it was because both of them had children who had been struck with that terrible disease. "I'm applying for a job here, and the butcher told me to wait outside."

"Are you a butcher?" Klara looked at Alina, her eyebrows raised in disbelief.

"No, I am a desperate woman. I left my husband, and I need work to earn money to take care of my son," Alina said, and as soon as she said it, she wished she hadn't. She wondered what Klara was thinking about her and Ugo.

There were a few minutes of silence. Then Klara said, "Come on, let me buy you a cup of the rotten stuff that we call coffee these days."

"But I have to wait here and see about this job."

"Come with me. I know this butcher. This is a man who doesn't want an employee. He wants a little fun with a woman, and he knows how desperate you are. He isn't going to hire you. All he'll do is put his hands all over you. Believe me, when it comes to men, I'm an expert."

For some reason, Alina knew Klara was right.

Alina shrugged. "Why not? Let's go and have a coffee."

The coffee was made from grains, but at least it was hot.

"You know what I do for a living? I am sure Ugo has told you."

Alina blushed. "Yes, I do know."

"Well, it's a living. At least I have a roof over my head and food in my belly. And when my daughter was alive, God rest her precious soul. We had a warm place to live in the winter. I know that you are probably going to be offended, but you need a job, right?"

Alina took a sip of the bitter hot water. Then she took a deep breath. Her mind was racing. She knew that Klara was suggesting she become a prostitute, but she had another idea. "How much money do you earn?" Alina asked.

"It's different all the time. It's a percentage. Twenty percent of what I bring in. The room where I sleep is taken out of my earnings. I share it with three other girls. But the food and water to bathe and wash clothes once a week are also covered by my earnings. Still, it's not so bad. What I do at the brothel is nothing I haven't done for free in the past, you know what I mean?"

Alina took a moment and studied Klara's beautiful gold-flecked eyes. They looked like the color of gemstones in the picture books Alina had seen as a child. "Are there a lot of girls in the house?"

"About twenty. Give or take. They come and go. We can always use another one, though."

"Yes. I am sure." Alina chewed on her lower lip. She had an idea.

"What would you and the other girls who work with you say to a thirty percent commission? And what if you only had to share your room with another girl? And, of course, you would have food and water to bathe twice a week and wash your clothes, the same as now."

"I'd say that would be wonderful. But no one is offering that much."

"I am."

"You?"

"Yes, me. If you and your friends will come to work for me, I will go today and buy a house. Then, as soon as I can open it, I will give you everything I just promised," Alina said, looking directly at Klara.

"You have enough money?"

"Yes, I think I do," Alina said.

"There is a big home with lots of rooms right down the street from here. It's a little run down, but if you promised to give us girls a ten percent increase and all the other benefits, I am sure most of the girls will come and help you fix the house up. But, the repairs will cost you too. Where are you going to get all of this money?"

"I already have it."

Klara tilted her head to one side. "You fooled me. I actually felt sorry for you. I thought you were a naïve and pitiful thing. But you're not."

"No, I certainly am not," Alina said.

sixty

Alina

THAT VERY SAME DAY, Alina went to look at the house Klara had told her about. It was large enough, and the foundation seemed solid. All it needed was some cosmetic work, a little paint, and some new curtains. When she was a child, Alina had watched her father bargain prices with customers. She had never done it, but she would now. In fact, she would dicker until she got the best possible price. Then, she would go see Klara and start her own business.

Alina had no intentions of being a prostitute, but owning this house might just be the opportunity she'd been searching for. It didn't matter what people thought of her. They didn't pay her bills. If she owned a brothel, she would have a place that brought in enough money for her to raise her son. She and Joey would have a roof over their heads, and she would see that the girls who worked for her were treated well. Would her parents be ashamed? Probably. But they weren't here to help her, and she had to stand on her own. This house would give her the income she and Joey needed to survive.

At first, the man who was selling the house thought Alina was a pushover. He tried to overcharge her. But she was tougher than he realized, and in the end, she got a better price than she'd originally anticipated.

With some difficulty, Klara arranged a meeting between Alina and several of her coworkers at a coffee shop. Fifteen young girls showed up, and Alina bought coffee and pastries for all of them. It was an investment, but trying to recruit these women was worth the output because each had an existing clientele. If they came to work for Alina, their customers would follow them. She would be earning money as soon as the doors opened. At first, the prostitutes were not interested in moving to a new brothel. They were afraid that if they left their current place of employment and Alina's house failed, they would have no place to work. But with Klara's influence and the offer of a higher percentage and better working conditions, Alina finally convinced most of them.

Twelve girls contracted to come to work for Alina.

"You will be more than employees at my house," Alina told them. "We will be like a family. I vow to treat all of you fairly. I will need your help to put the house together. But I promise you that you will be happy working for me. And I want you to know that this house will not fail, so you will never need to return to your former employer! I will treat you girls like sisters, not like employees. I want you to know that you come to me with any problems or needs you might have, and I will always do what I can for you."

The twelve girls agreed to help her put the house together. They all pitched in and painted the walls. At the secondhand store, Alina bought a bed for Joey. Then, she and Joey moved in before the house was even finished. He coughed from the smell of paint but never once complained. The following day, Alina stayed up well into the wee hours of the morning sewing curtains for each of the rooms. Then, when she was so exhausted that she couldn't keep her eyes open, she slept on an old blanket on the floor. Once she finished the painting and cleaning, she would buy all the rest of the furniture secondhand. If she bought it all at once, she would be making a large purchase, and therefore, she would have bargaining power regarding the price. One of the girls knew someone selling a used piano. The price was right, so Alina bought it for the living room. It was important to be frugal in case it took some time for the business to start earning money.

For two weeks, Ugo would come and wait for Alina at the corner where he and Alina usually met to go to class, but she didn't show up. He was worried. Although he hated to go to Maria's house uninvited, he was worried. All kinds of terrible scenarios played across his mind. Perhaps Trevor had done something to Alina, or maybe she was sick. It had gotten to the point where Ugo had trouble sleeping.

His feelings had been growing for Alina, and he couldn't deny it; he knew he was in love. He'd never felt this way towards any woman before. Not even Klara, who he'd believed he loved when they were married. Now he knew the difference, and the love he felt for Alina was consuming him. She wouldn't marry him; he'd asked her several times, but still, it wasn't like Alina to disappear like this. He had to go and find her in case she needed him.

Finally, Ugo went to Maria's apartment. She didn't know that Alina was opening a whorehouse, but she did know that Alina had purchased a home, and she knew where it was located. Alina had never told her not to disclose this information to Ugo, so she told him, not knowing that anything was wrong.

Ugo thanked her and left. He walked a mile to the house Alina had purchased and rang the bell. Alina had been upstairs sewing a bedspread when one of the girls came into her room to tell her that she had a visitor.

"Is it a man?"

"Yes," the girl said.

Well, it was probably Trevor or Ugo. They could have gotten the address from Maria. Or, it might be the previous employer of the girls who were now working for her. Alina was sure he was angry that she'd taken his prostitutes. Either way, she was going to have to handle the situation. Sooner or later, Trevor and Ugo would know what she had done. Alina walked down the stairs and saw Ugo's broad back. He was sitting on a chair facing away from her.

How was she ever going to make him understand why she had to do what she had done? It wasn't as if she didn't know how he felt about Klara becoming a prostitute. He'd told her. Once he knew that Klara worked for her, Ugo would probably hate Alina. It was for these very reasons that she'd been avoiding him. Now, he'd come to find her. Well, hadn't she expected this?

Joey was sitting on the floor and playing quietly. He was such a good boy. Since his recovery from polio, he was a quiet, introspective child who played calmly for short periods and then took long naps. Since they'd left Trevor's house, Joey rarely cried. It was as if the little boy felt he had no right to demand anything from life. His gratitude just to be alive and away from his terrible stepfather tore at Alina's heart. Sometimes, nightmares woke her at night. Nightmares that reminded her of the struggles Joey would have to face in his life.

As she came down to the last step, she said, "Hello, Ugo." Her heart was beating fast. She'd never wanted to disappoint him. And he looked so handsome and caring sitting there.

He stood up and whirled around to face her.

"Alina, are you all right? I've waited for you to come to class for the last two weeks. What's going on here?" Ugo's face was distraught. She saw the anguish and felt guilty for avoiding him and not being more straightforward.

Dread settled in her chest as she looked into his eyes. This was not going to be easy, but she knew that she had to tell him the truth today.

Since Alina knew that Klara might come in at any time, Alina thought it best to tell Ugo before he saw Klara and realized what was happening on his own.

"Can we go outside and talk?" Alina asked.

"Of course."

"Let me get my coat." Alina slipped her coat on and then asked one of the prostitutes who was sitting in the kitchen, "I hate to bother you, but can you keep an eye on Joey for a few minutes. I have to talk to Ugo. We're going outside, but I won't be long."

"Of course. Don't worry about Joey. I'll watch him," the girl said.

Ugo opened the door, and Alina walked outside. The chilly air felt sobering.

"I'm sorry I didn't come and talk to you. It wasn't fair of me."

"Alina, what is it? What's wrong? Are you ill? Did I do something to offend you?" He was so sincere that she almost started to cry.

She shook her head. "No, Ugo, no, it's none of those things. It's something that you aren't going to approve of, and I've been avoiding this conversation because I knew how you would react."

"What conversation, Alina? Please tell me what you're talking about."

"Ugo, I saw Klara at the butcher shop. And…"

"What did she tell you about me? Whatever she might have said, it's not true."

"Ugo, she didn't tell me anything about you. In fact, we never talked about you," Alina said.

"I don't understand."

"I needed a home for Joey. I couldn't find a job. So, Klara helped me." Even as the words left her lips, she saw the horror on his face. "I'm not a prostitute. I'm not going to be one."

He looked into her eyes, and she could see how confused he was.

"I bought this house. I am going to be a madam. This will be a brothel." There, she'd said the words, and instead of feeling better, she felt worse.

"You're going to run a whorehouse?" Ugo glared at her in total disbelief.

"Yes. I had a little money put away. But I had to make the money last. You see, I had to make sure that somehow I invested it in a business that would thrive regardless of whether there was a good or bad economy. Believe me, Ugo. I gave this a lot of thought. I could have opened a laundry, but when money is tight, people wash their own clothes. We are just coming out of a terrible depression. I don't want to be penniless and homeless if another one strikes the country. Regardless of how scarce money becomes, men always go to brothels."

"Who are you, Alina? I feel like I don't even know you. Like I never knew you at all."

"I am me, the same woman. Nothing has changed except that I can't continue without financial security, especially for my son." The more she explained, the worse she felt. Now, she was sick to her stomach.

"You want security? I'll give you security and decency. Marry me,

Alina. Okay, I'll admit it. I've always been in love with you. Maybe from that first day, I saw you. When you were nursing Johan's cut. I don't know. All I know is that if you give me a chance, I'll take care of you and Joey." He pulled her to him so he could look into her eyes, but she looked away.

"Ugo, if I've learned anything in my life, it's that marriage is not the answer. I have to have my own money to take care of Joey. I can't depend on you or anyone else."

"You can depend on me, Alina. I won't let you down," Ugo said. His eyes were glassy, and she was afraid he might cry.

Please don't cry, Ugo, she thought. *If you do, I might give in.*

"I understand, and I believe you. I care a lot about you, Ugo. But not enough to give up my freedom again. I will never be dependent on any man again," she said.

"This is a harsh world, Alina. In this country that is constantly changing, a woman needs a man to survive. You need a man to protect you. To become a madam of a whorehouse is not an answer. This is no life for a refined girl like you," Ugo said.

"I'm sorry, Ugo. But I've made my decision, and I already bought the house. In fact, Joey and I are living here."

"Let me see if I understand this. You are telling me that you live with your child in the house that you are turning into a brothel?"

"Yes, Ugo. I am renovating it, but Joey and I have moved in. I am hoping the brothel will be open by late spring."

"You already have girls hired?" He was angry. She could see it in his eyes, but she also saw something else. He was amazed that she'd done all of this without asking for anyone's help. "Without asking for my help? You hired Klara, didn't you?"

She nodded. "Yes."

"How could you do that?"

"I had to. She was the only person I knew in the business. She has been very good to me. She is giving me advice so I can put the business together."

"I can't believe this is all true." He shook his head. She saw his anger turn to disgust, and she felt the emptiness she had been fighting against every day of her life eating at her from the inside. There were days when the empty space in the pit of her stomach was as tiny as a pebble and other days when it was as big as a mountain. Standing beside Ugo and watching his face today, that empty space felt like the Grand Canyon.

"Don't you understand that you are putting a black mark on Joey too? Nobody is going to want to associate with him if his mother runs a whorehouse. Alina, you're making a big mistake. I want to be your husband. I will adopt Joey and raise him as if he were my own child. I'll help you get a legal divorce from Trevor, and you can be my wife. I'll be a good husband to you. You have my word. Please, think this through."

"It's not as if Joey is going to have it easy anyway. He's crippled. I know he will have a hard time finding a wife and work. When I took him to the park, the older children teased him because of the way he walked. The only thing that might make his life a little better is money. Besides, I have already had enough men for a lifetime, Ugo. I am aching inside. I am frightened of the future. I know you mean well. But I can't trust anyone, not even you, to take care of Joey. I have to do it. I have to earn enough money so that I am never in the same position that I was with Trevor."

"And you think I would ever be like Trevor?"

"What do you know of my marriage to Trevor? I never told you anything."

"You didn't have to. I saw the bruises on your face, your hands. I wanted to go and kill him. But because you didn't say anything, I kept my mouth shut. I knew you didn't want to talk about it. But, Alina, I am not Trevor."

"Johan was not Trevor either. He was a kind and gentle man, but he died, leaving me to find my own way. I can't go through that again. Not with a child, especially a child who has needs. I had to find a way to depend on myself, and this was the only thing I could do. Because of the Nazis in Germany, I wasn't able to finish my education and become a teacher. That was my dream. But dreams are just that: dreams. This is reality, Ugo. This is what I must do to close my eyes at night and sleep without worrying about where the money will come from to feed my son. And, God forbid, what if he needs extensive medical care later in life? After what he went through, there is no telling what he might need later."

"Alina, Alina..." he said, shaking his head. A tear slipped down his cheek.

"Stop it, Ugo." She felt tears forming in her eyes. Her hands were clenched into fists. In his eyes, she saw how much he cared, and it only made her angry because she cared, too. "Get out of here, Ugo. You don't understand, and you never will."

"I'll do as you ask, I am going, Alina. I don't know what to say to you. I am not sure that there is anything I could say that would make you put your trust in me and make you feel safe again. I just wish there was. God, I wish that there was." He turned and walked away.

She yearned to run after him. Maybe she was wrong. Maybe she should do what every other good woman did: marry and be a wife and mother. Part of her wanted to beg him to save her from this crazy choice she'd made. It was surely a decision that would ruin her reputation forever among decent people. She longed to feel his strong arms around her, protecting her, rescuing her. But she didn't chase him. Alina just stood there next to the house she'd bought, with the wind whipping through her hair and slapping her face with the tears that fell from her eyes. Her breath was ragged, and her hands were clenched at her sides.

"Goodbye, Ugo," she whispered as she watched him walk away.

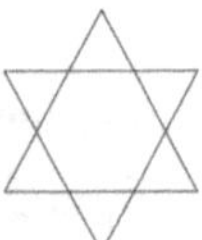

sixty-one

Ugo

UGO COULDN'T BELIEVE what he'd just heard. It was beyond his comprehension that a girl as sweet and innocent as Alina would stoop so low. How could Alina do what she was doing while knowing how he felt about what Klara had done? Did he mean that little to her? All the time they were together, he was careful to treat her with the utmost respect, like a lady. He'd never so much as made a remark she might find crude for fear he would offend her.

Perhaps he'd invented the Alina that he wanted her to be. Maybe he'd missed all the signs because he didn't want to see them. His stomach ached. He knew it was because he couldn't talk about his feelings with anyone. Ugo had always bottled things up inside. A man didn't fall apart. It was not acceptable. Yet, he felt like his world was shredding. First, his wife had humiliated him by turning to prostitution because he was not man enough to provide the life she wanted. Then, his precious daughter died of polio. And now he had lost his one last hope for happiness, his one true love, Alina.

Ugo had grown up enjoying Russian vodka but tried to save it for special occasions. It was no good for a man to become too dependent on the drink. But today, he needed a shot to soothe his nerves.

As soon as he got home, he took the bottle from the cabinet and took a swig. The taste of good Russian vodka made him long for home. America had not turned out as he'd expected. The streets certainly were not paved with gold as the legend went. He was poor, working a job that hardly paid him a living. It was true that things had gotten worse in Russia after the Reds came in. But the Russia of his memory was the land he had loved as a little boy. As a child, he'd known little about the war between the White and Red factions. He grew up on a farm far from the city, where he drank fresh cow's milk and ate vegetables grown in his mother's garden. But life couldn't go on that way. Too much political unrest.

He took another shot. The bottle of vodka was expensive; he should conserve what he had. And yet, it was the only thing that comforted him right now. So, he took another shot.

When Ugo was drunk enough that nothing really mattered, he lay down on his small, lumpy bed and fell asleep. But even in sleep, he couldn't escape his love for Alina. Her smile and her voice haunted his dreams.

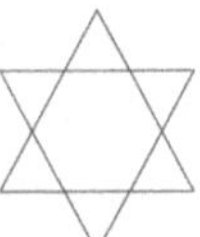

sixty-two

Alina

THE HOUSE of prostitution opened earlier than expected. With the help of the twelve women who would be her employees, Alina had everything ready to go by the end of February. She hired a pianist who played the popular big band songs. And then, the girls began to tell their customers where they were moving. Most of the customers were regulars, and as Alina had expected, the men followed the girls.

By the end of the first week that it was open, the house was hopping. Money was rolling in rapidly. The customers were mostly old men, too old to be in the war. But Alina had learned to read enough English to be able to scan the newspapers, and she had also purchased a radio. She knew that the Russians were on the brink of invading Berlin. Business would be even better when the war ended and the soldiers returned home. But more importantly, a spark of hope filled Alina's heart. Was it possible that she might see her parents, her sister, and her dear friend Lotti again? God, how she missed them. She said a silent prayer that they were alive. She missed Ugo and Maria too.

Then reality hit her like a splash of icy water as she looked around. What would her family think of her life, of what she'd done? Was Ugo right? Of course, he was. They would all be ashamed of her. They, like

Ugo. Would never understand. She wasn't proud of what she'd done. But she did what she needed to do to survive. And, unlike the owner of the previous brothel, she treated the girls fairly.

Joey was sitting on the floor, playing with one of the toys that she'd bought for him. Alina watched him, her heart aching. He was such a beautiful child, but his body leaned to one side, and his little legs were twisted. Alina would always put him first, no matter what anyone thought about her.

It was then that Alina decided she would never search for the people she'd loved and lost in the past. Because of what she'd done, she knew she must leave her family behind and move forward. Let them think she was dead. It was probably for the best. At least she would never hurt them. And Ugo?

Ugo was problematic for certain. He could sometimes be controlling. Even so, for some damned reason, she missed him terribly. But Alina didn't have the luxury of changing her mind, and Ugo couldn't be with her the way things were. So, he, too, was a part of her past. Another someone she must leave behind.

Alina knew what she would do in the future. She would build this business and make it thrive. She would be so rich that she would never have to worry about money again. So rich that even if Joey was a cripple, he would always have the best medical care and the finest education. And if he chose to marry, he would be able to find a wife.

sixty-three
Lotti

BOMBS THUNDERED down upon Berlin like the wrath of God. Day and night, they fell without any relief. The city lay in ruins. The rubble of destroyed buildings made the air thick with dust. People ran for shelter when the bombs fell, but it was impossible to avoid seeing the dead and dying everywhere. The hospitals were needed for the wounded. But, for now, perhaps because she was so young and pretty, the doctor had allowed Bernadette to stay in a hospital bed. It was obvious that he was trying desperately to save Berni's life. Lotti stopped going to work at the hotel. She did not leave her friend's side. Outside the hospital, the city shook as if the earth were about to split in two.

"She was pregnant. From what I can tell from examining her, someone performed a badly executed abortion on her. I can assure you that it was not a doctor," the doctor said to Lotti as she stood in the white hallway outside the hospital room where Bernadette had been transferred after surgery.

Even as they stood there speaking, Lotti could hear moaning from the other rooms where victims of the bombings lay writhing in pain. Lotti tried to avert her eyes from seeing any of them. She knew that if she caught a glimpse of the horrors that had befallen the people in the hospital beds, she might not sleep for a long time.

"Will she be all right? Will she live?" Lotti asked the doctor. She was holding on to the wall for support. Sweat beads had formed at her temple.

"Well, I hope so. But she has lost a lot of blood. The next day or so is crucial. She's young and strong. That's a good thing. If the bleeding stops, she'll have a good chance. All we can do now is wait and see how things go."

Lotti couldn't believe what she was hearing. Lotti had longed to have a child all her life, but that gift had been taken from her. It was hard to understand how any woman could intentionally end her pregnancy. Still, Lotti knew that there was a stigma to being an unwed mother. But Berni could have gone to a home for the Lebensborn and had the baby if she had wanted to. Unless, maybe, the father was Jewish or a political prisoner, or maybe this was why Berni had been so quick to befriend Lotti. Perhaps Berni, too, had a secret in her past that kept her from fitting in with the rest of the pure Aryan women.

The next two days passed in a blur. Lotti finally went to work. She explained to her boss that Berni was hurt badly in a bombing. He almost fired her, but he gave her another chance when she wept. Every day after her shift, Lotti returned to the hospital and went to Berni's bedside. The doctor said Berni had lost a lot of blood. She was tired and drifted in and out of sleep. When she was awake, Lotti spoon-fed her broth. At first, Berni vomited everything that went into her mouth, but then she began to keep a little bit of the liquid down. Lotti was hopeful. Sometimes, she read to Berni, who awakened for short periods of time but then drifted back to sleep.

"The bleeding has stopped. That's a good sign. And, she's taken some liquid and kept it down. I think she'll make it," the doctor told Lotti, who felt so grateful she began to cry.

"She is my only friend. She is all I have left in the world," Lotti said.

"Well, things look much better than I originally thought for her." The doctor smiled and patted Lotti's shoulder.

Berni spent the next seven days in the hospital, showing improvement every day. Although she had a million questions about what had happened and why, Lotti asked Berni nothing. They did not speak of the pregnancy. Did Berni know that Lotti had found out about Berni's abortion? Lotti had no idea. As Berni grew stronger, the two women talked, but nothing was ever brought up about the baby. Finally, the doctor declared Berni healthy enough to leave the hospital and return home. She was to be released in the morning. Lotti was relieved.

"You'll stay with me. I'll take care of you," Lotti said. She was sitting on the edge of Berni's bed.

"Are you sure?"

"Of course, I am sure. In fact, I insist." Lotti smiled and gently took the hair out of Berni's eyes.

"I can't ever thank you enough." Berni took Lotti's hand and squeezed it gently.

"You are my friend. This is what friends do for each other."

Lotti was preoccupied with getting things ready for Berni to move in. However, even as busy as she was, she couldn't escape the panic in the streets. Over the past few months, Dr. Goebbels had done his best to hide the truth, but now the Germans had no doubt that Germany was losing the war. Lotti was glad to see the Nazis fall, but she'd also heard terrifying things about how the Russians treated Germans, especially women. And to the Allies, Lotti was just another German, part of the enemy. They knew nothing of her past, her love for Lev, or her friends. The people in Berlin, mostly women, old men, and very young boys, were wobbling on the edge of a high wire, tense like cats in a thunderstorm. Everywhere Lotti went, there were whispers and speculation about what was to come. No one knew for sure what was to come, but they were living in constant fear. Stalin was known to be as heartless as Hitler.

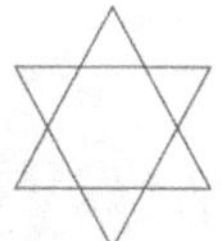

sixty-four
Berni

BERNI CAME HOME to Lotti's apartment, tired and weak. She couldn't help but see the world around her crumbling. Not that her life had ever been a good one. She'd lived through so much hell that she was unafraid to face whatever awaited her. One day soon, she would sit her dear friend Lotti down and tell her everything. Berni would tell Lotti why she'd had the abortion and why she had no fear of the Russians or even of death. Yes, someday, very soon, she would tell her. But for now, she would just do her best to recover for Lotti's sake and be grateful that she had such a wonderful friend.

sixty-five
Lotti and Berni

BERNI WAS STILL WEAK, but the terror of the Russians marching into Berlin gave Berni strength she didn't know she had. Until now, Berni had thought of herself as fearless. But, the smell of terror was contagious. It spread through the streets like the plague on the night of the first Passover.

She and Lotti clung to each other with the fear that the next breath they took might be their last. Lotti was sure it wouldn't make any difference even if she tried to explain to the invaders that she'd been anti-Hitler from the beginning. Somehow, she knew that the Russians wouldn't listen or care.

Rumors spread among the horrified women of the town like a fatal infection that the Russian soldiers were raping German women throughout the countryside as they pillaged their way into Germany's capital, which their *Führer* had abandoned and left to the mercy of the enemy. The only men left to defend the female population were boys under ten. But for Lotti, the most unnerving thing was that there was no way out. The destiny of Germany was coming at them like a freight train. And there was no way to escape what was about to befall the women left alone to face the enemy—the Russians who were rapidly descending upon Berlin.

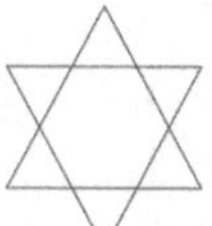

epilogue

IN JULY 1944, the Soviets liberated the first concentration camp, Majdanek, in Poland. Once the Nazis knew they were losing the war, they attempted to kill what was left of the prisoners, but they were unsuccessful at hiding the evidence of their crimes against humanity.

On April 30, 1945, Hitler and his bride, Eva Braun, committed suicide. The bombings in Berlin continued, and then the Russians descended upon the city. By May 2, Berlin had fallen, and her people lay trapped and desperate at the feet of the enemy. The Russian soldiers who invaded Berlin had watched their fellow soldiers die at the hands of the Nazis. They were going to make the Germans pay for Hitler's cruelty, and a dark, airless cloud covered Berlin.

The world was shocked and horrified by the liberation of Majdanek, but that was only the beginning. In the summer of 1945, Auschwitz, Belzec, Sobibor, and Treblinka were liberated. The horrifying conditions that were discovered in those camps seemed beyond human comprehension. The liberators were appalled, and they held all of Germany responsible, even those who were only innocent civilians. And then came the pictures that had been taken in the camps, with piles of dead bodies, women and small children lying in mass graves, and people who were so emaciated it was a miracle they were alive. When these photographs became public, a silent scream of shock and revulsion resonated, shaking the world.

The End.

a note from the author

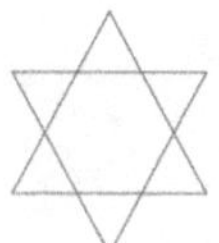

Dear All,

I always enjoy hearing from my readers, and your thoughts about my work are very important to me. If you enjoyed my novel, please consider telling your friends and posting a short review on Amazon. Word of mouth is an author's best friend.

Also, it would be my honor to have you join my mailing list. As my gift to you for joining, you will receive 3 **free** short stories and my USA Today award-winning novella! To sign up, just go to my website at www.RobertaKagan.com

I send blessings to each and every one of you,
Roberta

Email: roberta@robertakagan.com

about the author

I wanted to take a moment to introduce myself. My name is Roberta, and I am an author of Historical Fiction, mainly based on World War 2 and the Holocaust. While I never discount the horrors of the Holocaust and the Nazis, my novels are constantly inspired by love, kindness, and the small special moments that make life worth living.

I always knew I wanted to reach people through art when I was younger. I just always thought I would be an actress. That dream died in my late 20's, after many attempts and failures. For the next several years, I tried so many different professions. I worked as a hairstylist and a wedding coordinator, amongst many other jobs. But I was never satisfied. Finally, in my 50's, I worked for a hospital on the PBX board. Every day I would drive to work, I would dread clocking in. I would count the hours until I clocked out. And, the next day, I would do it all over again. I couldn't see a way out, but I prayed, and I prayed, and then I prayed some more. Until one morning at 4 am, I woke up with a voice in my head, and you might know that voice as Detrick. He told me to write his story, and together we sat at the computer; we wrote the novel that is now known as All My Love, Detrick. I now have over 30 books published, and I have had the honor of being a USA Today Best-Selling Author. I have met such incredible people in this industry, and I am so blessed to be meeting you.

I tell this story a lot. And a lot of people think I am crazy, but it is true. I always found solace in books growing up but didn't start writing until I was in my late 50s. I try to tell this story to as many people as possible to inspire them. No matter where you are in your life, remember there is always a flicker of light no matter how dark it seems.

I send you many blessings, and I hope you enjoy my novels. They are all written with love.

Roberta

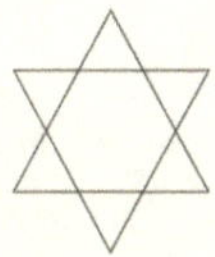

more books by roberta kagan
Available on Amazon

Margot's Secret Series

The Secret They Hid

An Innocent Child

Margot's Secret

The Lies We Told

The Blood Sisters Series

The Pact

My Sister's Betrayal

When Forever Ends

The Auschwitz Twins Series

The Children's Dream

Mengele's Apprentice

The Auschwitz Twins

Jews, The Third Reich, and a Web of Secrets

My Son's Secret

The Stolen Child

A Web of Secrets

A Jewish Family Saga

Not In America

They Never Saw It Coming

When The Dust Settled

The Syndrome That Saved Us

A Holocaust Story Series

The Smallest Crack

The Darkest Canyon

Millions Of Pebbles

Sarah and Solomon

All My Love, Detrick Series

All My Love, Detrick

You Are My Sunshine

The Promised Land

To Be An Israeli

Forever My Homeland

Michal's Destiny Series

Michal's Destiny

A Family Shattered

Watch Over My Child

Another Breath, Another Sunrise

Eidel's Story Series

And . . . Who Is The Real Mother?

Secrets Revealed

New Life, New Land

Another Generation

The Wrath of Eden Series

The Wrath Of Eden

The Angels Song

Stand Alone Novels

One Last Hope

A Flicker Of Light

The Heart Of A Gypsy